W9-CUC-191

THE WANDERER

Le Grand Meaulnes

with colored drawings by DIGNIMONT

ALAIN-FOURNIER

THE WANDERER

Le Grand Meaulnes

Translated from the French by
FRANÇOISE DELISLE

with an introduction by
HENRI PEYRE

and illustrations by
DIGNIMONT

THE HERITAGE PRESS

NEW YORK

Table of Contents

First Part

Second Part

Third Part

Introduction

The years immediately preceding the first World War count among the richest in the history of French culture. The Russian ballets were then giving a new impetus to painting and to music. Stravinsky scandalized the old and enchanted the young. Picasso opened the eyes of his contemporaries to a new vision with his 'Demoiselles d'Avignon.' Matisse, after a period of meditation on his art, was reaching a new harmony between the demands of the intellect and the *bonheur de vivre,* a harmony that was to fill painting with *luxe, calme et volupté*. The Cubists and the Fauves, aided by the keenest art critic of the century, the great poet Guillaume Apollinaire, were reaping the fruit of their early boldness. Claudel, Matisse's contemporary, published in 1911 a splendid version of his *L'Annonce Faite à Marie*. Gide gave his masterpiece *La Porte Étroite*. Giraudoux, Cocteau, Larbaud, Romains, Mauriac, Martin du Gard, Carco were voicing the aspirations of a new literary generation. In 1913 there appeared two novels of very unequal merit, Proust's *Du Côté de Chez Swann* and *Le Grand Meaulnes*, whose influence on French fiction was to be felt for several decades. Both were poetical novels of childhood, embodying what was most precious in the legacy of Symbolism and blending that airy fragrance with the earthy smells of Combray and of the valley of the Cher, respectively close to Chartres and to Bourges, perhaps the two most splendid among French cathedrals. Alain-Fournier disappeared one year after his only novel had seen the light; Proust lived on until 1922. Their true audience was to recognize their achievement only in the late nineteen twenties.

Le Grand Meaulnes is as autobiographical a work of fiction as was ever written in the third person singular. It can be interpreted only through its links with its creator: it is the summing up of a long quest after which the author, like Keat's Apollo, took 'leave of pale immortal death and with a pang died into life.' For Alain-Fournier had always felt himself a stranger on earth and had yearned for a fulfilment which was hardly possible in this existence. It happens that we can retrace his intellectual and spiritual evolution as completely as that of any French writer. Between the ages of eighteen and of twenty-eight he poured out the secrets of his fervent soul and confided the record of his long fictional labor to his sister Isabelle, to a friend, René Bichet, and most particularly to his closest friend, Jacques Rivière, who, after 1909, became his brother-in-law. To Rivière we owe an invaluable account of Fournier: the preface to the latter's *Miracles*

(1924) from which all biographers have drawn. The most recent and by far the best of these biographers is the Englishman, Robert Gibson, whose *Quest of Alain-Fournier* was published in England in 1954 and soon after in America by the Yale University Press.

Henri Fournier (for such was his Christian name before he christened himself Alain) was born in 1886 in a small village of central France, north of Bourges, where his father was a country schoolteacher. The village, La Chapelle-d'Angillon, is part of a rich and green province, the Berry, once portrayed in George Sand's rustic novels. Close by, the region of the Sologne stands in sharp contrast to the pasture lands and hedges of the Berry: it is a barren and sandy territory and has long served as a hunting-ground for wealthy Parisians. A few scions of the old families still live on their estates in Sologne. Other regions of France might have been, it seems, more propitious settings for the dreams of a boy athirst for adventure and in love with mystery: they are wilder, more grandiose and tormented. But Henri Fournier lent the sense of wonder of his own soul to the moderate scenery around him. The dirt road which marked the limit of his usual walks, the glade of the nearest forest, the islets surrounded by the meanders of the river Cher, appeared to the boy's imagination as the gate to an enchanted domain into which he might some day venture.

Henri loved the landscape amid which he grew with a fierce and exclusive passion. He peopled it with marvelous visions, transported into it the heroes of his favorite childhood stories, *Robinson Crusoe* and *David Copperfield*, and found inexhaustible poetry in a chestnut tree, an old farmhouse, a winding path between two hedges, a canal barge. He was secure and happy in his home, and he always went back to that child's universe as to a refuge. A brilliant pupil at school, he was sent to a Parisian *lycée* to continue his studies and eventually to prepare for the *Ecole normale supérieure*. There he never succeeded in passing the difficult competitive examination, for his heart was in recent literature rather than in the study of the past. But his years in the Parisian schools offered to him a double advantage. They deepened his love for his childhood scenery, which he fondly and vividly remembered while poring over Latin and French literary texts or analyzing philosophical systems. They brought him the friendship of Jacques Rivière, with whom he was to exchange some of the fullest and the most sincere letters ever written by an adolescent.

The revelation of contemporary literature came to the two young men in 1903, when their teacher read aloud in class a graceful poem by one of the Symbolists, Henri de Régnier. This decorative and languid poetry, somewhat lacking in imaginative power and much too self-conscious in its pursuit of naïveté, was nevertheless to them the intrusion of modernity into their lives. They soon outgrew their taste for the more facile aspects of Symbolism and became enamored of Jules Laforgue, then of Paul Claudel and of André Gide. Henri Fournier adored Debussy's *Pelléas,* its repressed and discreet emotion, its fluid melody. From Symbolism, he was able to retain only what would serve his own creation: a youthful wonder at the beauty of the world, the worship of dream preferred to reality, the obstinate need for idealization. But he also clung to his robust earthiness and to the concrete truth of his early years as a country boy. In a letter written in 1911 to Rivière, he clearly marked his differences from some of the apostles of a tinsel wonder-world and the dreamers of too pallid dreams: 'I like the world of wonder only when it is firmly bound up with reality, not when it overwhelms it or surpasses it.' Like Proust conjuring up the memories of Combray, the musty smells of

Aunt Léonie's bedroom, the golden and warm *brioches* bought, after Sunday mass, at the local bakery, Henry Fournier isolated himself from the bustle of Paris and the enticements of the concert hall and theatre to recapture his childhood sensations: the smell of the pasture lands and of the farm manure, the long brittle loaf emerging from the baker's oven, the home-made cherry liqueur of which he was allowed a swallow on great occasions, the hue of a rosy cloud and the voluptuous moistness of September rains. Of his childhood alone would he ever write, he decided early, and only with the utmost delicacy and restraint; for anything but tender and loving reverence for the paradise of his early memories would be a desecration:

> My creed in art and literature (he wrote to Rivière on August 15, 1906) is Childhood. To try to convey it with no childishness, with all its depth which touches on mysteries. My future book will perhaps be a constant and hardly perceptible coming and going between dream and reality: 'Dream' being understood as the immense and imprecise life of the child hovering above the other and perpetually set rumbling by echoes from the other.

Rivière, who was to become the inspirer and director of the *Nouvelle Revue Française* and one of the three or four leading French critics of the century, was more intellectual than Fournier. He perceived life through books and works of art, and even his two love novels and his analyses of personal feelings tended at times to be swayed by bookish impressions. By nature, he was inclined to systematic doubt and to disbelief. Like Gide, of whom he was later to make the same comment, he would lend himself and, soon after, like a kiss, withdraw. Fournier was much fiercer in his scorn for all rationalism, pitiless in his rejection of all the scaffoldings of systems which imprison life. Impetuously, and without having fed on Bergson or on the art of the Fauves, he proclaimed to his family on February 7, 1906:

And I say that the unknowable is life which rolls us along in its divine waves; that reason is but one of its miserable toys . . . I say that wisdom lies in renouncing one's thought, the house of cards of one's thought and in surrendering to life. Life is contradictory and fluid—yet it is intoxicating—and wherever it leads us, there lies truth.

Fournier, however, was not merely voicing juvenile romantic declamations or echoing, unknown to himself, the Nietzschean and Bergsonian hymns to life of which the nascent twentieth century was fond. At twenty or twenty-five, he was already aware of his originality, determined to allow it to mature slowly, and unforgiving of all that failed to come up to his demands: books, friends, women, and life itself. He never felt certain that he was made to dally long in this all too real world. A sentence of Benjamin Constant which he had stumbled upon haunted him as expressing with singular aptness his own conviction: 'I am perhaps not quite a real being.' The English romantics had, even more felicitously than the French, blended the dream and dark reality, the visionary world hailed by Wordsworth and Shelley and an intuitive penetration into the spiritual essence of things; their poetry, cherished by young Fournier, was the cry of wounded souls disenchanted by the impurity of life and yearning for 'a land of heart's desire.' The young student spent a summer in England in 1905, was attracted by the exquisiteness of a few English girls, but found them lacking in mystery, too inclined to prompt and mere comradeship. The English landscape threw his nostalgic memory back to his native province, which he felt he would betray if he became too attached to the parks and forests near London. Besides, already, at nineteen, Henri Fournier had been marked by the sign of a great and impossible love. The conjunction of that adventure of his soul and of his passion for his native land was slowly to give birth to his masterpiece.

There is something childish in many great loves: that of Dante for Beatrice, that of Tristan for Isolde, that of Novalis for his thirteen-year-old fiancée soon ravished by death. And yet we accept the revelations afforded these lovers as grave turning-points in their lives and in ours. Like most authentic, and most Platonic, lovers, Henri Fournier was in love with love and a worshipper of the eternal feminine. Such lovers, who insist upon setting the loved one upon an inaccessible pedestal and transfiguring her through poetry, art and their inwardly cherished ideal, are commonly the most embarrassing ones to women and, with all their contentment with chastity, the most demanding of all. Already, in his twentieth year, the Parisian student knew that no real woman could ever answer all he would expect of her, and that he would have to become, regretfully, resigned to his loves as to his life, forsaking glimpses of many a lost paradise.

Still, the souls of women, as he was fond of saying, alone were attuned to his need for poetry and to the inner landscape which he would one day consent to share with them.

To me (he confessed to his friend on June 18, 1909) the soul of woman is like a limitless valley which opens up: a gesture of her arms, a look, a tone of voice inspires me with the vertiginous thrill of entering it . . . I have experienced this with the least virtuous and most impure among them. They imparted to me, more humbly than the others, but just as mysteriously, the nostalgic longing for those wide unknown lands shaped like their souls, to which they return through sleep and death.

To his friend, who discerned some exaggeration in his chivalrous cult, he explained on May 2, 1909:

That is why I have that delicate cult for women with which you gently find fault: with them, the slightest appearances, the frailest envelope leave the soul almost bare and, as it were, tangible. It is when I am close to them that I feel my own soul weighing most heavily.

The great love of Meaulnes in the novel is naturally an expansion and a transfiguration of the momentous encounter which, from 1905 to his death, had determined his whole life. Fournier's letters, the oral reports of his friends, his notebooks utilized by his biographer Robert Gibson, have revealed to posterity the purity and the tragedy of that romantic adventure.

On Ascension Thursday, June 1, 1905, Fournier visited an art exhibition in the Grand Palais, near the Champs-Elysées. A slender and elegant girl, tall, blue-eyed, came down the steps as he was leaving. The young man experienced an immediate *coup de foudre*. The girl, her companion, an older lady, and Fournier, the shy student, boarded a boat on the Seine. He saw the two ladies land and enter a house on the Boulevard Saint-Germain. From then on, his one obsession was to see the fair-haired princess again. He succeeded against unbelievable odds in seeing her once in the church at Saint-Germain-des-Prés, in walking out with her; she told him her name, Yvonne, and that she came from afar, from Toulon. She kept repeating: 'What's the use? I forgive you, of course. But we are two children, we have acted foolishly.' That was all. He watched her depart as he remained, leaning on the Alexander III Bridge. From that fateful day of June 1905 he decided that his life could receive meaning only through that fleeting, impossible love.

Two years later, he learned, through patient detective work, that Yvonne had married and was forever lost for him; much later, in 1913, while he was completing the novel in which she was enshrined, he met Yvonne's sister and heard that his inaccessible love was the mother of two children. He confided to Rivière:

xx

I sobbed all evening in my room. I am suffering abominably. Under my window is a provincial courtyard, all sunny. In front of the door, under wistaria, a woman is sewing. As each hour moves across the face of the church clock nearby, I wonder if I can still endure to go on living . . . It is terrible to confess that I am not totally despairing, in spite of all. I cannot believe that God has showed me so much, promised so much and will grant me nothing—in this world or in the next, it is true!

He visited Yvonne in Rochefort, pondered lovingly, in utmost grief over the might-have-been, and admitted that his life henceforth could be only a bleak desert. His novel appeared a few months later. For her sake, he would have liked to receive the Goncourt prize, which he barely missed being awarded. But even literary creation and success were of scant avail. His sorrow and his solitude deepened. Within ten more months, he had himself disappeared, lost in one of the early battles of World War I. Ever since he had known his great love to be 'begotten by despair upon impossibility,' to be, perhaps, although he never admitted it, a phantom of his imagination – he had found most earthly joys tainted with bitterness and, like the poet, he had been 'more than half in love with death.'

Yet it would be wrong to imagine Fournier as a mere effete idealist, pitying himself, embracing clouds, Ixion-like, and taking refuge in literature in order to shun living. After his studies, he served in the French army for two years and enjoyed the companionship of simple, even coarse men from the farms, their clumsiness in expressing themselves, their good-natured simplicity. He then entered a journalistic career, taught (he was, for a period in Paris, the private tutor of young T. S. Eliot), travelled, but worked always at his novel. His early verse and prose poems, collected under the title of *Miracles,* are very minor works, insubstantial and deficient in imaginative vigor.

He jotted down fragments of a narrative, *The Land without a Name,* which vaguely but clumsily prefigured the novel he dreamed of. Wisely, he soon realized that he had to break away from the recording of his childhood memories, to forsake the perilous mold of the prose poem and to personify his emotions and obsessions in characters which would be the more true to their creator because they differed from him. The elaboration of his novel, he now realized, would be a slow maturation. More suffering endured and perhaps inflicted was no doubt necessary. 'A man who is unable to despair,' Goethe once said, 'has no need to be alive.'

Henri Fournier nurtured his inner desolation. The temptation of 'entering the Catholic Church intact,' as he called it, even to join a monastery, occurred to him repeatedly. But he was not yet ready to yield to it. He still preferred an obstinate fidelity to his own self. He had affairs with several women, one of whom, Jeanne (called Valentine in the novel), was utterly devoted to him. But, to the imperious demands of Fournier, she soon proved inadequate: she was not totally pure, she seemed too resigned to prosaic happiness, and she was powerless to obliterate the other radiant and impossible image. The young man treated her harshly and in the end sacrificed her to his dream. A philosopher once remarked that if artists and other creators are so frequently unhappy, it is merely because happiness does not interest them. Fournier wrote in one of his letters in 1909, the very year that *La Porte Étroite* was to appear with its message of happiness spurned: 'Happiness is the greatest of all sins.' It is strange that a similar message, characterizing renouncement as greater and secretly more pleasurable than fulfilment, should have been echoed at the same time by such diverse writers as Claudel in *L'Annonce Faite à Marie* as, in truth, in all his works ('There is nothing to which man is less attuned than happiness, nothing of which he wearies faster'), Valéry in *La Jeune Parque,* Proust, who sacrificed the enjoyment of the present to the remembrance of the past, Gide, and Alain-Fournier! How blind must be the superficial observers of France who see in French art, literature and life nothing but a *joie de vivre* and the Epicurean plucking of to-day's flowers and fruit!

The characters of three boys stand out in *Le Grand Meaulnes.* François, the narrator, is of necessity the palest of the three, for his role is to reflect the love for the natural scenery which is the passion of all the actors in the story and the admiration of the schoolboys for Big Meaulnes, their mysterious hero. François Seurel's frail health shut him off from action and adventure. His zest for living was somewhat vicarious and manifested itself through Meaulnes, the leader, to whose impetuousness François serves as a foil. His behavior at the denouement of the story is neither felicitous nor convincing. But, through the humble schoolmaster's son, the reader is afforded one of the most faithful portrayals of a French country school in literature. The glimpses we get of M. Seurel and of his wife constitute a free and touching picture of what French literature between 1900 and 1920, after the glamorous excesses of naturalism, was striving to express: the life of simple and humble people.

François has not a few features of Fournier's own childhood and adolescence as they appeared on the surface of his life. But a boy's truest life is in his secret and repressed violence, in the dreams which he grafts upon placid reality. Fournier's own spiritual exaltation and imaginative violence were not lent to the narrator of the novel but rather to Meaulnes, seventeen years old, impulsive and obstinate, wrapped in his dreams, who entered school one day. Adventure was his goal, and he soon imparted his passion for it to his schoolfellows. One afternoon, having borrowed without permission a carriage and a mare, he lost his way at dusk, slept at night in an old sheepfold and the next day discovered a Sologne manor where a strange festival was being held for children. As he found later, the occasion was the expected return of Frantz de Galais who had gone off to fetch his betrothed. Meaulnes, the wanderer, boarded a little pleasure boat which toured a lake and, like Henri Fournier on his Ascension Day, met a ravishingly beautiful girl accompanied by an older lady. He told her how much he admired her. Then she disappeared. She was Yvonne de Galais, the daughter of the manor.

Frantz, her brother, returned at last as the feast was coming sadly to an end. His fiancée was not with him. She had lacked faith. She was no princess, but a modest seamstress, who did not feel up to the part her fanciful fiancé had wished her to play. Before he ran off dramatically, Frantz confided his sorrow to the unknown guest, Meaulnes, who, as he was riding back to his village school in a carriage, heard a shot in the woods and caught sight of a wounded man carried in the arms of a clown. It was the fickle and romantic adolescent, Frantz de Galais, who had tried to kill himself after the failure of his dream and after he had joined himself to the band of clowns and gypsies who had attended his tragic wedding party.

Later, his head bandaged, slowly recovering, Frantz appeared at the country school where he and Meaulnes, both obstinately trying to retain the dreams of their childhood, both refusing the realities of life, became the leaders of an adventurous group of boys. They swore to remain ever loyal to one another and to answer promptly every appeal which either, if ever in distress, might make to his comrade.

Having grown into a young man, Meaulnes went to Paris, still obsessed by the memory of Yvonne de Galais. He had heard it rumored that she was married and he entered into an amorous liaison with Valentine. Valentine was Frantz's love, and Meaulnes suffered from having thus betrayed his friend unknowingly. However, Yvonne was not married, and Meaulnes, through the intervention of François, returned, declared his love to her and became her husband.

Domestic happiness was not for them. Meaulnes still yearned for the past and grudgingly accepted a reality which could only fail to equal his immense adolescent dreams. Frantz, the fickle and imperious friend, incurably nostalgic for his shattered vision of happiness, jealous of the peace which Meaulnes was on the verge of finding in security, roamed about the countryside and at last uttered his call to Meaulnes, who heeded his appeal, perhaps out of romantic and childish loyalty, more probably out of a peevish impulse to destroy the fabric of his domestic peace and to choose adventure rather than quietude. François Seurel remained to talk with Yvonne gently about the departed Meaulnes and to bid her be patient. Months went by without word of Meaulnes. Yvonne gave birth to a baby daughter, but the delivery was difficult and she died a few days later. Meaulnes, in Paris, had at last succeeded in reuniting Frantz and Valentine. He returned to find his young wife dead, and, forlorn, departed with the daughter she had left him in his arms.

No bare outline can convey the tragic pathos of the best scenes of *Le Grand Meaulnes*. The characters do not stand in sharp outline as they would in a novel by Mauriac, with clear-cut problems which they might try to solve by wallowing in sin and finally answering the supreme appeal of grace. They are not analyzed in all the recesses of their desires and regrets; nor are all their facets portrayed through a method of saturation such as Balzac and Zola used. Yvonne de Galais is nowhere analyzed and she is hardly ever described: she is not of this world, but rather the personification of Fournier's impossible feminine dream. Yet the reader accepts her presence and feels it to be authentic. Frantz and Meaulnes are both embodiments of the author's youthful passion for a world of spiritual adventure and of 'childhood recaptured at will.' Frantz is a petulant and spoilt child, sensitive, egocentric, bent upon living a dream which he knows to be destructive of others and of himself. Meaulnes is more balanced and earthy, self-assured but unforgiving of the life of adults which is a compromise and a slow decadence from the adolescent ideal of purity and of total faith. Yvonne is to him, as he is well aware, but the symbol of his own childhood. To her he behaves with apparently inexplicable cruelty, not unlike a saint who repudiates earthly bonds; he is athirst for an absolute, to the threshold of which woman holds the key, but only if she remains inaccessible, idealized, and thus easily molded at will by the dreamer's phantasy.

In a letter to Rivière written as early as April 4, 1910, Fournier had lucidly explained the significance of his hero and the reason for his cruelty toward all attachment which is a form of imprisonment:

Meaulnes, Big Meaulnes, the hero of my book, is a man whose childhood was too beautiful. During the whole of his adolescence, he trails it behind him. At times, it seems as if that imaginary paradise which was the world of his childhood is going to arise at the end of his adventures or to be conjured up by one of his gestures . . . But he knows already that that paradise can no longer be. He has given up happiness. He is in this world like one who will soon depart. Therein lies the secret of his cruelty. He uncovers the falsehood and reveals the deceit of all the little paradises which open up before him. And on the day when the undeniable and ineluctable happiness stands suddenly in front of him and leans its human face against his, Big

xxvi

Meaulnes flees, not out of heroism, not out of terror, but because he is not of this world.

A number of critical works in various languages have already been composed on *Le Grand Meaulnes,* some interpreting it as a pre-Surrealist masterpiece, as did Christian Dedeyan, others almost as a portrait of an Existentialist hero as did Robert Champigny. Both interpretations are tantamount to a betrayal of the truest essence of a book in which the author spurned all ideology and insisted upon embracing life in its most precious function: that of the creation of dreams. 'The more poetical a thing is, the truer it is,' Alain-Fournier might have said with another one of those 'inheritors of unfulfilled renown,' the short-lived Novalis. The great art of this novel, which appears artless in its simplicity, is that all ideological developments *à la* Proust or *à la* Dostoevsky, all digressions pointing to a message, all pretentious claims to a superposition of symbolic layers of meaning have been sedulously and wisely eschewed by the young author.

His originality, in the first years of the twentieth century, was to reintegrate the child into French literature. For centuries, French men and, regrettably, French women writers also had banished the child from the literature and from the painting of their country. The child was most frequently considered a creature of small interest because he was incapable of self-analysis, a little being with whom something was amiss, because he could not as yet express himself clearly on adult subjects ranging from love to politics. Even among the French romantics, who were in this respect less faithful sons of Rousseau than were Wordsworth or Goethe, the little world of childhood with its memories, its illusions, its dreams and its immense childish griefs, from which the future originality of the man is derived, remained a closed book to novelists and poets. André Gide, Colette (contemporaries of Freud, though scarcely influenced by him) stressed the perverseness of that new scapegoat of modern psychology, the child, enmeshed in sexual conflicts and in impure urges. Alain-Fournier, whom Giraudoux and other French portrayers of a purer kind of childhood were to follow, gave us a different, and perhaps a truer portrayal of the child. The adolescents in *Le Grand Meaulnes* do not indulge in infantilism or in boyish adventures; they do not feed on brutal crudities or on fake violence. They live in a real everyday world, that of the valley of the Cher and of a few simple dwellings of humble and very real farmers and gentlemen-farmers of Central France. They do not distort reality through Surrealist devices or through forcing themselves to believe in ghosts and in supernatural creatures. *Le Grand Meaulnes* is naturally and very simply joined to real life and is granted our credence even more readily than is Coleridge's *Ancient Mariner*. Its tragic quality is that of the lives of many adults: an inability of men and women to transcend a haunting sense of guilt; a sin of angelism, as theologians like to call it, of cherishing the dream of an impossible purity incompatible with this life; a relentless impulse to destroy happiness as soon as they have attained it.

Alain-Fournier refrained from appending any religious message to his artistic achievement. It would be a distortion of the life of one who was often obstinate and imperious, capricious and fierce, prone to despair and lacking in mercy to all that failed to come up to his demands, to caricature such a life by stressing its saintliness. Yet we know from Alain-Fournier's letters how powerfully he was tempted by the Gospels and by thoughts of a total surrender to Christian faith, while he was

xxviii

composing his novel. His hunger for an absolute was equaled by his conviction that the process of living is a betrayal of one's ideal, or, worse, still, a ceasing to cherish it. There might be one authentic escape: to throw oneself into the arms of God and find a mystical joy in the sacrifice of all earthly happiness. On September 28, 1910, Fournier announced, commenting on the strange behavior of 'that great cruel angel,' Meaulnes:

> There will be in my book a renouncement which I want more beautiful than that of *La Porte Étroite*. Because it will not be without reason. Because, behind that gesture of human renouncing, the whole Kingdom of joy conquered will be felt.

The success of his novel, in the last months of 1913, did not heal in Fournier the wound with which, in the phrase of Lamennais, his soul was born. Even the creation of Meaulnes, Frantz and François, these three beings of his own person, of Yvonne de Galais, the poetical transmutation of the apparition of 1905, failed to act as a sublimation or as a catharsis, as the creation of Werther had done for Goethe. More and more, the young man in his middle twenties, disconsolate because his childhood had been too beautiful, had the premonition that death alone held the key to the escape toward those ardently desired lands. He saw much of Péguy in his last years, and both felt that the time was approaching when the lights would go out over Western Europe.

In the first days of August 1914, Péguy, Rivière and Fournier were mobilized as infantry officers. On August 24, Rivière was taken prisoner. Two weeks later, Péguy was killed at the battle of the Marne. On September 6, 1914, a young officer, Pierre Maury, who later became a Protestant minister, overheard a conversation held at the battlefront, while shells were raging and men were falling, wounded and dead. A sceptical captain asked his fervent subordinates in banter: 'And where is that God of yours in the midst of all this?' Lieutenant Fournier's voice replied: 'I do not know where God may be in this war and who are we to solve such enigmas? But I do know this: when, where and however God wishes, I shall be called.'

On September 22, 1914, trenches had been dug on both sides of the fighting line and a few skirmishes were carried on to seize the no-man's-land between the French and the Germans. The captain of Fournier's unit, a fiery officer who thought that his duty was to discover where the enemy was and to push them back, ordered a reconnaissance. Two companies rushed out of the trenches, soon to be rolled back by machine-gun fire. The officers tried to leap forward. Fournier was one of them. He never reappeared. For four years, a feeble hope was cherished that he might some day be found among the prisoners of war, but after 1918, all hope had to be given up. He had found the path to the Land without a Name of which he had dreamed so much. He had joined his Yvonne de Galais in death.

HENRI PEYRE

First Part

THE BOARDER

He arrived at our home on a Sunday of November, 189–. I still say 'our home,' although the house no longer belongs to us. We left that part of the country nearly fifteen years ago and shall certainly never go back to it.

We were living in the building of the Higher Elementary Classes at Sainte-Agathe's School. My father, whom I was in the habit of calling M. Seurel as did other pupils, was head of the Middle School and also of the Higher Elementary classes where pupils worked for the preliminary teacher's examination. Mother taught the infants.

At the extreme end of the small town a long red house with five glass doors and a Virginia creeper upon its walls; an immense courtyard with shelters, a washhouse and a huge gateway, on the side looking towards the village; on the north side, a small gate opening on the road leading to the station three kilometres off; on the south, at the back of the house, fields, gardens, meadows joining the outskirts . . . such is the simple plan of this dwelling where I spent the most troubled but the most happy days of my life – the house from which we launched our adventures and to which they returned to break themselves like waves on a bare rock.

At the time of some new 'appointments,' a whim of fate, due to some inspector or to the Prefect, had led us there. Towards the end of the summer holidays, a long time ago, a peasant cart, preceding our household goods, deposited my mother and myself before the little rusty gate. Urchins who were stealing peaches in the garden silently escaped through holes in the hedge . . . My mother, whom we used to call Millie and who was the most methodical housekeeper I ever knew, had at once gone into the rooms full of dusty straw, and had declared with much consternation – as was her custom at each 'removal' – that our furniture would never fit in a house so badly built . . . She had come out to impart her trouble to me. While speaking she had, with her handkerchief, gently wiped my face blackened by the journey. Then she had gone back to consider what doors and windows would have to be blocked to make the place habitable . . . As for me, wearing a big straw hat with streamers, I was left alone on the gravel of that strange playground, waiting for her, prying shyly around the well and under the cart-shed.

Thus to-day I picture our arrival. For as soon as I wish to bring back the distant memory of that first evening when I waited in our playground at Sainte-Agathe, at once it is another kind of waiting which I recall, at once I see myself again, both hands pressed to the bars of the front gate, anxiously watching for some one who will soon come down the High Street. If I try to imagine that first night which I must have spent in my attic, amidst the lumber-rooms on the upper storey, I recall other nights; I am no longer alone in that room; a tall, restless, and friendly shadow moves along its walls and walks to and fro. And that quiet countryside – the school, old Father Martin's field, with its three walnut trees, the garden daily invaded on the stroke of four by women paying calls – all this is, in my memory, forever stirred and transformed by the presence of him who upset all our youth and whose sudden flight even did not leave us in peace.

Yet we had already been ten years in that district when Meaulnes arrived.

I was fifteen. It was a cold Sunday of November, the first day of autumn to make one think of winter. All day Millie had waited for the station omnibus to bring her a hat for the bad weather. That morning she missed Mass, and right up to the sermon, from my place in the choir with the other children, I looked anxiously towards the door to see her come to church wearing her new hat.

In the afternoon, I had to go to vespers alone. 'Anyhow,' she said to comfort me, brushing my little suit with her hand, 'even if it had come, this precious hat, I should have had to spend my Sunday making it up again.'

This is how our winter Sundays were often spent. In the early morning Father went off to some misty pond to jack-fish from a boat, and Mother retired till nightfall into her dark bed-room, to remake her simple dresses. She shut herself up in that

5

way for fear some lady visitor, as poor as herself and as proud, might surprise her at the job. As for me, vespers over, I waited, reading in the cold dining-room, until she opened the door to show me how she was getting on.

That Sunday, a little excitement in front of the church kept me out-of-doors after vespers. A christening, under the porch, had attracted a crowd of urchins. In the square a few villagers had put on their firemen's jackets and piled their arms; stiff and stamping their feet with cold, they were listening to Boujardon, the corporal, losing himself in theory . . .

The christening bells stopped suddenly, like festive chimes at a mistaken time and place. Boujardon and his men, rifles slung over their shoulders, dragged off the fire engine at a slow trot, and I saw them disappear at the first turning, followed by four silent urchins, crushing under their heavy boots the twigs on the frozen road, down which I dared not follow them.

In the village the only place left alive was the Café Daniel, from which I heard the murmurs of the drinkers' talk rise and fall, and hugging the low wall of the big playground which separated our house from the village, I came, rather anxious at being late, to the small gate.

It was ajar and I saw at once that something unusual was happening.

In fact, there stood, outside the dining-room door – the nearest of the five glass doors opening on the playground – a grey-headed woman, leaning forward and trying to look through the curtains. She was small and wore a black old-fashioned velvet bonnet. Her face was thin and refined, but worn with anxiety, and, at sight of her, I do not know what misgiving made me stand still on the first step, in front of the gate.

'My goodness, where's he gone!' she was muttering to her-

6

self. 'He was with me a moment ago. He must have gone all round the house already. Perhaps he's run away . . .'

And after each sentence she gave three barely perceptible little taps on the window-pane.

No one came to let in the unknown visitor. Without any doubt Millie had received her hat from the station, and, hearing nothing, at the end of the red bedroom, before a bed bestrewed with old ribbons and uncurled feathers, she was stitching, undoing, and remaking her modest headgear. In fact, as soon as I came into the dining-room, followed closely by the visitor, Mother appeared, both her hands to her head, holding wires, ribbons, and feathers which were not yet perfectly secured.

She smiled at me, from blue eyes tired with working till dusk, and exclaimed: 'Look! I was waiting to show you . . .'

But noticing that woman sitting in the big armchair at the other end of the room, she stopped, disconcerted. She quickly removed her hat, and during the whole scene that followed, held it against her breast, inside out, like a nest resting in the bend of her right arm.

The woman with the old-fashioned bonnet had begun to explain herself. She held between her knees an umbrella and a leather handbag, slightly nodding her head the while, and clicking her tongue as do village women when paying a call. She had regained full assurance, and when she spoke of her son she even assumed a superior and mysterious manner which puzzled us.

They had both driven from La Ferté d'Angillon, fourteen kilometres from Sainte-Agathe. Herself a widow – and very rich, as she gave us to understand – she had lost the younger of her two children, a boy called Antoine, who had suddenly died one evening, on returning from school, after bathing with his brother in a dirty pond. She had decided to let Augustin,

7

the elder boy, board with us, that he might take the Higher Course.

And forthwith she began to praise this boarder whom she was bringing us. I could no longer recognise the grey-headed woman whom, only a minute ago, I had seen stooping in front of the door, with the piteous and haggard bearing of a hen who has lost the wildest chick in her brood.

What she was relating with admiration about her son was surprising enough; he loved doing things to please her, he had often gone along the river-bank for miles barelegged, to bring her wild ducks' and moor hens' eggs hidden amongst the reeds . . . He could set nets . . . The other night, he had found a pheasant caught in a snare, in the wood . . .

I, who hardly dared to enter the house if I had torn my overall, looked at Millie with astonishment.

But Mother was no longer listening. She even motioned to the woman to be quiet; and putting down her 'nest' on the table with great care, she got up silently as if to take some one by surprise . . .

Above us, indeed, in a box-room where the blackened remains of the last fourteenth of July fireworks were piled up, an unknown step trod confidently to and fro, shaking the ceiling, crossed the huge dark lumber-rooms of the upper storey and passed at last towards the unused assistant masters' rooms, where lime tree leaves were put to dry and apples to ripen.

'A little while ago,' said Millie in a low voice, 'I heard that noise in the rooms downstairs; I thought it was you, François, come back . . .'

No one answered. We stood, the three of us, with beating hearts; then the attic door which led to the kitchen was heard to open; some one came down, crossed the kitchen, and appeared in the dim entrance of the dining-room.

'Why! It is you, Augustin!' said the visitor.

He was a tall boy of seventeen, or thereabout. At first, as night was falling, I saw only his peasant felt hat, pushed to the back of his head, and his black overall tightly belted in the fashion of schoolboys. I could see, too, that he was smiling . . .

He saw me, and before any one had had time to demand an explanation: 'Aren't you coming into the playground?' he asked.

I hesitated for a moment. Then, as Millie did not keep me back, I took up my cap and went towards him. We left by the kitchen door and went into the yard under the shelter where darkness was already gathering. In the dim evening light I watched, as I walked, his sharp-featured face with its straight nose and downy lip.

'Look,' said he, 'I found this in your box-rooms. You couldn't have looked at these things.'

He was holding in his hand a little wheel of blackened wood; a string of partly burnt squibs was twisted round it; evidently a Catherine wheel from the fireworks display on the fourteenth of July.

'Two of them didn't go off. We will set them alight,' said he, in the tone of voice of one who hopes to make better finds later on.

He threw his hat to the ground, and I saw that his hair was cropped like a peasant's. He showed me two squib lighters with their paper tapers which the flame had singed, before going out. He stuck the axle of the wheel into the sand and – to my astonishment, as such things were strictly forbidden me – pulled out of his pocket a box of matches. Bending down with care, he lighted the squib. Then, taking hold of my hand, he quickly drew me back.

A moment, later, as she came out of the door with Meaulnes'

mother after having discussed and settled the boarding fees, my mother saw two sheaves of red-and-white stars rising up under the shelter, hissing like bellows. For a moment's space she caught a glimpse of me as I stood in this magic light, holding by the hand the tall strange boy and showing no fear . . .

Once again, she dared not say anything.

And that evening, at dinner, there sat at our table a silent guest who ate with lowered head, paying no attention to the three pairs of eyes fixed upon him.

AFTER FOUR O'CLOCK

Until then I had never loafed about in the streets with the other village boys. An affection of the hip from which I had suffered up to this year of 189– had made me nervous and wretched. I still see myself chasing the nimble schoolboys in the alleys round our home, hopping wretchedly on one leg . . .

So I was seldom allowed to go out, and I recall that Millie, who was very proud of me, more than once brought me home and boxed my ears for having been caught hopping thus with some village urchins.

The arrival of Augustin Meaulnes, at the very time of my cure, marked the beginning of a new life.

Before his coming, a dreary evening of loneliness began for me when lessons were over at four. Father was in the habit of carrying into the dining-room grate the fire remaining in the classroom stove; and, little by little, the last boys who had lingered behind left the chilled building, thick with clouds of smoke. There were still a few games, some galloping races in the playground, then night came; the two pupils who had swept the classroom fetched their hoods and cloaks, and with their baskets under their arms went away quickly, leaving the big gate open . . .

Then, as long as there was a ray of light, I stopped in the record-room at the town hall, with its dead flies and posters that flapped in the draught, and I read, sitting on an old weighing-machine, close to a window looking on the garden.

When it was quite dark, and the dogs of the neighbouring farm began to howl and a light was seen at the window of our little kitchen, then I went home. Mother had begun to get supper ready. I climbed three steps of the attic stairs, sat down without a word and, leaning my head on the cold rails of the bannisters, watched Millie light her fire in this narrow kitchen where the flame of one candle flickered . . .

But some one has come who has taken from me these peaceful, childlike delights. Some one has blown out the candle which lit up for me the gentle motherly face bent over the evening meal. Some one has extinguished the lamp around which, at night, we were a happy family, when Father had fixed the wooden shutters over the glass doors. And he was Augustin Meaulnes, whom the other fellows soon called 'Admiral Meaulnes.'

As soon as he became a boarder with us, that is, from the early days of December, the school was no longer deserted in the evening after four. Every day then, in the classroom, despite the cold from the swinging door and the shouts and clatter of the cleaners with their pails of water, a score of the big boys, both those from the countryside and the village, gathered round Meaulnes. Long discussions followed, never-ending arguments, into which I was drawn restlessly but with pleasure. Meaulnes never said anything, but it was because of him that repeatedly one chatterbox or another, making of himself the centre of the group, and taking in turn each of his noisily approving friends as witness, would relate some long story of poaching, which the others followed with gaping mouths and inward laughter.

Sitting on a desk and swinging his legs, Meaulnes was thoughtful. At exciting moments he used also to laugh, but softly, as though he reserved his real laughter for some better story known only to himself. Then, as night fell and no more light came from the classroom windows on the throng of boys, Meaulnes used suddenly to get up, and pushing his way through, call out: 'Come on! Let's go!'

Then all followed him and until pitch dark one could hear them shouting, towards the heights of the village.

It came about now that I went with them. With Meaulnes, I went at milking-time to barn doors just outside the village. We entered shops, and the weaver, between two clicks of his loom, used to say out of his darkness: 'Ha! the schoolboys.'

Generally, at dinner-time, we were to be found near the Higher Elementary School with Desnoues, the wheelwright, who was also a blacksmith. His shop was an old inn with big double-leaf doors, always kept open. From the street you could hear the squeak of the forge bellows, and you could sometimes make out, by the glow of the forge fire, in this dark and noisy place, the country folk who had stopped their cart to have a chat, or a schoolboy like us, his back to a door, a silent onlooker.

And it is there that everything began, about eight days before Christmas.

I HAUNTED A BASKET-MAKER'S SHOP

Rain had fallen all day; it did not stop till evening. The day had been deadly tedious. No one went out at recreation, and all the time M. Seurel could be heard calling to the form: 'Don't make such a row, boys!'

After the last recreation of the day or, as we called it, the last 'quarter,' M. Seurel, who for a while had been walking to and fro lost in thought, suddenly stopped, banged vigorously on the table with a ruler to put an end to the confused buzz with which the last hour of a boring day ends, and, in the attentive silence, asked: 'Who will drive to the station to-morrow with François to fetch Monsieur and Madame Charpentier?'

These were my grandparents; Grandfather Charpentier with his grey woollen burnous; an old man, a retired gamekeeper wearing a rabbit fur bonnet which he called his képi . . . Little boys knew him well. In the morning, to wash himself, he would draw a pail of water and slosh his face in the manner of old troopers, vaguely rubbing his small pointed beard. A group of children, hands behind backs, watched him with respectful curiosity . . . They also knew Grandma Charpentier, the small peasant woman and her knitted cap – as Millie never failed to bring her, at least once, into the infants' class.

Each year, a few days before Christmas, we were in the habit of going to the station to meet the 4.2 train which brought them. To come to us they had crossed the length of the 'départe-ment', dragging with them baskets full of chestnuts and other Christmas fare rolled up in napkins. The moment the two, muffled up, smiling, and rather shy, had crossed the threshold, we shut all doors on them, and a glorious week of happiness began for us all . . .

To drive them from the station I needed a steady fellow with me, one who would not upset us into a ditch, and yet a gay lad, too, because Grandfather Charpentier was pretty free with swear words and Grandma rather talkative.

In answer to M. Seurel's question a dozen voices called out together: 'Admiral Meaulnes! Admiral Meaulnes!' But M. Seurel pretended not to hear.

Then they shouted: 'Fromentin!' Others: 'Jasmin Delouche!'

The youngest, Roy, the boy who rode across the fields on a sow at full gallop, called out in a piercing voice: 'Can I go? Can I go?'

Dutremblay and Mouchebœuf rather shyly put up their hands.

I should have liked it to be Meaulnes. This little drive, in a donkey cart, would have become a more important event. He also longed for it, but remained scornfully silent. All the big boys seated themselves, as he did, on the table, the wrong way round, feet on the bench, as we used to do in times of rest or great rejoicing. Coffin, his overall rolled up round his belt, was hugging the iron pillar which supported the beam of the classroom and, in his excitement, was beginning to climb it.

But M. Seurel damped every one by saying: 'Good! I choose Mouchebœuf.' And each went back to his seat silently.

14

At four o'clock, in the big icy playground, hollowed into channels by the rain, I found myself alone with Meaulnes. Without speaking, we both stood looking at the shining village drying under the high wind. Soon little Coffin, wrapped in his hooded cloak and holding a piece of bread in his hand, came out of his home; walking close to the walls and whistling, he went straight for the door of the wheelwright. Meaulnes opened the big gate, hailed the boy, and a moment later the three of us were settled at the back of the hot red shop, across which icy gusts of wind swept. Coffin and I sat close to the forge fire, our muddy feet amongst the white shavings; Meaulnes, hands in pockets and silent, leaned against the leaf of the door. From time to time a village woman, stooping to brave the wind, passed by in the street on her return from the butcher, and we looked up to see who she was.

No one spoke. The blacksmith and his assistant – one blowing the bellows, the other beating the hot iron – threw big sharp shadows upon the wall . . . I recall that evening as one of the great evenings of my youth. I felt both pleasure and anxiety; I was afraid my companion would deprive me of the small happiness of driving to the station, yet, without daring to own it to myself, I expected some extraordinary scheme from him which would upset everything.

From time to time the peaceful and regular work of the forge momentarily paused. The smith let his hammer fall onto the anvil in a series of clear, strong blows. He held the piece of iron on which he had been working close to his leather apron and looked at it. Then, raising his head, he said to us, by way of taking an easy breath: 'Well, my lads! How goes it?'

His man kept his right hand high up on the chain of the bellows, put his left hand on his hip, looked at us with a smile.

Then the din of hard work began again.

During one of these pauses, we caught sight of Millie through the swinging door, as she passed in the high wind, closely wrapped in her shawl and laden with small parcels.

The blacksmith asked: 'I suppose Monsieur Charpentier will be coming soon?'

'To-morrow, with Grandmother,' said I. 'I am going to meet the 4:02 train.'

'In Fromentin's cart, eh!'

I replied at once: 'No, in Father Martin's.'

'Ah! then you won't be back in a hurry!'

Both he and his man began to laugh.

His man, to say something, remarked slowly: 'With Fromentin's mare you could have fetched them from Vierzon. There's an hour's wait there. It is fifteen kilometres from here. You could have got there and back afore Martin's donkey's harnessed.'

'Ah!' said the other, 'that mare has got some go in her, and surely Fromentin would gladly lend her.'

The conversation ended there. The forge, once again, became the place of sparks and din where each had his own thoughts.

But when the time had come to leave and I got up to attract Meaulnes' attention, he did not notice me at first. Leaning against the door, his head bent down in deep thought, he seemed absorbed in what had just been said. Seeing him thus lost in thought, looking as though across leagues of fog at these quiet folk at their work, I was reminded suddenly of that picture in 'Robinson Crusoe,' where the young Englishman is seen on the eve of his great adventure 'haunting the shop of a basket-maker'. . .

And I have often thought of it since.

16

THE ESCAPE

At two o'clock in the afternoon next day, in the centre of the freezing country, the form-room stands out clear as a ship on the ocean. There is no smell of brine or tar as on a boat, but of herrings fried on the stove and of the scorched woollens of the boys who, on coming back, got too close to the fire.

As the end of the year is drawing near, the exercise books for term examination have been given out. And while M. Seurel is setting problems on the board silence prevails, only disturbed by whispered conversations, or broken into by stifled exclamations and with sentences of which the first words alone are uttered to frighten one's neighbour: 'Sir! So and So is . . .'

M. Seurel, writing out the problems, is thinking of something else. From time to time he turns round and looks at us in a stern but vacant way. And this covert disturbance stops entirely for a moment, to begin again immediately, softly at first like a purr.

I alone keep quiet in the midst of this turmoil. I am sitting at the extreme end of one of the tables on the juniors' side and close to the high windows, and I need only raise myself a little to get a view of the garden, the stream at the lower end of it, and then the fields.

From time to time I stand on tiptoe and look anxiously towards the farm of the Fair Star. As soon as the class opened I had noticed that Meaulnes had not come back after the dinner hour. The boy next him certainly could not have failed to notice it too. Too busy with exam work he has not yet said anything. But as soon as he looks up the news will spread at once, and someone, as usual, will certainly call out, in a loud voice, the first words of the sentence: 'Sir! Meaulnes . . .'

I know that Meaulnes has gone. To be more exact I suspect him of having run away. As soon as dinner was over he must have jumped over the low wall, taken his course through the fields, and crossed the stream on the old plank for the Fair Star. He must have asked for the mare to go to the station for Monsieur and Madame Charpentier. They are harnessing her this very moment.

The Fair Star, on the other side of the stream, where the hill slopes down, is a large farm hidden from our view in the summer by the oaks and elms in its yard and also by quick-set hedges. It is situated in a little lane which joins the Station Road on one side and on the other an outlying district of the village. The big feudal building is surrounded by high walls, the buttresses of which stand in pools of manure. In the month of June it is buried in leafage, and from the school the rumbling of carts and the shouts of the cowherds alone can be heard at nightfall. But to-day, out of the window and between the stripped trees, I can see the tall grey wall of the farmyard, the entrance gate and then, through gaps in the hedge, a strip of road, white with frost, parallel to the stream and leading to the Station Road. Nothing moves yet in that clear wintry landscape. Nothing has yet changed.

In the classroom M. Seurel has almost finished writing out the second problem. Generally he set down three. If he only set two to-day . . . He would go back to his desk and notice the absence of Meaulnes. He would send two boys to look for him in the village and they would find him before the mare was harnessed . . .

M. Seurel, once the second problem is on the board, drops his tired arm. Then, to my great relief, he goes to the next line and begins to write again, saying:

'This one is only child's play!'

. . . Two little black streaks showing over the top of the wall at the Fair Star, certainly the upturned shafts of a cart, have now disappeared. I feel sure that over there everything is being made ready for Meaulnes' departure. Soon the head and the fore parts of the mare emerge between the posts of the gateway, then stop, while, no doubt, behind the cart, they are fixing a second seat for the travellers whom Meaulnes proposes to fetch. At last the complete equipage slowly comes out of the yard, disappears for a moment behind the hedge, and, going at the same slow pace, shows itself again on the strip of white road visible between breaks in the fence. Then I recognise, in the black figure holding the reins, one elbow lazily resting on the side of the cart in peasant fashion, my friend, Augustin Meaulnes.

A moment later everything disappears behind the hedge. Two men who have remained by the gate, looking at the departing cart, begin to converse with increasing liveliness. One of them at last decides to make a speaking-trumpet of his hands and to call after Meaulnes and then to run a few paces along the road in his direction. But then, in the cart, which slowly has reached the Station Road and can certainly no longer be seen from the lane, Meaulnes suddenly changes his attitude. Standing up like the driver of a Roman chariot, one foot resting on the front bar and both hands shaking the reins, he sets his beast going at a gallop and in a moment disappears on the other side of the slope. On the road the man who has been calling begins to run again, and the other, starting at full speed across the fields, seems to be coming towards us.

In a few minutes, just as M. Seurel having left the blackboard is rubbing the chalk off his hands and at the very moment when three voices call out together from the back of the classroom: 'Sir! Admiral Meaulnes has gone!' the man with the blue smock is at the door, which he suddenly throws wide open and lifting his hat asks from the doorstep: 'Excuse me, sir, is it you as sent that pupil to ask for the cart to drive to Vierzon to meet your parents? We began to suspect . . .'

'Certainly not!' replied M. Seurel.

And at once all the class is in frightful disorder. The three boys close to the door, whose usual job is to chase away with stones the goats or the pigs which stray in the playground and browse the March Pride, rush out. Following the loud clatter of their hobnailed clogs on the flagstones of the room are heard their muffled and hurried steps crushing the sand of the yard and skidding as they sharply turn by the little gate opening on the road. The other boys have crowded to the garden windows. Some have climbed on the table to see better . . .

But it is too late. Admiral Meaulnes has escaped.

'You will go to the station with Mouchebœuf all the same,' says M. Seurel to me. 'Meaulnes does not know the way to Vierzon. He will lose himself at the Cross-Roads. He will not meet the train at three.'

Millie pokes her head in at the door of the infants' classroom to ask: 'What on earth is the matter?'

In the village street people have begun to form groups. The peasant stands there, hat in hand, obstinate, motionless, like a man demanding justice.

THE CART COMES BACK

When I had brought home my grandparents from the station and after dinner, seated in front of the large hearth, they began to relate in full detail all that had happened to them since the last holidays, I soon realised that I was not listening.

The little gate of the playground was quite near the dining-room door. It used to squeak as it opened. Generally at nightfall, during the long country evenings, I sat secretly waiting for this squeaking of the gate. It was usually followed by the noise of clogs clattering or being wiped outside the door, and sometimes by whispers as of people making some plan before coming in. There was a knock. It was a neighbour, the women teachers . . . anyhow, some one who was coming to cheer us during these long hours.

But that evening I had nothing to hope for from outside, since all those I loved were met together in our house; and yet I continued to be alert to all the noises of the night and to wait for some one to open our door.

Old Grandfather was there, hairy and bushy in appearance like some big Gascon shepherd, his two feet firmly planted as he sat, his stick between his legs, and with the usual slant of his right shoulder when he stooped to tap the ashes from his pipe against his shoe. He was approving with his kind moist eyes what Grandmother was saying about their journey, their neighbours, and the peasants who had not yet paid their rent. But I was no longer with them.

I was imagining the rumbling of a cart which would suddenly stop at our door. Meaulnes would jump from it and walk

in as if nothing had happened . . . Or perhaps he had first gone
to take back the mare to the Fair Star, and I should soon hear
his step sounding on the road, and the gate opening . . .

But nothing happened. Grandfather was gazing fixedly in
front of him and his winking eyelids kept closing over his eyes
as at the approach of sleep. Grandmother awkwardly repeated
her last sentence, which no one was listening to.

'Is it about that boy that you are worried?' she said at last.

As a matter of fact, I had questioned her at the station to
no purpose. She had seen no one at Vierzon who might have
been Admiral Meaulnes. My friend must have been delayed on
the way. His attempt had failed. During our return journey I
had brooded over my disappointment, while Grandmother was
chatting with Mouchebœuf. On the road whitened with frost,
small birds had been fluttering around the hoofs of the trotting
donkey. From time to time above the stillness of the wintry
afternoon had arisen the far-away call of a farm girl or of a lad
hailing a comrade from one clump of firs to another, and each
time that long call over the desolate hills had made me shudder
as if it were the voice of Meaulnes inviting me to follow him
from afar . . .

While I was going over all this in my mind, bedtime came.
Already Grandfather had gone into the red room, the bed-
sitting-room so damp and icy cold from having been closed
since last winter. To make him at home the lace antimacassars
of the armchairs had been removed, the rugs folded up and all
the knick-knacks put away. He had placed his stick on a chair,
his thick shoes under an armchair, he had just put out his candle
and we were standing saying good-night, ready to retire to bed,
when the noise of a cart silenced us.

It almost sounded as if two vehicles slowly followed each
other at a very slow trot. The noise finally came to a stop under

the dining-room window which overlooked the road, but was never used.

Father had taken up the lamp and, without waiting, went to open the door which had already been locked. Then pushing open the gate, he walked to the edge of the steps and raised his light above his head to see what was happening.

Two carts had in fact stopped, the horse of one fastened behind the back of the other. A man had jumped down and was hesitating . . .

'Is this the town hall?' said he, coming near. 'Could you direct me to M. Fromentin, the farmer at the Fair Star? I have found his cart and mare without a driver, going along the lane, close to the road of Saint-Loup-des-Bois. I was able to read his name and address on the plate, with my lantern. As it was on my way, I brought back his trap round here to avoid accidents, but it has delayed me no end all the same.'

We stood there stupefied. Father approached and lit up the cart with his lamp.

'There were no traces of a driver,' went on the man. 'Not even a rug. The animal is tired and slightly lame.'

I had got quite at the front and, with the others, I was looking at this lost vehicle which had come back to us like wreckage washed ashore by the high tide—the first and perhaps the last wreckage of Meaulnes' adventure.

'If it's too far to Fromentin's,' said the man, 'I'll leave the cart with you. I've lost too much time already and they must be anxious at home.'

Father agreed. In this way we could take back the trap to the Fair Star that very evening without saying what had happened. Then we could decide what we were to tell the village people and to write to Meaulnes' mother . . . And the man whipped up his horse, refusing the glass of wine we offered.

23

As we were coming in without uttering a word and Father was leading the cart towards the farm, Grandfather, who had lit his candle again, called out from his room: 'Has that traveller come back then?'

The women consulted each other's faces by looks for a moment.

'Yes, he's been to his mother's. Go to sleep. Don't worry.'

'That's all right. Just what I thought,' said he.

And, reassured, he put out his light and turned over in bed to sleep.

That was the explanation which we gave to the village people. As to the mother of the runaway, it was decided to wait before writing to her. And during three long days we kept our anxiety to ourselves. I still see my father coming home from the farm towards eleven, his moustache damp with the evening mist, talking with Millie in a very low voice, anxious and angry . . .

SOME ONE KNOCKS AT THE WINDOW

The fourth day was one of the coldest of that winter. From early morning the first comers to the playground kept warm by sliding round the well. They were waiting for the stove to be lit to rush into the classroom.

Behind the front gate several of us waited for the arrival of the boys from the countryside farther off. They came with

eyes quite dazed from having crossed hoar-sparkling fields and looked on frozen ponds and coppices from which hares ran . . . Their overalls had a smell of hay and stables which made the air of the classrooms heavy, as they crowded round the red-hot stove. And that morning one of them had brought in a basket a frozen squirrel which he had found on the way. He tried, I remember, to hang up the long stiff animal by its claws to a pillar of the playground shelter . . .

Then the dull class-work of winter began.

A sharp knock on the window made us look up. Upright against the door we saw Admiral Meaulnes shaking off the frost from his overall before he came in, standing there head erect and as if dazzled with rapture!

The two boys of the bench nearest to the door hurried to open it: they had a little confabulation, which we did not hear, just outside, and at last the truant made up his mind to come into the school.

That breath of fresh air coming from the deserted playground, the bits of straw which could be seen clinging to Admiral Meaulnes' clothing, and above all the look he had of a traveller, tired, hungry, but thrilled by wonders, all gave us a strange feeling of pleasure and curiosity.

M. Seurel had come down the two steps of his desk where he had been giving us a dictation, and Meaulnes walked towards him looking aggressive. I recall how handsome he seemed to me then, that big friend of mine, in spite of his battered look and of his eyes reddened by nights spent, most likely, in the open.

He went up to the master's desk and said, in the assured voice of a man who brings news: 'I have come back, sir.'

'So I see,' replied M. Seurel, looking at him with curiosity . . . 'Go to your seat.'

The boy turned towards us, his back slightly bent, smiling in a mocking way, as do big unruly fellows when punished, and, catching hold of the end of the table with one hand, he let himself drop on his bench.

'You are going to take out a book and read as I tell you,' said the master – all heads were turned then towards Meaulnes – 'while the others finish their dictation.'

And the lesson went on as before. From time to time Admiral Meaulnes turned my way, then looked out of the windows from which the white garden was visible, downy and motionless, and the bare fields on which a crow sometimes descended. In the classroom the heat was heavy around the reddened stove. My friend settled himself to read, holding his head in his hands: twice I saw his eyelids close and I thought he was falling asleep.

'I'd like to go to bed, sir,' said he at last, half lifting his arm. 'I've not slept for three nights.'

'Then go!' said M. Seurel, anxious above all to avoid a scene.

We sat up, all of us, pens in the air, and sadly watched him go, his overall rumpled at the back and his shoes earthy.

How slow that morning was in passing! Towards mid-day we heard the traveller, upstairs in the attic, preparing to come down.

At dinner time I found him sitting by the fire near our puzzled grandparents, and as the clock struck twelve the boys, big and little, scattered over the snowclad playground, made off like shadows before the dining-room door.

Of that dinner I recall only a great silence and a great distress. Everything was icy; the oilcloth without a tablecloth, the cold wine in the glasses, the red flagstones under our feet. It had been decided to put no questions to the truant so as not to rouse him to revolt. And he availed himself of that truce to say not a word.

At last, dessert ended, and we two were able to make a dash for the playground. A school playground in the afternoon, with the snow trampled away by clogs . . . a playground black all round with drips from the roofs of the shelters . . . a playground thick with games and screams! Meaulnes and I pelted along by the school buildings. At once two or three fellows from the village left their game and ran up to us with shouts of joy; hands in pockets, scarves unloosed, and mud squirting from under their clogs. But my friend burst into the big classroom where I followed; he shut the glass door just in time to stop the rush of the fellows in pursuit. There was instant uproar loud and clear; glass panes shaken, clogs stamping on stone; one shove bent the iron bar holding the two leaves of the door; but Meaulnes had already turned the little key in the lock, at the risk of cutting himself on its broken ring.

We used to think it maddening to behave like that. In summer, fellows who were locked out in this way, would tear round at full speed into the garden and managed often to climb in at one of the windows, before you could shut them all. But it was then December and everything was shut up. For a little while the boys kept shoving against the door; they yelled insults at us; then, one by one, they turned tail and went off crestfallen, doing up their scarves as they went.

Only two boys were in the classroom, which smelt of chestnuts and sour wine, two sweepers who were shifting the tables. I went up to the stove to warm myself lazily till lessons time, while Meaulnes searched the master's desk and the lockers. He soon found a small atlas which he studied with eagerness as he stood on the platform, his elbows on the desk and his head in his hands.

I was just about to go up to him; I should have placed my hand on his shoulder and, no doubt, we should have followed together, on the map, the route which he had taken, when suddenly the door leading to the infants' room opened with a crash under a violent push, and Jasmin Delouche, followed by a village boy and three fellows from the neighbouring countryside, emerged with a shout of triumph. One of the windows in the infants' classroom had probably been half shut; they had pushed it open and jumped through.

Jasmin Delouche, although rather small, was one of the elder boys of the top form. He was very jealous of Admiral Meaulnes, though he pretended to be his friend. Before our boarder's arrival, Jasmin himself had been cock of the form. He had a pale, rather sallow face, and pomaded hair. He was the only son of widow Delouche, the innkeeper, and he played the man, trotting out with self-conceit what he had heard in the billiard-room and at the bar.

At his entry Meaulnes looked up frowning and called out to the boys, as they scrambled to the stove: 'So one can't have a minute's peace here!'

'If you don't like it, you should have stopped where you were,' said Jasmin Delouche, without looking up.

I think that Augustin was in that state when temper comes and gets you so that you cannot control it.

'Now then, you!' he said, a little pale, rising and shutting his book, 'get out of it!'

The other sneered.

'Oh!' he cried, 'because you ran away for three days, you think you are going to be boss now!' he went on, dragging in the others. 'A chap like you can't turn us out, I tell you that much!'

But Meaulnes was already on him. A scrap began; a wild

28

scrimmage; sleeves of overalls split and tore at the seams. Martin alone – one of the boys of the neighbourhood who had come with Jasmin – interfered.

'Leave him alone!' he called out, with quivering nostrils, shaking his head like a ram.

With a violent jerk Meaulnes threw him reeling, arms out, to the middle of the room; then gripping Delouche by the neck with one hand and opening the door with the other, he tried to throw him out. Jasmin clung to the tables and dragged his feet, making his hobnailed shoes grate on the flagstones, while Martin, having regained his balance, came back with measured steps, head forward and furious. Meaulnes let go Delouche to collar this idiot, and would soon have found himself in a fix if the door of the living-room had not partly opened. M. Seurel was seen standing there at the door, his back turned towards us, to finish, before he came in, a conversation he was having with some one . . .

At once the battle stopped. Some boys collected round the stove, none too proud of themselves, having, right to the end, avoided taking sides. Meaulnes sat down in his place, his sleeves undone and torn at the gathers.

As for Jasmin, purple in the face, during the few minutes before the ruler rapped for form-work to begin, he could be heard calling out: 'He can't stand anything now. He puts on side. Does he suppose we do not know where he's been!'

'You ass! I don't know myself,' replied Meaulnes, in the immediate silence.

Then, shrugging his shoulders and burying his head in his hands, he began to do his work.

THE SILK WAISTCOAT

Our room was, as I have said, a big attic – half attic, half room. The other rooms, meant for assistant masters, had windows; no one knows why ours was lighted only by a skylight. It was impossible to shut the door fast, as it scraped the floor. When we went up in the evening, sheltering with one hand the candle which the draughts of the big house threatened to blow out, every time we tried to shut this door and every time we had to give it up. And the whole night long we felt all round the silence of the three lumber-rooms penetrating our bedroom.

There we met again, Augustin and I, on the evening of that same winter day.

I swiftly took off all my clothes and threw them in a heap on a chair at the foot of my bed, but my companion, without saying a word, began to undress slowly. I watched him undress from the iron bed in which I already lay – looking through cretonne hangings adorned with a wine-stalk pattern. One moment he sat down on his low curtainless bed; the next he got up and paced to and fro as he undressed. The candle, which he had placed on a wicker table, the work of gipsies, threw his moving and gigantic shadow upon the wall.

Quite unlike me he was folding and arranging his school clothes in a bitter and distracted way, but with much care. I still see him drop his heavy belt on a chair, over the back of which he folded his black overall extremely creased and soiled, then take off a kind of dark blue tunic which he wore under his overall, and stooping with his back to me, spread the garment at the foot of his bed . . . But when he stood up again and turned to face me, I saw that in place of the brass button uniform waistcoat that should be under the tunic, he was wearing a queer silk waistcoat, cut very open and fastened by a row of small and closely set mother-of-pearl buttons.

It was a garment of fantastic charm, such as must have been worn by the young men who used to dance with our grandmothers, in the days of the dandies.

I distinctly recall, at that moment, the tall peasant boy, bareheaded – for he had carefully placed his cap on his other clothes – his face so young, so gallant, and already so firmly set. He was once more pacing the room when he began to unbutton this mysterious article of a costume which was not his. And it was strange to see him, in shirt-sleeves, with short trousers and muddy shoes, handling this waistcoat of a marquis.

He had no sooner touched it than, starting from his reverie, he turned his face towards me with a look of anxiety. I rather wanted to laugh. He smiled with me and his face brightened.

'What's that? Do tell me,' I said in a low voice, emboldened. 'Where did you get it?'

But his smile vanished at once. Twice, with his heavy hand, he brushed back his closely cropped hair, and suddenly, like a man unable to resist desire, slipped his tunic back over the dainty jabot, buttoned it up tightly, and slipped on his rumpled overall; then he hesitated a moment, looking at me sideways . . . Finally he sat on the edge of his bed, took off his shoes, which fell noisily onto the floor, stretched himself on the bed, fully dressed like a soldier ready for the fray, and blew out the candle.

About midnight I woke up suddenly. Meaulnes was standing in the middle of the room, his cap on his head, and was looking for something on one of the pegs – a cloak which he threw on

31

his back . . . The room was very dark. Not even that gleam of light which snow sometimes gives. A black and icy wind was blowing in the garden and over the roof.

I raised myself a little and called to him softly: 'Meaulnes! Are you going away again?' He did not reply. Then, quite beside myself, I said: 'Very well, I shall go with you. You must take me.' And I jumped out of bed.

He came close to me, took hold of my arm, forcing me to sit on the edge of the bed, and said to me: 'I can't take you, François. If I knew my way well, you should come with me. But I must first of all find it on the map, and I can't.'

'Then you can't go either!'

'That's true. It's utterly useless,' he said, discouraged. 'Well, go back to bed. I promise not to go without you.'

And he again began to pace to and fro in the room. I dared say nothing more. He kept walking, stopping and then setting off again more quickly like a man in search of memories which he sorts out, challenges and compares, ponders on, thinks he has discovered, and then the thread breaking the search begins once more . . .

That was not the only night on which, awakened by the sound of his steps, I found him thus, about one in the morning, treading the attic and lumber-rooms, as do sailors who cannot lose the habit of pacing the deck on night watch and who, in the quiet of their Breton holding, get up and dress of a night, at the regulation hour, to keep a land watch.

Two or three times, during the month of January and the first fortnight of February, I was roused out of my sleep in that way. Admiral Meaulnes was there, on foot, all equipped, his cloak on his back, ready to start, and every time, on the edge of that mysterious country into which he once already had ventured, he stopped, he hesitated. At the moment of lifting

the latch of the door to the stairs and of slipping off by the kitchen door, which he could easily have opened without being heard, he would shrink back once more . . . Then, during the long midnight hours he paced feverishly the disused lumber-rooms, lost in thought.

At last one night, towards the fifteenth of February, he woke me up by gently placing his hand on my shoulder.

The day had been very disturbed. Meaulnes, who had now entirely dropped out of all the games of his former comrades, had remained seated at his bench during the last recreation of the evening, busily sketching out a mysterious plan, following it with his finger and elaborately measuring it out on the atlas of the Cher. There was an incessant going and coming between the playground and the classroom. Clogs kept clattering. Boys chased one another from table to table, taking benches and plat-form at a jump . . . Every one knew that it was not wise to come near Meaulnes when he was working thus; yet, as recreation continued past regulation time, two or three boys from the village advanced towards him for a joke, without any noise, and looked over his shoulder. One of them was bold enough to push the others on top of Meaulnes . . . The latter hastily closed his atlas, hid his sheet of paper, and caught hold of the last of the three boys while the other two managed to escape.

It was that surly Giraudat, who began to whine, tried to kick, and at last was pushed out of doors by Admiral Meaulnes, to whom he shouted in a rage: 'You great coward! No wonder they are all against you and want to make war on you! . . .' and a lot of insults, to which we replied without having quite under-stood what he meant. I was the one to shout the loudest, because I had sided with Admiral Meaulnes.

There was now a kind of pact between us. The promise

which he had given to take me with him, instead of saying, like everybody else, that I should not be able to stand the walking, had bound me to him forever. And I never ceased thinking of his mysterious journey. I had become convinced that he must have met a girl. She, no doubt, was infinitely more beautiful than Jeanne, who could be seen in the nuns' garden by looking through the keyhole; or Madeleine, the baker's daughter, so pink and so fair; or Jenny, the daughter of the lady of the manor, so handsome, but insane and living in seclusion. It was certainly of a young girl he was thinking at night, like the hero of a novel. And I bravely decided to speak to him about it the first time he wakened me . . .

After four o'clock, on the evening of that new fight, we were both busy putting away garden tools, pickaxes, and spades which had been used to dig trenches, when we heard shouts on the road. It was a troop of young boys and urchins, formed in fours, marching quickly like a well-drilled squad, led by Delouche, Daniel, Giraudat, and another whom we did not know. They had spotted us and hooted like anything. So all the village was against us, and some fresh soldier stunt, from which we were excluded, was being planned.

Meaulnes, without saying anything, put away in the shed the pickaxe and the spade which he had on his shoulder. But at midnight I felt his hand on my arm, and I woke up with a start.

'Get up,' he said, 'we are going.'

'Do you know the right way to the very end?'

'I know a good part of it. And we shall have to find the rest,' he replied, with clenched teeth.

'Listen, Meaulnes,' I said, sitting up, 'listen to me; there's only one thing to be done! – and that is to look for the bit of the way we don't know in full daylight with the help of your map.'

'But that bit is far away from here.'

'All right, we'll drive there this summer, when the days are longer.'

There was a prolonged silence, which meant that he agreed.

'As we shall try together to find again the girl you love, Meaulnes,' I said at last, 'tell me who she is, talk to me about her.'

He sat down at the foot of my bed. I could see in the darkness his lowered head, his folded arms and his knees. Then he took a deep breath, as some one who has had a weight upon his heart for a long time and who is, at last, going to tell his secret . . .

THE ADVENTURE

My friend did not tell me that night all that had happened to him on the way. And even when he decided to confide everything to me, during days of anguish of which I shall speak later, it remained for a long time the great secret of our youth. But to-day when all is ended, and there remains only dust of so much good and so much evil, I can relate his strange adventure.

At half-past one in the afternoon on the Vierzon road, during that freezing weather, Meaulnes set his beast at a brisk pace, because he knew he was late. At first he thought, with amusement, only of our surprise when, at four o'clock, he brought back Grandfather and Grandmother Charpentier. For certainly, at that moment, he had no other intention.

35

Little by little, the cold being piercing, he wrapped his legs in a rug, which at first he had refused, but which the folk at the Fair Star had thrown into the cart.

At two o'clock he passed through the village of La Motte. He had never gone through a small hamlet at school-time and was amused to see this one so empty, so asleep. Here and there a curtain was moved, revealing the inquisitive face of a housewife.

Leaving La Motte, immediately after the schoolhouse, he hesitated between two roads, but seemed to remember that the left road led to Vierzon. Nobody was there to tell him. He once more put the mare to a trot, though the road became narrower and badly in need of repair. He skirted a fir wood for some time, but at last, meeting a carter, he used his hands as a trumpet to inquire if he really were on the right road for Vierzon. The mare pulled on the reins, without stopping her trot; the man must have failed to understand the inquiry; he called out something with a vague gesture, so Meaulnes chanced it and went on.

Once more there was the vast frozen plain without incident or distraction; only at times a magpie startled by the cart flew off to perch on a stunted elm in the distance. The traveller had wrapped the big rug round his shoulders like a cloak. He must have dozed for a long while with his legs stretched out and one elbow resting on the side of the cart . . .

. . . When Meaulnes recovered his wits, thanks to the cold penetrating the rug, he noticed a change in the countryside. There was no longer the far horizon, no longer that stretch of pale sky in which sight was lost, but little meadows, still green, with high hedges. On both sides water flowed under the ice in the ditches. Everything showed the neighbourhood of a river. And the road between the tall hedges was nothing more than a narrow rutted lane.

36

A moment before the mare had stopped trotting, Meaulnes tried to whip her up to the same pace again, but she persisted in walking with extreme slowness, and the big schoolboy, leaning forward, his hands resting on the dashboard, noticed that she was lame in one hind leg. He was much troubled and at once jumped out.

'We shall never reach Vierzon in time for the train,' he said half aloud.

And he did not dare to own to himself the thought which upset him most, that perhaps he had lost his way and was no longer on the road to Vierzon.

For a long time he examined the beast's foot and could find no trace of a wound. The mare was frightened and lifted her foot directly Meaulnes tried to touch it, pawing the ground with her heavy clumsy hoof. At last he realised that she had simply got a stone in her shoe. As a boy who was expert in the handling of beasts he sat on his heels and tried to grasp her right foot with his left hand and put it between his knees, but he was bothered by the cart. Twice the mare got away and went on a few yards. The step struck his head and the wheel hurt his knee. He would not give in and ended by mastering the timid beast, but the stone was so embedded that Meaulnes was obliged to use his peasant's knife before he could get it out.

When he had finished the job and at last looked up, rather giddy and dim-eyed, he noticed with horror that night was falling . . .

Any one else but Meaulnes would immediately have turned back. That was the only way not to get more badly lost. But he reflected that he must be very far from La Motte. Besides, the mare might have taken a byway while he was asleep. Anyhow, this lane must lead to some village in time . . .

In addition to all these reasons, the big boy, with his foot

on the step and the mare already pulling on the reins, ached
with exasperation to achieve something and to get somewhere,
in defiance of every obstacle!

He whipped up the mare, who started and set off at a quick
trot. The darkness grew. In the deep-cut lane there was now
only just room for the cart. Sometimes a dead branch from the
hedge caught in the wheel and broke with a snap . . . When it
was pitch dark Meaulnes thought suddenly with a pang of our
dining-room at Sainte-Agathe in which, by this time, all of us
ought to be together. Then rage took him; then pride and the
deep joy of having at last run away without premeditation . . .

A HALT

Suddenly the mare slowed down as if her foot had stumbled
in the dark; Meaulnes saw her head sink and rise twice; then
she stopped dead, her nostrils close to the ground, appearing
to sniff at something. The trickle of water could be heard by
her feet. A stream barred the way. In summer that spot was
certainly a ford. But at this time of the year the current was
so strong that ice had not formed and it would have been
dangerous to push on.

Meaulnes gently pulled on the reins to go back a few yards
and stood up in the cart full of perplexity. It was then that
he noticed a light between the branches. Only two or three
meadows seemed to separate it from the lane . . .

The schoolboy jumped down from the cart and backed the mare, talking to her to quiet her and to stop the frightened tossing of her head.

'Come on, old girl, come on. We shan't go any farther now. We shall soon know where we've got to.'

And pushing open the half-shut gate of a small meadow by the lane, he went through with the trap. His feet sank deep into the soft grass. The cart jolted silently. His head was by the mare's head and he could feel her warmth and her hard breathing . . .

He took her to the far end of the meadow and threw the rug over her back; then thrusting aside the branches of the hedge, he again noticed the light which came from an isolated house.

None the less he had to cross three meadows and jump over a treacherous brook into which he nearly fell with both feet . . . At last, after a final leap from the top of a bank, he found himself in the yard of a rustic farm. A pig was grunting in its sty. At the noise of footsteps on the frozen ground a dog began to bark furiously.

The shutter over the door was open, and the light which Meaulnes had seen came from a wood fire burning on the hearth. There was no other light but that of the fire. In the house, a country woman rose from a chair and came to the door, with no sign of fear. At the same moment the grandfather clock struck half-past seven.

'Excuse me, ma'am,' said the big boy, 'I believe I have trodden on your chrysanthemums.'

She waited, basin in hand, looking at him.

'The fact is,' she said, 'it's that dark in the yard you can't see your way.'

There was a moment's silence, during which Meaulnes stood

39

looking at walls papered with pages out of illustrated papers, as they are in inns, and at the table on which lay a man's hat.

'He's not in, the boss,' he said, sitting down.

'He'll be back in a moment,' she replied, quite at her ease now, 'he's gone to fetch wood.'

'I don't exactly want him,' went on the young fellow, bringing his chair nearer to the fire, 'but out there a few of us – sportsmen, you know – are keeping a lookout. I came to ask if you could spare us a little bread.'

Admiral Meaulnes knew quite well that with country folk, above all in an isolated farm, one must speak with caution, even with diplomacy, and above all never show that one does not belong to the district.

'Bread,' said she, 'we shan't be able to give you much. The baker who always calls on a Tuesday hasn't come to-day . . .'

Augustin, who for a moment had hoped he was near a village, took fright.

'The baker, from where?' he asked.

'Why, of course, the baker from Vieux-Nançay,' replied the woman, astonished.

'How far is it exactly from here to Vieux-Nançay?' went on Meaulnes, very anxious.

'By the road I couldn't tell exactly; but by the short cut it is three leagues off.'

And she began to relate that her daughter was there in service, that she always walked all the way home on the first Sunday of the month, and that her master and mistress . . .

But Meaulnes, completely put out, interrupted her to say: 'Vieux-Nançay, would that be the nearest village from here?'

'No, the nearest is Les Landes, five kilometres off here. But

there are no shops and no baker at Landes, only just a small fair each year on Saint Martin's Day.'

Meaulnes had never heard of Les Landes. He saw himself so much lost that he was almost tickled. But the woman, busy at the sink washing her basin, turned round, inquisitive in her turn, and said slowly, looking at him quite straight: 'Don't you, then, belong to these parts? . . .'

At that moment an elderly peasant appeared at the door, carrying an armful of wood, which he threw on the stone floor. The woman explained to him, in a very loud voice, as if he were deaf, what was required by the young man.

'Well, that's easy,' said he simply. 'But come nearer, you're getting no warmth from the fire.'

A moment later both were settled by the hearth; the old man breaking his wood to put on the fire, Meaulnes enjoying a bowl of milk and some bread which had been offered him. Our traveller, delighted at finding himself in that humble dwelling after so many worries, and thinking that an end had come to his strange adventure, was already making plans for bringing friends with him in the future, to visit these kind people. He did not know that this was only a halt, and that presently he was to resume his journey.

He soon asked to be shown the road to La Motte. And, little by little, coming back to the truth, he related that he had been cut off, with his cart, from the other guns and now found himself completely lost.

Then the man and the woman insisted so much on his putting up at the farm and not starting before broad daylight, that Meaulnes in the end accepted, and walked out to fetch his mare and put her up in the stable.

'Mind holes in the path,' said the man.

Meaulnes dared not confess that he had not used 'the path.'

He nearly brought himself to ask if the good fellow could come with him. For a second he hesitated on the threshold and so great was his indecision that he almost staggered. But he went out into the gloom of the yard.

THE SHEEPFOLD

To find where he was he climbed on the bank from which he had jumped.

Slowly and with difficulty, as when he came, he made his way between swamps, through willow hedges, and went to fetch his cart at the farther end of the field where he had left it. The cart was no longer there. Standing still, with throbbing temples, he strained hard to catch all the sounds of the night, sure that he heard, each moment, the jingle of the horse's collar close at hand. Nothing . . . He went all round the meadow; the gate was partly open, partly dilapidated as if a cart wheel had passed over it. The mare must have escaped that way, alone.

Turning back, he walked a little way and caught his feet in the rug which no doubt had slipped from the mare onto the ground. This decided him that the beast had gone off in that direction. He started to run.

Obsessed by the obstinate and insane resolve to overtake the cart, his face on fire, a prey to this panic wish, which resembled fear, he went on running . . . Sometimes he stumbled in a rut. In the utter darkness he ran into hedges when the lane turned, and too tired to stop in time he crashed into brambles, his arms stretched out, his hands torn in the effort to protect his face. Sometimes he stopped and listened and went on again. Once he thought he heard a cart, but it was only a jolting wagon going along a road, in the far distance on the left . . .

Came a time when the knee which he had grazed against the step of the cart hurt so much that he had to stop, his leg quite stiff. Then he realised that unless the mare had run off at a quick gallop, he would long ago have caught her up. He told himself, too, that a cart could not get lost in that way, and that some one would surely find it. At last he retraced his steps, worn out, scarcely able to drag himself along.

After a while he believed that he was again in the neighbourhood of the place he had left, and soon he noticed the light of the house he was looking for. A path opened in the hedge.

'That's the path the old man spoke of,' thought Augustin.

And he entered this passage, glad to have no more hedges and banks to get over. Next moment, the path turning to the left, the light appeared to slip to the right, and Meaulnes reaching a cross-road, in his hurry to regain the poor lodging, without thinking took a path which seemed to lead straight there. But he had hardly walked ten steps along it when the light disappeared, either because the hedge was hiding it, or else because the peasants were tired of waiting and had closed their shutters. Bravely the schoolboy took to the fields and made for the place where the light had just been shining. Then, leaping once more over a hedge, he landed on a new path . . .

Thus, little by little, Admiral Meaulnes' trail was tangled and

43

the thread broke which was connecting him with those he had left.

Discouraged, almost exhausted, in despair he resolved to follow this path right to the end. A hundred yards farther he emerged into a vast grey meadow, where here and there he could distinguish shadows appearing to be juniper trees and a dark shed in a fold of the ground. Meaulnes drew near. It was only a kind of large cattle pen or forsaken sheepfold. The door yielded with a groan. The light of the moon came through chinks in the woodwork, when the high wind chased the clouds.

Without searching farther, Meaulnes stretched himself on the damp straw, one elbow on the ground, his head on his hand. Having removed his belt he curled up, knees bent in his overall. He then thought of the mare's rug which he had left in the lane and felt so wretched and so cross with himself that he had a strong desire to cry . . .

So he forced himself to think of something else. Frozen to the bone, he recalled a dream – or rather a vision which he had had when quite a child and of which he had never spoken to any one; one morning, instead of waking up in his room where his trousers and coat were hanging, he had found himself in a long green room with walls like foliage. The light streaming into this place was so sweet that you could simply taste it. Close to the first window a young girl was sewing with her back to him; she seemed to be waiting for him to wake. He had not had strength to creep out of bed into this enchanted dwelling. He had fallen asleep again. But next time he swore he would get up. To-morrow morning, perhaps! . . .

THE MYSTERIOUS MANOR

At dawn he began to walk again. But his swollen knee hurt him; he had to stop and sit down every moment, the pain was so sharp. The place where he was happened to be the most desolate in Sologne. During all the morning he saw, in the distance, only a farm girl bringing in her flock. In vain he called to her and tried to run; she disappeared without hearing him.

Nevertheless he went on walking in her direction with a distressing slowness . . . Not a roof, not a soul. Not even the cry of a curlew in the reeds of the marshes. And above this complete solitude shone a December sun, clear and icy.

It might have been three o'clock in the afternoon when he noticed at last, above a fir wood, the spire of a grey turret.

'Some old forsaken manor,' thought he; 'some deserted dovecot!'

And without hurrying he went on his way. At the corner of the wood, in between two white posts, appeared a drive which Meaulnes entered. He walked up a few yards and stopped startled, disturbed by inexplicable feelings. He walked with the same fatigue, the icy wind cut his lips and took his breath away, and yet a strange contentment urged him on, a perfect and almost intoxicating peace, the assurance that his goal had been reached and that he had now nothing but happiness to expect. In the same way he once used to feel faint with excitement on the eve of great summer festivals, when fir trees, whose branches overshadowed his bedroom window, were set up at nightfall along the village streets.

'So much joy,' he said to himself, 'just because I am coming to this old dovecot full of owls and draughts! . . .'

And angry with himself he stopped, wondering if it would be better to turn back and go on to the next village. He had been thinking thus for a while, with head lowered, when he suddenly noticed that the drive had been swept clean in big regular circles as was usual at his home at festival time. He was really in a lane which looked like the High Street of La Ferté on the morning of Assumption Day! . . . Had he noticed at the bend of the drive a crowd of holiday-makers raising up the dust as in the month of June, he could not have been more surprised.

'Would there be a fête in this lonely spot?' he said to himself.

Advancing as far as the first bend, he heard the sound of approaching voices. He stepped behind some bushy young firs, crouched and listened, holding his breath. They were childish voices. A group of children passed close to him. One of them, probably a little girl, was speaking in a way so wise and so decided that Meaulnes, although he hardly caught the sense of her words, could not help smiling.

'One thing alone worries me,' she was saying, 'that is the question of the horses. No one will ever prevent Daniel riding on the big bay pony.'

'No one will ever prevent me!' replied the mocking voice of a young boy; 'are we not allowed to do just as we please? . . . Even hurting ourselves, if we like . . .'

And the voices grew distant as another group of children approached.

'If the ice thaws,' said a little girl, 'to-morrow morning we shall go boating.'

'But shall we be allowed?' said another.

'You know very well that we are arranging things in our own way.'

46

'But suppose Frantz was to come back this very evening with his fiancée?'

'Well! he would do as we wish! . . .'

'No doubt a wedding,' thought Augustin. 'But the children lay down the law here! . . . Strange land!'

He wanted to come out of his hiding-place and ask them where he could find something to eat and drink. He stood up and saw the last group going away. There were three little girls with pinafore dresses reaching to their knees. They wore pretty hats with strings. Down the neck of each hung a white feather. One of them, half turning round and slightly leaning towards her friend, was listening to long explanations the other was giving with one finger raised.

'I should frighten them,' thought Meaulnes, looking at his ragged peasant overall and the queer belt of the schoolboys at Sainte-Agathe.

Fearing that the children would meet him on their way back along the drive, he passed on through the firs in the direction of the 'dovecot,' without considering at all what he could ask for there. He was soon stopped at the edge of the wood by a low mossy wall. On the other side, in between the wall and the outhouses of the estate, was a long narrow courtyard as full of carriages as the yard of an inn on the day of a fair. These carriages were of all kinds and shapes: some elegant and small four-seaters with their shafts up in the air; wagonettes; coaches quite out of date with their moulded cornices, and even some old berlins with windows raised.

Meaulnes, hidden behind the firs for fear of being seen, was examining the disorder of the place when he noticed, on the other side of the yard, just above the driver's seat of a tall wagonette, a window in one of the outhouses, half open. Two

47

iron bars, such as are often seen on stable shutters behind old manors, were meant to close this aperture, but time had loosened them.

'I will go in through there,' thought the schoolboy. 'I shall sleep in the hay and leave at daybreak without having frightened these lovely little girls.'

He climbed over the wall, painfully because of his wounded knee, and jumping from one carriage to another, from the coachman's box of a wagonette to the roof of a berlin, he hauled himself up to the window, which noiselessly opened under his push, like a door.

He found himself, not in a hayloft, but in a big room with low ceiling, which must have been a bedroom. In the winter twilight one could make out that the table, the mantelpiece, and even the armchairs were covered with tall vases, objects of value, ancient weapons. At the other end of the room hung curtains to conceal an alcove.

Meaulnes had closed the window, both because of the cold and for fear of being seen from outside. He went to raise the curtains at the back of the room and disclosed a big low bed covered with old gilded books, lutes with broken strings, and chandeliers all thrown in a heap. He pushed all these things to the back of the alcove, then stretched himself on this couch to rest and to ponder over the strange adventure which had befallen him.

A deep silence reigned over this domain. Only at intervals the moaning of the high December wind could be heard.

And Meaulnes, stretched out, began to wonder if in spite of these strange meetings, in spite of the voices of the children in the drive, in spite of the carriages huddled together, the place was not simply, as he had thought at first, an old disused building in the winter wilderness.

48

Soon the wind seemed to bring him the sound of distant music. It was like a memory full of charm and of regret. He recalled the days when his mother, still young, used to come in the afternoon, and sit at the drawing-room piano and he, silently, from behind the door leading to the garden, listened to her until night . . .

'Surely it seems as if some one were playing the piano somewhere?' he thought.

But leaving his question without an answer, worn out with fatigue, he was soon asleep . . .

WELLINGTON'S ROOM

It was night when he awoke. Chilled with cold he turned from side to side in his bed, crumpling and rolling his black overall under him. A faint yellow light bathed the curtains of the alcove.

Sitting up on the bed he pushed his head between the curtains. Some one had opened the window and had hung two green Chinese lanterns in the aperture.

But Meaulnes had scarcely time for one look around before he heard soft footsteps on the landing and whispers. He started back into the alcove and his hobnailed shoes rang against one of the bronze ornaments which he had pushed close to the wall.

For an instant he held his breath in anxiety. The footsteps were approaching and two shadows glided into the room.

49

'Don't make any noise,' said one.

'Well!' replied the other, 'it's high time he woke up!'

'Got his room ready?'

'Of course, just like the others.'

The wind made the window swing.

'Look,' said the first, 'you didn't even shut the window. The wind has blown out one of the lanterns already. We shall have to light it again.'

'Bah!' replied the other, suddenly lazy and discouraged, 'what's the good of these illuminations on the countryside, the desert side so to say? There is nobody to see them!'

'Nobody? But more people will be coming most of the night. Down there, on the road, in their carriages, they will be glad to see our lights!'

Meaulnes heard a match struck. The one who had spoken last, and who appeared to be the leader, went on in a drawling voice, like a gravedigger in Shakespeare:

'You are putting up green lanterns in the Wellington room. You would just as soon put red ... You know no more about it than I do!'

Silence.

'... Wellington, he was an American chap? Well! Is green an American colour? You're the travelled comedian, you ought to know that.'

'Oh! Come off it!' replied the 'comedian.' 'Me, travelled? Oh, yes! I have travelled! But I've seen nothing! What can you see in a caravan?'

Meaulnes looked between the curtains with caution.

The manager was a fat bareheaded man, buried in a huge overcoat. He held in his hand a long pole hung with lanterns of many colours, and with his legs crossed he quietly watched his companion work.

50

As for the comedian, he had the most woeful body imaginable. Thin, tall, and shivering, with squinting greenish eyes, a moustache drooping over a toothless mouth, he called to mind the streaming face of a drowned man stretched on a slab. He was in his shirt-sleeves and his jaws chattered. He displayed in speech and gesture absolute contempt for his own person.

After a moment given to thought – both pitiful and laughable – with arms outstretched, he approached his partner and confided to him:

'Shall I tell you what? . . . I can't understand why they should have fetched rotters like us to help in such a fête! Got that, my lad? . . .'

Disregarding this outburst of emotion, the fat man continued to watch the work with his legs crossed, yawned, quietly sniffed, and then turning his back went away with the pole on his shoulder, saying: 'Come on! It's time to dress for dinner.'

The bohemian followed him, but as he passed in front of the alcove:

'Sir Sleeper!' said he, with courtly bows and a clown's diction, 'it's up to you now to wake up and dress like a marquis even though you're only a pot-boy like me, and you will descend to the fancy-dress ball, since that is the good pleasure of these little gentlemen and of these little ladies.'

He added, in the tone of a quack at a fair, with a final bow: 'Our friend Maloyau, of the kitchen department, will present the character of Harlequin and your humble servant that of tall Pierrot . . .'

THE STRANGE FESTIVAL

As soon as they had disappeared, the schoolboy came out of his hiding-place. His feet were frozen, his joints stiff, but he was rested and his knee seemed healed.

'Come down to dinner?' thought he, 'I certainly shall. I shall simply be a guest whose name every one has forgotten. Besides, I am not an intruder here. It is quite clear that M. Maloyau and his companion were expecting me . . .'

Coming out of the absolute darkness of the alcove, he managed to see fairly well about the room, by the light of the green lantern.

The bohemian had 'decorated' it. Cloaks had been hung from curtain hooks. On a heavy dressing-table, with its broken marble top, was displayed all that was necessary to transform into a beau any lad who might have spent the previous night in a forsaken sheepfold. A matchbox lay on the mantelpiece by the side of a tall candlestick. But they had neglected to polish the floor, and Meaulnes was aware of sand and rubbish under his shoes. Again he had the impression of being in a house which had been disused for a long time. Going towards the fireplace he nearly stumbled over a pile of cardboard boxes large and small; he reached out an arm, lit the candle, then lifted the lids of the boxes and stooped down to look.

He found young men's costumes of days long gone by, frock coats with high velvet collars, dainty waistcoats cut very open, interminable white cravats, and patent-leather shoes dating from the beginning of the century. He dared not touch a thing even with his finger-tips; but shivering as he cleaned himself, he put one of the long cloaks over his schoolboy overall and raised its

pleated collar; he changed his hobnailed shoes for elegant pumps and prepared to go downstairs bareheaded.

He reached the bottom of a wooden staircase in a dark corner of the yard, without meeting any one. The icy night air blew on his face and raised one side of his cloak.

He took a few steps and thanks to the faint clearness of the sky he was at once able to get an idea of his surroundings. He was in a little yard formed by outhouse buildings. Everything appeared old and ruined. Gaps yawned at the bottom of the staircase, for the doors had long since been removed; nor had the panes been replaced in the windows, which made black holes in the walls. Yet all these buildings had a mysterious holiday aspect. A coloured reflection hovered about in the low rooms, where also lanterns must have been lit looking on the countryside. The ground had been swept, invading weeds pulled up. Meaulnes, listening, thought he heard something like a song, like children's and young girls' voices down there towards the shadowy buildings where the wind shook the branches in front of the pink, green, and blue opening of the windows.

There he was, in his long cloak, like a hunter, stooping to listen, when an extraordinary little fellow came out of a neighbouring building any one would have thought deserted.

This little fellow wore a top hat very much curved in, which shone in the night as if made of silver, a frock coat with its collar reaching his hair, a low-cut waistcoat, and peg-top trousers . . . This dandy, who might have been fifteen, was walking on tiptoe as though lifted up by the elastic straps of his trousers, but very swiftly.

He greeted Meaulnes as they met without stopping, automatically bowing low, and disappeared in the darkness in the direction of the central building, farm, castle, or abbey, the turret of which had guided the schoolboy early in the afternoon.

After a moment's hesitation, our hero followed in the wake of the strange little personage. They crossed a wide open space, half garden, half yard, passed in between clumps of bushes, went around a fenced fish-pond, then a well, and found themselves at last at the entrance of the central building.

A heavy wooden door, rounded at the top and studded with nails like a church door, was half open. The dandy hurried in; Meaulnes followed him and from his first steps in the corridor, he found himself, without seeing any one, in the midst of laughter, songs, shouts, and chases.

A passage ran across the end of the corridor. Meaulnes was hesitating whether to push on to the end or open one of the doors behind which he could hear voices, when he saw two little girls, at the end, chasing each other. He ran to see them and catch them up, moving noiselessly in his pumps. A sound of opening doors, two faces of fifteen which the freshness of the evening and the chase had made quite rosy under their poke bonnets, and everything disappeared in a sudden glare of light.

For an instant they twirled round in fun, their wide light skirts rose and bellied up; one could see the lace of their long quaint drawers; then, after this pirouette, they bounced into the room together and shut the door again.

Meaulnes remained for a moment dazed and staggering in this dark corridor. He now feared to be discovered. His clumsy and hesitating gait might lead him to be mistaken for a thief. He deliberately retraced his steps towards the front door, when again he heard a sound of steps and children's voices at the end of the corridor. Two little boys were talking as they approached.

'Will dinner be ready soon?' Meaulnes asked them with assurance.

'Come with us,' replied the bigger of the two, 'we'll take you in.'

And with that ease and need of friendliness which children have before a great party, they each took hold of one of Meaulnes' hands. Most likely they were two little peasant boys. They had been dressed in their best clothes: short knickers above the knees, which showed their thick woollen stockings and their heavy boots, a small blue velvet jacket, a cap of the same colour, and a white necktie.

'Do *you* know her?' asked one of the children.

'Me,' said the smaller one, who had a round head and naïve eyes; 'Mummy says that she had a black dress and a round collar and that she looked like a pretty Pierrot.'

'Whom do you mean?' asked Meaulnes.

'Why! Frantz's fiancée, whom he has gone to fetch . . .'

Before Meaulnes could say anything, the three of them reached the door of a large room where a big fire was burning. For table, boards had been placed on trestles; white tablecloths had been spread and people of all kinds were dining with ceremony.

THE STRANGE FESTIVAL
(*continued*)

It was a meal spread in a great room with a low ceiling, like those offered on the eve of a country wedding to relatives who had come from a distance.

The two children had let go the schoolboy's hands and had

rushed into an adjoining room from whence could be heard childish voices and the clatter of spoons on plates. Meaulnes climbed over a bench boldly and calmly and found himself seated beside two old peasant women. He at once began to eat with fierce appetite; and only after a while did he raise his head to look at other guests and listen.

Little, as a matter of fact, was being said. These folk seemed but slightly acquainted. They must have come, some from far off in the country, others from distant towns. Scattered about along the tables were some old men with side whiskers and others clean-shaven, who might have been old sailors. Dining near them other old men looked very much like the first: the same tanned faces, the same sharp eyes under bushy eyebrows, the same narrow ties like shoestrings. But it was easy to see that these had never voyaged farther than the other end of the parish, and if they had been tossed and beaten by winds and storms it had occurred on that rough yet undangerous voyage in cutting the furrow to the field end and guiding back the plough. Few women were to be seen; only some old peasants with round faces as wrinkled as apples under their goffered caps.

With every one of these guests Meaulnes felt confident and at ease. Later he came to explain that feeling by saying: If you have ever done something unpardonable you sometimes think, in the midst of much bitterness: 'Yet there are people in the world who would forgive me.' You imagine old people, in-dulgent grandparents, who are, beforehand, certain that all you do is well done. Undoubtedly the guests in the hall had been chosen from good folk of that kind; the rest were young people and children.

Meanwhile, two old women were chatting close to Meaulnes.

'Even if all is for the best,' said the elder, in a very shrill comi-

cal voice which she vainly tried to soften, 'the lovers will not be here before three o'clock to-morrow.'

'Be quiet! or you'll make me angry,' replied the other in the most peaceful manner.

She was wearing over her forehead a knitted hood.

'Let's work it out!' replied the first, undisturbed. 'An hour and a half by train from Bourges to Vierzon and seven leagues by coach from Vierzon here . . .'

The talk went on. Meaulnes lost not a word. This friendly squabble helped to clear matters up a little. Frantz de Galais, the son of the house – who was a student or a sailor or perhaps a cadet in the Navy, one could not be sure – had gone to Bourges to fetch a young girl and marry her; strange to say, this boy, who must be very young and very fantastic, arranged everything in his own way at the manor. He had wanted the house where his fiancée was to live to look like a festive palace. And to welcome the young girl he had himself invited these children and these kind-hearted old people. Such were the points which the discussion of the two women elucidated. They left everything else in mystery and always came back to the question of the lovers' return. The one insisted on to-morrow morning, the other on to-morrow afternoon.

'Poor old Moinelle, you always are so stupid,' said the younger quietly.

'Poor Adèle, you're always so obstinate. I haven't seen you for four years and you haven't changed an atom,' replied the other with a shrug of her shoulders, but in the most peaceful voice.

And thus they had it out together, without the least bad feeling.

Meaulnes joined in with the hope of learning more: 'Is she as pretty as people say, Frantz's sweetheart?'

They looked at him bewildered. No one but Frantz had seen the girl. Coming home from Toulon one evening, he had found her wandering in great distress in one of the gardens of Bourges which are called Les Marais. Her father, a weaver, had turned her out of the house. She was very pretty and Frantz had decided at once to marry her. It was a strange story, but had not his father M. de Galais and his sister Yvonne always allowed him to do as he liked!

Meaulnes was cautiously going to put other questions when a charming couple appeared at the doorway; a girl of sixteen wearing a velvet bodice and a skirt with deep flounces, a young fellow in peg-top trousers and a frock coat with a high collar. They crossed the room dancing a *pas de deux*; others followed, then again others rushed through screaming and chased by a tall ghastly Pierrot in dangling sleeves, who wore a black cap and smiled from a toothless mouth. He was running in big clumsy strides, as if each step preceded a jump, and he flapped his long empty sleeves. The girls were a little frightened of him, the young men shook him by the hand, and he appeared to be the delight of the children, who chased him with shrieks and laughter. As he passed he looked at Meaulnes with his glassy eyes, and the schoolboy thought he recognised, now completely clean-shaven, the companion of M. Maloyau, the bohemian who a little while before was hanging up the lanterns.

The meal ended. Every one rose.

In the corridors round games and country dances began. A band played a minuet somewhere. Meaulnes, with his head half hidden by the collar of his cloak, as by a ruff, felt himself a different person. He, too, caught the fun of it all and began to chase the tall Pierrot through the corridors, now like the wings of a theatre where the play had overflowed from the stage, in every direction. He thus found himself part of a gay crowd in

58

extravagant fancy dress. Sometimes he opened a door and was in a room with a magic lantern. Children clapped loudly. Sometimes, in a corner of the room devoted to dancing, he talked with some dandy and tried hastily to find out the sort of dress to be worn on the days following.

Rather troubled at last by all this gaiety offered him, and every moment fearing lest his partly open cloak would reveal his schoolboy overall, he sought refuge for a while in the quietest and darkest part of the dwelling. No other sound could be heard there but the muffled music of a piano.

He entered another door and found himself in a dining-room lit by a hanging lamp. There also fun was on, but fun for the children. Some of these, seated on hassocks, were busy turning over the pages of albums open on their knees; others, squatting on the floor in front of a chair, were gravely engaged in displaying pictures on the seat; others, again, near the fire said nothing and did nothing but listen to the hum of the fête audible throughout the great house.

One door of this dining-room was wide open. In the next room could be heard the piano being played. Meaulnes, inquisitively, put his head in. It was a sort of drawing-room parlour; a woman or a young girl, with a brown cloak thrown over her shoulders and her back turned, was very softly playing tunes of round games and nursery rhymes. Close to her, on the sofa, six or seven little boys and girls sat in a row as in a picture, good as children are when it grows late, and listened. Only now and again one of them, using his wrist as prop, lifted himself up, slid down to the ground, and passed into the diningroom; then one of those who had finished looking at the pictures came to take his place.

After the ball where everything was charming but feverish and mad, where he had himself so madly chased the tall Pierrot,

Meaulnes found that he had dropped into the most peaceful happiness on earth.

Noiselessly, while the girl played on, he went back to sit in the dining-room, and opening one of the big red books scattered on the table, he absent-mindedly began to read.

Almost at once one of the little boys crouched on the floor came up to him, and catching hold of his arm, climbed on his knee to look over; another settled on the other side. Then began a dream like his old dream. His mind could dwell on the fancy that he was married and in his own home during a beautiful evening and that this lovely unknown person playing the piano, close to him, was his wife.

THE MEETING

Next morning Meaulnes was one of the first to be ready. He put on, as he had been told, a simple black old-fashioned suit; a tight-waisted jacket with sleeves puffed out at the shoulders, a double-breasted waistcoat, trousers so wide at the bottom that they hid his dainty shoes, and a top hat.

The courtyard was deserted when he came down. He took a few steps and felt projected into a day of spring. It proved, indeed, to be the most lovely morning of that winter, sunny as in the first days of April. The frost was giving way and the damp grass shone as with dewdrops. In the trees many small birds were singing, and from time to time a warm breeze touched his face as he walked.

He behaved as guests do who wake before their host. He went out into the courtyard, thinking that, at any moment, a friendly and gay voice would call from behind him: 'Up already, Augustin?'

But he walked alone for a long time in the garden and in the courtyard. Over there, in the main building, nothing stirred, either in the windows or in the turret. Yet the two wings of the heavy-studded door were already open. And at one of the top windows a ray of sunshine shone as in summer in the early morning.

Meaulnes for the first time saw the grounds of the manor in broad daylight. Remains of a wall separated the unkept garden from the courtyard, where quite recently sand had been spread and smoothed over with the rake. At the end of the annex where his room was stood stables built in quaint disorder, which multiplied corners thick with ramping bushes and Virginia creeper. The fir woods, which hid the manor from all the flat country around, encroached onto the very grounds – except towards the east where could be seen blue hills covered with rocks and yet more firs.

For one moment, in the garden, Meaulnes leaned over the shaky fence enclosing the fish-pond; near the edges there remained a little thin ice in folds like froth . . . He saw himself reflected in the water, as if bending over the sky in his romantic student's costume. And he fancied it was another Meaulnes; no longer the schoolboy who had run away in a peasant's cart, but a charming youth of romance from the pages of some handsome prize-book . . .

He hurried towards the main building, for he was hungry. A peasant woman was laying the table in the large hall where he had dined the previous evening. As soon as Meaulnes sat down in front of one of the bowls set in a line on the cloth,

61

she poured him some coffee and said: 'You are the first down, sir?'

He did not wish to answer lest he should suddenly be recognized as a stranger. He only asked at what time the boat would leave for the morning excursion which had been announced.

'Not for half an hour, sir. No one has come down yet,' was the reply.

So he continued to wander in search of the landing-stage, all around this long castle-like house, built with unequal wings in the style of a church. When he turned round the south wing, he suddenly saw the reeds which, as far as the eyes could reach, formed the landscape. Water from the ponds bathed the foot of the walls on that side, and in front of several doors little wooden balconies overhung the rippling wavelets.

The youth, idly, rambled at leisure along a shore sandy as a towing-path. He peered through the dusty panes of large doors into dilapidated or forsaken rooms and sheds encumbered with wheelbarrows, rusted tools, and broken flower pots, when, suddenly, at the other end of the building, he heard footsteps crunching the sand.

Two women were approaching, one very old and bent, the other a young girl, fair and slender, whose charming dress, after all the fancy costumes of the previous evening, at first appeared strange to Meaulnes.

They stopped a moment to look at the view, while Meaulnes said to himself, with an astonishment which he later viewed as vulgar: 'That girl must be what is called eccentric – perhaps an actress who has been asked for the fête.'

Meanwhile, the two women passed close to him, and Meaulnes, motionless, watched the girl. Often, in after days, when falling asleep, after having tried in vain to recall the beautiful elusive face, rows of young women, not unlike this one, would pass before him in his dream. One had a hat like hers, another her slightly drooping head; this one her clear gaze, this other her small waist and yet another her blue eyes; but none of these women was ever the tall young girl.

Meaulnes had time to notice under the mass of fair hair a face, rather short but with features outlined with almost painful delicacy. And when she had passed, he observed that she wore what was certainly the most simple and sensible of dresses.

In some perplexity he was asking himself if he should accompany them, when the girl, turning imperceptibly towards him, said to her companion: 'Surely the boat will soon be here, now? . . .'

And Meaulnes followed them. The old lady, shaky and worn with age, never ceased chatting and laughing. The girl answered her gently. And when they walked down to the landing-stage she once again had that innocent grave look which seemed to say: 'Who are you? What are you doing here? I don't know you. And yet it seems to me that I do know you.'

Other guests were now scattered amongst the trees, waiting. Three pleasure boats came to the shore, ready to take the holiday-makers on board. One by one, as the women, who seemed to be the lady of the manor and her daughter, passed by, the young men bowed low and the girls curtsied. Strange morning! Strange pleasure party! It was cold, in spite of the winter sun, and the women were twisting round their necks those feather boas which were then fashionable.

The old lady remained on shore and, without knowing how, Meaulnes found himself in the same boat as the young lady of the manor. He leaned at the side of the deck, one hand holding on his hat in the high wind, and he was able to watch at his ease the girl who sat in shelter. She watched him, too. She answered her friends, smiled, and then gently let her blue eyes rest on him, biting her lip a little.

There was deep silence on the near banks. The boat glided on with a quiet sound of engine and water. It was easy to imagine one was in the heart of summer. They were going to land, so it seemed, in the beautiful garden of some country house. There, the girl would walk about under a white sunshade. Until evening the moan of doves would be heard . . . But suddenly an icy blast came to remind the guests at this strange fête that it was December.

They landed in front of a fir wood. On the landing-stage, the passengers had to wait a moment huddled, one against the other, while one of the boatmen unlocked the gate. With what joy, in after days, Meaulnes recalled the one minute when, on the shore of the lake, he had felt, close to his own, the girl's face, since lost! He had gazed at that profile, so pure, until his eyes had nearly filled with tears. And he remembered having seen, like a delicate secret she had confided to him, a little powder on her cheek . . .

On land everything happened as in a dream. While the children ran about with shouts of joy, while groups formed and scattered through the woods, Meaulnes entered a path where ten paces ahead of him the girl was walking.

He was close to her without having had time to think. 'You are lovely,' he said simply.

But she hurried on and without replying turned off along another path. Other people were playing and running about the avenues, each wandering where the fancy took him. The young man sharply reproached himself with what he called his

64

thick-headedness, his grossness, his stupidity. He rambled on aimlessly, convinced that he would never again set eye on this gracious being, when suddenly he saw her approaching and forced to pass close to him in the narrow path. With two bare hands, she pushed the folds of her long cloak out of the way. She wore black shoes cut very open. Her ankles were so slender that at times they appeared to bend and you feared they might break.

This time, the young man took off his hat and said very softly: 'Will you forgive me?'

'I forgive you,' she said gravely. 'But I must go back to the children, as they are the masters to-day. Good-bye.'

Augustin begged her to stay a moment longer. He spoke to her awkwardly, but in a voice so agitated and so disturbed, that she walked more slowly and listened to him.

'I do not even know who you are,' she said at last.

She spoke in an even tone, dwelling on each word in the same way, but saying the last one more softly . . . Then she regained her steady look, still biting her lips a little, and her blue eyes looked into the distance.

'I do not know your name either,' replied Meaulnes.

They were following a lane no longer under the cover of the woods, and some way off the guests could be seen crowding around an isolated house in the open country.

'Here is "Frantz's House," said the girl. 'I must leave you . . .'

She hesitated, looked at him a moment, and smiling, said: 'My name? . . . I am Mademoiselle Yvonne de Galais . . .'

And she hurried away.

"Frantz's House" was then uninhabited. But Meaulnes found it invaded, up to the attics, by the crowd of guests. He had scarcely leisure, however, to examine the spot where he now stood; they all hastened to eat a cold lunch which had been brought in the boats and which was hardly seasonable, but most likely the children had decided on it; then they set off again.

Meaulnes came close to Mademoiselle de Galais as soon as he saw her leave the house, and in answer to what she had said previously: 'The name I had given you was much nicer,' he said.

'How is that? What was the name?' she replied, always with the same seriousness.

But he was afraid of having said something silly, and he did not answer.

'Well, my own name is Augustin Meaulnes,' he went on, 'and I am a student.'

'Oh! you are studying?' she said.

And they spoke a moment longer. They spoke slowly with happiness – with friendship. Then the girl's attitude changed. Less haughty and less serious, she now also seemed more uneasy. She seemed to be dreading what Augustin might say and was troubled beforehand.

She was close to him, trembling like a swallow alighted for a moment on the ground and already quivering with the longing to resume its flight.

'What is the good? What is the good?' she replied gently to the plans which Meaulnes proposed.

But then at last he dared to ask her permission to come back one day to this delightful manor.

'I will wait for you,' she replied simply.

They came in sight of the landing-stage.

She stopped suddenly and said thoughtfully: 'We are two children, we have behaved foolishly. We mustn't get into the same boat this time. Good-bye; do not follow me.'

66

For an instant Meaulnes remained dumbfounded, watching her go away. Then he continued his walk. And the girl in the distance, stopped at the moment of disappearing in the crowd of guests, and turning, for the first time, took a long look at him. Was that a last farewell? Was it to forbid him to follow her? Or had she perhaps something else to tell him? . . .

As soon as they returned to the manor the pony-race started in a big meadow that sloped down at the back of the farm. It was the last item of the fête. According to the arrangements the fiancés were to arrive for it and Frantz was to manage it all.

Yet they had to begin without him. The boys in their jockey suits and the little girls as horsewomen led in some frisky ponies decked with ribbons as well as very old docile horses, amid shouts, children's laughter, betting, and prolonged sounding of the bell. One could have fancied one's self on the green and newly mown turf of a miniature race-course.

Meaulnes spotted Daniel and the little girls with feathers in their hats whose voices he had heard the day before in the drive near the wood. . . . The other part of the show was lost on him, so great was his anxiety to find, among the crowd, the charming hat trimmed with roses and the long brown cloak. But Mademoiselle de Galais never appeared. He was still looking for her when a full peal of the bell and joyful hurrahs announced that the race was over. A little girl mounted on an old white mare had won the prize. She proudly passed by on her mount, the feather of her hat fluttering in the wind.

Then suddenly all was still. The games were ended and Frantz had not come back. There was a moment of hesitation; people consulted uneasily. At last, in groups, the guests went back to the house to await in silence and anxiety the homecoming of the engaged couple.

FRANTZ DE GALAIS

The race had ended too soon. It was half-past four and still daylight when Meaulnes found himself again in his room, his head full of the events of this extraordinary day. He sat down idly at the table, waiting for the dinner and the fête which would follow.

The great wind which had blown on the first evening blew again. It could be heard roaring like a torrent or passing by with the insistent hiss of a waterfall. Every now and then the damper in the grate shook.

For the first time Meaulnes felt the little pang that gets you at the close of too lovely a day. It occurred to him to light a fire, but he tried vainly to raise the rusted damper. Then he began to tidy the room; he hung up his handsome clothes on the pegs, arranged the disordered chairs in a row along the walls, as if he were anxious to make preparations for a long stay.

Remembering, however, that he ought to be ready to leave at a moment's notice, he carefully folded his overall and his other school things like travelling clothes on the back of a chair and put his hobnailed shoes, still thick with mud, under the chair.

Then he sat down again and, feeling calmer, inspected his dwelling-room now set in order.

From time to time a drop of rain left a streak on the window which looked on the stable-yard and the fir wood. At peace since he had tidied his room, the big boy felt perfectly happy. There he was, mysterious, a stranger in the midst of this unknown world, in the room he had chosen. What he had found surpassed all his hopes. And it was enough now for his joy to recall, in the high wind, the face of that girl who turned towards him . . .

Night had fallen during this reverie, and he had not given a thought even to lighting the tall candles. A gust of wind banged the door of the dressing-room adjoining his, which also looked on the stable-yard. Meaulnes was about to close it when he noticed, in that room, a faint light as of a candle burning on the table. He put his head through the half-open door. Some one had got in there, by the window, no doubt, and was walking up and down with silent tread. So far as one could see it was a very young man with a long travelling cloak on his shoulders. Bareheaded, this young man paced up and down without a stop, like one distracted by some unbearable grief. From the window, which he had left wide open, the wind made his cloak flutter, and each time he passed close to the light a glint of brass buttons on his handsome frock coat caught the eye.

He was whistling between his teeth a kind of chanty such as sailors and prostitutes sing, to keep up their spirits in the pot-houses of seaports.

He stopped for an instant in the midst of his troubled walk, leaned over the table, searched in a box, took out several sheets of paper . . . By the light of the candle Meaulnes saw in profile very fine and very aquiline features, clean-shaven, under a thick head of hair which was parted on one side. He had stopped whistling. He was very pale; his lips were half open and he seemed short of breath as if he had received a violent blow on the heart.

Meaulnes wondered whether it would be wise to retire or to go in and put a hand on his shoulder like a friend and talk

69

to him. But the other raised his head and saw him. He looked at him for a moment; then, without surprise, came up and said, steadying his voice:

'I do not know you, sir, but I am pleased to see you. As you are here it is to you I will explain . . . Listen! . . .'

He appeared completely broken. After he had said 'Listen,' he caught hold of Meaulnes by his coat lapel, as though to fix his attention. Then he turned his head towards the window, as if to collect his thoughts, blinked – and Meaulnes realized that he badly wanted to cry.

But suddenly he swallowed back this childlike grief and, still gazing at the window, he went on in an altered voice:

'Well! listen; it's all ended; the fête is ended. You can go down and tell them. I've come back alone. My fiancée will not come. Scruples, fear, lack of faith . . . besides, sir, I must explain to you . . .'

But he could not go on. His face screwed up. He explained nothing. He suddenly turned away and went, in the dim light, to open and then close drawers full of clothes and books.

'I am going to get ready to go away again,' he said. 'Let no one disturb me.'

He placed various things on the table, a dressing-case, a revolver . . .

And Meaulnes walked out, full of dismay, not daring to say a word or to shake hands.

Downstairs everybody seemed to have guessed something already. Nearly all the girls had changed dresses. In the main building dinner had started, but people ate in haste, anyhow, as at the moment of starting on a journey.

There was a constant going to and fro from this large kitchen hall to the bedrooms and stables. Those who had done eating formed groups and said 'Good-bye' to each other.

'What's happening?' asked Meaulnes of a peasant boy who was making haste to finish his meal, a felt hat on his head and a table napkin tucked into his waistcoat:

'We are leaving,' he said. 'It's been decided very suddenly. At five o'clock we found ourselves quite alone, all the guests together. We had waited as long as we possibly could. Too late for the lovers to turn up. Somebody said, "Let's go"... And everybody made ready to leave.'

Meaulnes made no reply. He did not mind going now. Had he not reached the end of his adventure? ... Had he not this once obtained all that he wished for? Scarcely had he had time even quietly to go over in his mind the beautiful conversation of the morning. At the moment the only thing was to go. And soon he would come back – without trickery this time ...

'If you like to come with us,' went on his companion, who was a boy of his own age, 'look sharp and get ready; we are going to harness up at once.'

Meaulnes hurried out, leaving his meal unfinished and omitting to tell the guests what he knew.

The park, the garden, and the yard were now plunged in total darkness. There were no lanterns that evening at the windows. But as this dinner was, after all, not unlike the meal at the conclusion of a wedding, the less considerate of the guests, who had perhaps been drinking, began to sing. As he went off, Meaulnes heard their cabaret songs fill the air of the park which for two days had held so much grace and so much wonder. And it proved the beginning of confusion and chaos. He passed close to the fish-pond into which he had looked, that very morning, at his own reflection. How everything seemed changed already ... with this song, sung in chorus, which reached him in snatches:

Where have you come from, little wanton?
Your cap is in two
Your hair all askew . . .

And this one, too:

My shoes are red . . .
Good-bye, my lover . . .
My shoes are red . . .
Good-bye forever!

As he reached the foot of the stairs leading to his isolated lodging, some one came down and bumped into him in the dark, saying: 'Good-bye, sir!' – and wrapping himself in his cloak as if it were very cold, disappeared. It was Frantz de Galais.

The candle which Frantz had left in his room was still burning. Nothing had been touched. Only, written on a conspicuous sheet of note-paper, were these words:

'My fiancée has disappeared, letting me know that she cannot be my wife; that she was a dressmaker and not a princess. I do not know what will become of me. I am going away. I no longer wish to live. May Yvonne forgive me for not saying good-bye to her, but she could not do anything for me . . .'

It was the end of the candle, the flame of which guttered, flickered a moment and went out. Meaulnes returned to his own room and shut the door. In spite of the darkness he made out all the things which he had tidied, in full daylight and in full happiness, a few hours before. Garment after garment, all intact, he found again his old wretched suit, from his hobnailed shoes to his clumsy belt with the brass buckle. He undressed and dressed again swiftly, but distraught, placing his borrowed clothes on a chair, putting on the wrong waistcoat . . .

Under the windows, in the stable-yard, the bustle of departure had begun. Pulling, shouting, and pushing, each one wanted to get his vehicle out of the confused crowd in which it was hemmed. From time to time a man would climb on the driver's seat of a trap or on the hood of a big covered cart and search about with his light. The reflection of the lantern came in at the window; for a brief moment the room around Meaulnes, once familiar and where everything had been so friendly, breathed again, lived again . . . And thus it was that, carefully closing the door, he left this mysterious place which no doubt he was never again to see.

THE STRANGE FESTIVAL
(*concluded*)

Already, night as it was, a string of vehicles wound slowly towards the gate at the entrance of the wood. A man, in a goat-skin, holding a lantern, led the first horse of the procession.

Meaulnes was anxious to find some one to give him a lift. He was anxious to go away. Deep within him he dreaded finding himself suddenly alone at the manor and his trick discovered.

When he arrived in front of the main building, he found the drivers assigning their occupants to the last carriages. The travellers were made to stand while the seats were brought forward or pushed backward, and the girls, swathed in shawls, got up clumsily, the rugs slipping to their feet, and one could distinguish the anxious faces of those whose heads were lowered towards the carriage lights.

One of these drivers Meaulnes recognised as the young peasant who had offered to see him home a while ago.

'May I get in?' he called out.

'Where are you going, my lad!' replied the other, not recognising him.

'Sainte-Agathe way.'

'Then you should ask Maritain for a seat.'

And the big schoolboy started in search of this unknown Maritain amongst the guests who were late in leaving. The man was pointed out to him amongst the convivial spirits in the kitchen.

'He's a slacker,' they told him; 'he'll be here till three in the morning.'

Meaulnes thought for a moment of the poor worried girl who, in the midst of her grief and anxiety, would hear the songs of these tipplers filling the place far into the night. In which room was she? Where was her window amongst these mysterious buildings? But there was no point in stopping. He must go. Once back at Sainte-Agathe everything would become clearer; he would no longer be a runaway schoolboy; he would once more be able to dream of the young mistress of the manor.

One by one the vehicles left; the wheels grated on the sand of the drive. One could see them turn to disappear in the night with loads of muffled-up women and children wrapped in shawls and already dropping asleep. One more big covered cart; then passed a wagonette in which women were huddled shoulder to shoulder, and Meaulnes was left standing bewildered on the steps of the house. Soon, only an old berlin, driven by a peasant in a smock, would be left.

74

'You can get in,' he replied to Augustin's inquiries. 'We are going your way.'

With some difficulty Meaulnes opened the door of the rickety old vehicle, while the panes rattled and the hinges creaked. On the seat, in a corner of the carriage two quite small children, a boy and a girl, were asleep. The noise and the cold woke them. They stretched, looked vaguely about them shivering, nestled back in their corner and dropped off to sleep again.

Now the old carriage set off. Meaulnes closed the door more gently, and carefully settled in the other corner; then, hungrily, he tried to make out, through the window, the place he was about to leave and the road by which he had come: he guessed, in spite of the darkness, that the carriage was crossing the courtyard and the garden, passing in front of the stairway leading to his room, going through the gate and leaving the manor grounds to enter the woods. The trunks of the old fir trees could be distinguished moving by the window.

'Perhaps we shall meet Frantz de Galais,' Meaulnes said to himself with beating heart.

Suddenly, the carriage swerved in the narrow lane to avoid collision with an obstacle. From its heavy appearance, as far as one could tell in the night, it was a caravan, almost in the middle of the road, which had stopped there during these last days in proximity to the fête.

Having passed that obstacle, the horses started again at a trot, and Meaulnes was beginning to tire of looking out of the window in a vain effort to pierce through the surrounding darkness, when suddenly, in the depths of the woods, there was a flash of light followed by a report. The horses set off at full gallop and Meaulnes could not make out, at first, whether the peasant who drove was attempting to hold them back or on the contrary urging them on. He wanted to open the door. As the handle was on the outside, he tried without success to lower the window; he shook it . . . The children waking up in a fright huddled against each other without saying a word. And while he shook the window, his face close to the glass, a bend in the road enabled him to see a white figure running. It was the tall Pierrot of the fête, the bohemian in his fancy costume, but haggard and distracted and carrying in his arms a human body clasped closely to him. Then all disappeared.

In the carriage, tearing on at full gallop in the night, the children were once more asleep. No one to whom to speak of the mysterious happenings of the past two days. After reviewing at length all he had seen and heard, the young man, himself tired, his heart heavy, dropped off to sleep like a sad child . . .

. . . It was scarcely dawn when the carriage stopped on the road and Meaulnes was awakened by some one knocking at the window. With some difficulty the driver opened the door and shouted, while the icy wind froze the schoolboy to the bone: 'You get out here! It's almost daylight. We are going to take the short cut. You're quite near Sainte-Agathe.'

Half asleep, Meaulnes obeyed, felt about in the darkest corner of the carriage for his cap which had rolled under the feet of the sleeping children; then he got out, stooping.

'Well, good-bye,' said the man, climbing back to his seat; 'you've only got six kilometres to do. Look, there is the milestone by the roadside.'

Meaulnes, still heavy with sleep, dragged himself up to the milestone and sat down with his arms folded and his head bent forward as though to fall asleep again.

'No, no!' called out the coachman; 'you mustn't think of sleeping there. It's too cold. Come on, up you get, walk a bit . . .'

Staggering like a drunken man, the big boy with his hands in his pockets and his shoulders hunched up, went slowly along the road to Sainte-Agathe, while the old berlin, the last trace of the mysterious festival, quitted the highroad and jolted silently off over the grass track. Now only the hat of the driver could be seen, dancing above the hedges . . .

Second Part

THE GREAT GAME

*W*ind and cold, rain or snow, the impossibility of making any long expedition prevented Meaulnes and me from mentioning again the Lost Land before the end of the winter. There was nothing worth beginning during these short February days – these Thursdays broken up by squalls which invariably ended, about five, in a dismal freezing downpour.

Nothing recalled Meaulnes' adventure except the strange fact that since the afternoon of his return we no longer had friends. At recreation time the same games were got up as before, but Jasmin never spoke to Admiral Meaulnes. In the evenings, as soon as the classroom was swept, the playground became deserted, as in the days when I was alone, and I now watched my friend strolling to and fro from the garden to the shed and from the playground to the dining-room.

On Thursday mornings each of us settled at the master's desk in one of the two classrooms to read Rousseau and Paul Louis Courrier whom we had dug out of the cupboards from amongst English textbooks and copybooks of carefully transcribed music. In the afternoon some caller or other often caused us to leave the house and return to the school . . . Sometimes we used to hear some of the senior boys stop for a moment, as if by chance, in front of the big gate, bang against it during some unintelligible military games, and then go away. . . . This melancholy life went on until the end of February. I was beginning to think that Meaulnes had forgotten everything when an adventure, stranger than the others, came to prove to me that I had been mistaken and that a violent storm was brewing under the dreary surface of this winter life.

It happened to be a Thursday evening towards the end of the month, that the first news of the mysterious manor, the first ripple of that adventure of which we never spoke, reached us. We were all snug for the evening. My grandparents having left, there remained only Millie and my father, who had not the least idea of the secret quarrel by which the form was split into two clans.

At eight o'clock Millie, who had opened the door to shake out the crumbs after the meal, exclaimed: 'Ah!' in a voice so clear that we all came near to look. On the doorstep there was a layer of snow . . . As it was very dark, I walked a few steps into the playground to see if the layer was thick. I felt light flakes touch my face, to melt at once. I was quickly made to come in, and Millie, feeling chilly, hastened to shut the door.

82

At nine o'clock we prepared to go to bed; Mother was already holding the lamp in her hand when we quite distinctly heard two violent bangs hammered with great fury against the big gate at the other end of the playground. Millie put down the lamp on the table and we all stood there alert, listening.

No one dreamed of going to see what was the matter. Before getting halfway across the playground the lamp would have been out and the glass broken. There was a short silence and Father was beginning, 'It must have been . . .' when right under the dining-room window looking on the Station Road, as I have said before, sounded a shrill prolonged whistle which must have been heard as far as the church. And immediately behind the window, scarcely softened by the glass, and coming from people who seemed to have hoisted themselves up to the window-sill, burst loud shouts of: 'Fetch him along! Fetch him along!'

At the other end of the building other loud shouts responded. These people must have gone through Father Martin's field and climbed on the low wall separating the field from the playground.

Then cries of 'Fetch him along,' shouted on every side by eight or ten unknown persons disguising their voices, burst out from the roof of the larder which they could only reach by climbing over a heap of faggots leaning against the outside wall; from a little wall which ran from the shed to the big gate and on which being rounded you could sit comfortably astride; from the railed wall along the Station Road, quite easy to climb . . . Finally a number of stragglers came up from the garden behind, making the same din, but shouting: 'Let 'em have it!'

And we heard the sound of their yells echoing in the empty classrooms where they had opened the windows.

Meaulnes and I knew so well all the corners and corridors of the big building that we could clearly see, as on a plan, the positions from which the unknown people were launching their attack.

To tell the truth, it was only just at first that we were frightened. The shrill whistle had made the four of us think of tramps and gipsies breaking in. As a matter of fact, for the last fortnight, a tall rogue and a youngster with his head bandaged up had been about in the square behind the church. There were strange workmen, too, at the wheelwright's and the blacksmith's.

But as soon as we heard the cries of the assailants we were convinced that we had to do with people – probably youngsters – from the village. Absolute little scalawags – you could spot them by their piercing voices – were among the crowd who stormed our house as they would board a ship.

'Well, I never . . .' exclaimed my father.

And Millie asked in a faint voice: 'What on earth does it all mean?'

Suddenly the voices near the big gate and the adjoining wall stopped, then those near the window. Two blasts of a whistle came from behind the French window. The cries of those hanging on the larder roof and of those attacking from the garden grew fainter and fainter, then ceased; we heard along the dining-room wall the scuttering steps of the whole gang in hasty retreat, getting lost in the snow.

Some one obviously was disturbing them. At an hour when all slept, they thought they could easily storm a house isolated at the far end of the village. But here was some one upsetting their plan of campaign.

We had scarcely time to recover – for the attack had been sudden as a well-planned boarding of a ship – and prepared to sally out, when we heard a voice we knew call out at the same gate:

'Monsieur Seurel! Monsieur Seurel!'

It was M. Pasquier, the butcher. The fat little man scraped his clogs on the doorstep, shook his short smock powdered with snow, and came in. He put on the knowing and startled air of one who has surprised the secret of a mystery.

'I was in my yard which faces the Cross-Roads. I was going to lock up the goats' shed. Suddenly, standing there in the snow, what d'ye think I saw? Two tall lads as looked posted like sentries or on the watch for something. They were standing by the cross. I went towards them, just two steps. – Lord! there be these lads starting off at full-speed towards here. I didn't wait; not me. I picked up my lantern and I said: I be off to tell M. Seurel of this . . .'

And once more he begins his story. 'I was in my yard at the back of my place . . .' So we offer him a drink, which he accepts, and we ask him details which he cannot give.

He had seen nothing on reaching our house. All the bands, warned by the two sentries whom he had disturbed, had at once vanished. As for knowing who the rascals could be . . .

'Gipsies, quite likely,' he suggested. 'For a month they've been about in the square waiting for fine weather to give us a play, and must have been hatching some mischief.'

This did not help us much, and we all stood there very puzzled while the man sipped his drink and once more started his story, when Meaulnes, who so far had listened attentively, took the butcher's lantern from the floor and exclaimed: 'We must go and see!'

He opened the door and we followed him, M. Seurel, M. Pasquier, and myself.

Millie, quite herself again after the attackers' departure, and,

85

like all orderly and careful people, very uninquisitive by nature, said: 'Well, go if you like, but close the door and take the key. As for me, I am going to bed; I'll leave the lamp burning.'

WE FALL INTO AN AMBUSH

We went out over the snow in absolute silence. Meaulnes walked ahead, raying out the light from his storm lamp, like a fan. We had scarcely set foot outside the big gate when two figures in hoods sprang up like startled partridges from behind the town weighing-machine. Either to cheek us, or from pleasure at the game they were up to there, or from nervousness and fear of being caught, they spoke a few words and laughed as they ran away.

Meaulnes dropped his lantern in the snow, calling out: 'Follow me, François! . . .'

And leaving behind the two elderly men who could not stand the pace, we rushed in pursuit of the two shadows, who, after skirting the lower part of the village by the Old Plank Road, deliberately went back towards the church. They ran steadily, without hurrying, and we kept up with them easily. They crossed Church Street, where all was asleep and silent, and passed into a maze of by-streets and blind alleys at the back of the churchyard.

This was the quarter of the journeymen, sempstresses, and weavers known as 'The Nookery.' We did not know it well

86

and we had never been there at night. The place was deserted in the daytime: the journeymen being away, the weavers working indoors; and during this night of absolute silence it appeared even more forsaken, more asleep than other parts of the village. So there was no possible chance of any one unexpectedly coming to lend us a hand.

I knew only one way amongst these small houses, scattered about at random like cardboard boxes, and that was the one leading to the dressmaker known as the 'Dumb Girl.' You had to go down a rather steep slope paved here and there; then, taking two or three turns amongst weavers' back yards and empty stables, you came to a wide blind alley closed up by a farmyard long since deserted. I used to visit the Dumb Girl with my mother, and while they talked on silently with flashing fingers and grunts common to people with her affliction, I could look out from the window at the high wall of the farm – the last house on that side of the village – and the closed gate of a disused yard destitute of straw, where nothing ever passed by . . .

That is exactly the way the two unknown persons took. At each turning we feared to lose them, but, to my surprise, we always reached the corner of the next alley before they had left it. I say to my surprise, because this could not possibly have been done, so short were these alleys, had they not slowed down whenever we were out of sight.

At last, without hesitating, they took the street leading to the Dumb Girl's, and I called out to Meaulnes: 'We've got them. It is a blind alley!'

The truth is, they had got us . . . They had led us exactly where they wanted. When they reached the wall, they resolutely turned on us, and one of them let out that shrill whistle which we had already heard twice during the evening.

87

At once a dozen fellows came out of the abandoned farmyard where they had apparently been posted to await us. They had pulled their hoods over their heads and hidden their faces in their scarves.

We knew beforehand who they were, but we had decided not to tell M. Seurel, as our affairs were not his concern. There were Delouche, Denis, Giraudat, and all the others. We recognised each one during the skirmish by his way of fighting and by snatches of talk. But one worrying thing remained and seemed almost to frighten Meaulnes: some one was with them whom we did not know and who seemed to be their leader . . .

He never touched Meaulnes; he watched the work of his men, who, being dragged in the snow and their clothes torn, had all they could do to tackle the great breathless chap. A couple of them had gone for me, and had had a job to put me out, as I fought like a demon. I was on the ground, knees bent, sitting on my heels; they twisted my arms behind my back, and I watched it all with intense curiosity mingled with terror.

Meaulnes shook off top-form boys by twisting violently round on himself and throwing them headlong into the snow . . . And the Unknown, standing very straight, followed the fight with interest, but perfect calm, saying now and again in a clear voice: 'Go on . . . Courage . . . Once more . . . Go on, my boys . . .'

Obviously he was in command . . . Where had he sprung from? Where and how had he trained them for the fight? This remained a mystery to us. His face, like the others', was hidden in a scarf, but when Meaulnes shook off his adversaries and advanced towards him, the gesture the Unknown made to see clearly and face the position, exposed some white linen with which his head was swathed as in a bandage.

At this moment I cried out to Meaulnes: 'Look out behind! There's another.'

He had scarcely turned round when a lanky fellow, springing from the gate at Meaulnes' back, cleverly twisted a scarf around my friend's neck and threw him backward. At once the four boys who had fallen in the snow came back to the fray to pin Meaulnes down, tying his arms with a cord, his legs with a scarf, while the young man with the bandaged head searched his pockets . . .

The late comer, the thrower of the lasso, had lit a small candle which he protected with his hand, and at each find of some new piece of paper the leader went to this light to examine what it contained. He, at last, unfolded the kind of map covered with inscriptions at which Meaulnes had worked since his return, and exclaimed with glee: 'This time we've got it! There's the plan! That's the guide! We are going to see if this gentleman has really been where I imagine.'

His accomplice blew out the candle. Each one picked up his cap or his belt. And all disappeared as silently as they had come, leaving me free to hasten to release my friend.

'He won't go far with that plan,' said Meaulnes, rising on his feet.

And we went off slowly, as he walked rather lame. In Church Street we came upon M. Seurel and M. Pasquier.

'You didn't see anything, I bet!' they said . . . 'Neither did we.'

Thanks to the pitch darkness they noticed nothing queer. The butcher left us and M. Seurel went in quickly and then to bed.

But once upstairs in our room, by the light of the lamp which Millie had left us, we both remained a long time mending our overalls and quietly discussing all that had happened, like two brothers in arms on the evening of a lost battle . . .

89

THE BOHEMIAN AT SCHOOL

Waking up next morning was painful. At half-past eight, just as M. Seurel was giving the signal to enter school, we arrived, quite out of breath, to line up. As we were late, we crept in wherever we could, though generally, during M. Seurel's inspection, Admiral Meaulnes headed the long row of boys who stood elbow to elbow, loaded with lesson-books and pencil-boxes.

It surprised me to see the silent alacrity which every one displayed to make room for us in the middle of the column; and while M. Seurel delayed opening school by a few seconds to inspect Meaulnes, I inquisitively looked around to right and left to see the faces of our enemies of the previous day.

The first one I noticed was that same fellow who had been in my mind ever since, but who was the very last person I expected to see here. He was in Meaulnes' usual place, at the head, one foot on the stone step, one shoulder and the corner of the satchel he carried on his back, resting against the door-post. His fine face, very pale and slightly freckled, was turned towards us with a sort of disdainful and amused interest. The top of his head and one side of his face were bandaged in white linen. I recognised the leader of the gang, the young bohemian who had robbed us on the preceding night.

But we were now entering the classroom and each one took his seat. The new pupil sat close to the pillar, on the left of the long bench where Meaulnes occupied the first seat on the right. Giraudat, Delouche, and the three other first-bench boys sat quite close to each other to make room for him, as if this had been arranged beforehand . . .

The winter often brought us in this way casual pupils, lads in apprenticeship, sons of bargees held up by the ice on the canal, or of pedlars delayed by the snow. They remained at school from two days to a month, rarely more . . . Objects of great interest at first, they were soon unheeded and quickly forgotten in the crowd of ordinary pupils.

But this one was not to be forgotten so soon. I still remember that strange fellow and the queer treasures he used to bring, in the satchel strapped on his back. First there were 'sight-seeing' penholders which he took out to write his dictation with. Through a peephole in the handle, by shutting one eye you could see the church of Lourdes or some unknown building, dim and magnified. He chose one, and the others passed from hand to hand. Then came a Chinese pencil-box, full of compasses and exciting implements which travelled along the bench on the left, being silently and furtively thrust on from hand to hand under the desks, so that M. Seurel might not see.

Then came round some perfectly new books, the titles of which I had often read with longing on the covers of the few books in our library: 'The Blackbird on the Heath,' 'The Sea-gull's Rock,' 'My Friend Benedict.'. . . Some of the boys, resting a story-book on their knees, used one hand to turn over the pages of these volumes procured no one knew how, probably by theft, and with the other hand wrote their dictation. Others played with compasses inside their lockers. Others, while M. Seurel's back was turned and he dictated walking from desk to window, quickly closed one eye and applied the other to the greenish hollow view of Notre Dame of Paris. And the unknown pupil, pen in air and his refined profile outlined against the grey pillar, winked his eyes, happy at all the furtive play which had started around him.

Little by little, however, the class became anxious: the objects which were passed round had one by one come to Meaulnes' hands, but absent-mindedly and without looking at them, he carelessly placed them by his side. They soon mounted up to an angular and diversely coloured heap such as may be seen at the feet of the woman symbolising Science in allegorical pictures. M. Seurel would inevitably discover this unusual display and notice the game. Then he would remember to inquire into the events of the night. The presence of the bohemian would facilitate his task.

Soon, indeed, he stopped, surprised, in front of Meaulnes.

'To whom does all this belong?' he asked, pointing to 'all this' with the back of the book folded over his forefinger.

'I don't know,' replied Meaulnes surlily and without raising his head.

But the unknown pupil intervened. 'They are mine,' he said.

And at once he added, with a young aristocrat's ease and freedom of manner which the old schoolmaster could not resist: 'But I place them at your disposal, sir, if you wish to look at them.'

Then, in a few seconds, without any noise, as if not to disturb the new atmosphere just created, the whole class gathered inquisitively around the master whose head, half bald, half curly, bowed over the treasures, while the pale youth, serenely triumphant in the middle of the group, gave all necessary explanations. Meanwhile, seated silently at his desk and completely forsaken, Admiral Meaulnes had opened his rough notebook and with brow knitted was absorbed in a difficult problem . . .

The 'last quarter' found us thus occupied. The dictation was not finished and disorder reigned in the classroom. To tell the truth, it had been recreation all the morning.

So, at half-past ten, when the dark and muddy playground became invaded by the pupils, a new leader was soon observed to be running the games.

Of all the new plays which the bohemian introduced amongst us that morning, I remember only the most violent: a sort of tournament where the bigger boys were horses with the younger ones hoisted on their shoulders.

Divided into two camps at either end of the playground, they charged each other, seeking to upset the enemy by the force of the shock, and the cavaliers using scarves as lassos or their outstretched arms as spears, tried to unhorse their opponents. Sometimes the charge was dodged, and the cavalier, losing his balance, was sent sprawling in the mud under his mount. Some fellows, half dismounted, were kept up by the horse gripping their legs; they scrambled up again and charged into the fray. The slim cavalier with the bandaged head, mounted on Delage, who had lanky limbs, red hair, and flapping ears, urged on the two rival troops and steered his mount adroitly, shouting with laughter. At first Augustin, in a bad temper, watched from the classroom step as this play started. And I was waiting by his side, uncertain.

'He's a clever rascal,' he said between his teeth, his hands in his pockets. 'To come here the very next morning, that was the only way to avoid suspicion. And M. Seurel got taken in!'

He remained there a long while, his cropped head bare, fuming at the comedian who would bring to some harm these lads of whom, not so long ago, he, Meaulnes, was the captain. And I, peaceful youngster as I was, entirely agreed with him.

Everywhere on the playground, in the absence of M. Seurel, the fight went on: the smaller boys had now climbed on each other's backs; they were running and tumbling about even before they received the enemy's charge . . . Soon, in the middle

93

of the playground, there remained only one savage whirling group out of which emerged, now and again, the white bandage of the new leader.

Then Admiral Meaulnes could no longer keep back. Lowering his head and placing his hands on his thighs, he called out: 'Now for it, François!'

Surprised at this sudden decision, I none the less jumped upon his shoulders without a moment's hesitation, and in a second we were in the thick of the fray, while most of the combatants, scared, fled away shouting: 'There's Meaulnes! There's Admiral Meaulnes!'

He began to turn sharply round among those who remained, saying to me: 'Reach out your arms; collar 'em as I did last night.'

And I, intoxicated by the fray and certain of victory, gripped the youngsters as they went by; they struggled a little on the big boys' shoulders, then toppled off into the mud. In less than no time only the newcomer on Delage remained unthrown; but the latter, not too keen to stand up to Augustin, pulled himself up with a violent jerk of the hips and forced the white rider to dismount . . .

Thus dismounted, the young fellow, with one hand on his mount's shoulder as a captain holds his horse's bridle, looked at Admiral Meaulnes with some astonishment and immense admiration.

'Good work!' he said.

But at that very moment the bell rang, dispersing the pupils who had crowded round us in expectation of a queer scene. And Meaulnes, vexed at not having thrown his enemy, turned upon his heels, saying with some temper: 'Next time you're in for it!'

Up to noon the class went on as at the end of the term, full

94

of comic incidents and chat, the centre of which was the pupil-comedian.

He explained that, being held up by the cold on the square and not even dreaming of arranging evening shows to which no one would come, they had decided he should go to school to amuse himself during the daytime, while his companion looked after the tropical birds and the performing goat. Then he related their wanderings in the neighbourhood, when the rain pelts on the wretched tin roof of the caravan and you have to get out on steep hills and put your shoulder to the wheel. The pupils at the back of the room left their bench to come nearer and listen. The less romantic took that chance of warming themselves at the stove. But soon curiosity got the better of them, and they also drew near the chatting throng to listen, keeping one hand on the top of the stove not to lose their place by it.

'And what do you live on?' asked M. Seurel, who had followed the proceedings with the rather childish curiosity of a schoolmaster and was asking a lot of questions.

The youth hesitated a moment as if he had never bothered about that detail.

'Well,' he replied, 'on what we earned last autumn, I suppose. It's Booby who keeps the accounts.'

No one asked him who Booby was. But I thought of the tall rascal who, on the previous evening, had treacherously attacked Meaulnes from behind and thrown him.

WHICH DEALS
WITH THE MYSTERIOUS MANOR

During the afternoon the same distractions occurred again; all through every class disorder persisted and the same trickery. The bohemian produced other exciting things: shells, games, songs, and even a little monkey who stealthily scratched inside his satchel . . . At every moment M. Seurel was obliged to interrupt work to inspect something the clever rogue had pulled out of his bag . . . Four o'clock came and Meaulnes was the only one to have finished his problems.

No one was in a hurry to leave. It seemed as if, between school hours and recreation, there no longer existed that sharp distinction which renders school life as simple and as regular as the succession of night and day. We even forgot to tell M. Seurel, as we usually did about four o'clock, the names of the two boys who had to stay to sweep the room. Yet we had never before failed to do so, as it was a way of announcing the end of school and hastening it.

As luck would have it, that day it was Meaulnes' turn; and that very morning, while talking with him, I had warned the bohemian that newcomers as a matter of course were always appointed second sweeper on the day of their arrival.

Meaulnes came back to the classroom as soon as he had fetched his bread for the usual four o'clock snack. But we had to wait a long time for the bohemian; he arrived at last, running, just as night was falling . . .

'Stop in the form-room,' my friend had said to me, 'and while I hold him, you must bag that plan he stole. '

So I sat down on a small table, close to the window, and read by the last glimmer of daylight, while I saw them both silently shifting the school benches – Admiral Meaulnes glum and cross, his black overall well buttoned up at the back and tightly belted at the waist; the other delicate and nervous, his head bandaged up like a wounded soldier. He wore an old jacket which showed tears I had not noticed during the day. Full of a sort of savage zeal, he lifted and pushed the desks in feverish haste, smiling a little. You would have said he was playing some queer game, the secret of which escaped us.

Thus they reached the darkest corner of the room, to move the last desk.

At that spot Meaulnes could have knocked down his adversary at one blow and no one outside could have seen or heard anything through the window. I could not understand why he missed such a chance. The other fellow, back at the door, could at any moment escape, pretending the work was finished and we should never see him again. The map and all the information which Meaulnes had taken such a time to discover, to unravel and piece together, would be lost for us . . .

At any moment I was expecting a signal from my friend, a gesture warning me of the start of the fight, but the big schoolboy did not stir. Now and again, however, he fixed strange questioning eyes on the bohemian's bandage which, in the falling light, appeared profusely stained with black spots.

The last desk was moved without anything happening.

But at the moment when both were going up the classroom about to end their job by sweeping the threshold, Meaulnes lowered his head, and without looking at our enemy said in a low voice: 'Your bandage is red with blood and your clothes are torn.'

97

The other looked at him a moment, not surprised at what he said, but deeply moved at hearing him say it.

'A little while ago, on the square,' he replied, 'they tried to take your plan away from me. When they heard that I wanted to come back here to sweep, they understood that I was going to make peace with you and they all went for me. But still, I did save it,' he added proudly, holding forth to Meaulnes the precious folded paper.

Meaulnes slowly turned towards me.

'You hear?' he said. 'He's just been fighting and getting hurt on our account, while we were laying a trap for him!'

He spoke rather formally, but then, throwing aside all ceremony, unusual with the boys at Sainte-Agathe: 'You are a good chap,' he said, and held out his hand.

The comedian took hold of it and for a second remained speechless, very much moved, words failing him . . . But soon, keenly interested, he went on:

'And so you laid a trap for me! What a lark! I'd guessed it and I was thinking: Won't they be surprised, when they get back their plan to see that I've completed it . . .'

'Completed it?'

'Hold hard! Not entirely . . .'

Leaving off this flippant manner, he added gravely and slowly, coming nearer to us:

'Meaulnes, it's time to tell you: I, too, have been where you went. I was present at that extraordinary fête. It occurred to me, when the other boys told me about your mysterious adventure, that it concerned the old forsaken manor. To make sure of it I stole your map. But, like you, I don't know the name of the manor; I couldn't go back to it; I don't know the whole of the way to it from here.'

With what eagerness, with what intense curiosity, with what

98

friendliness we drew close to him! Greedily Meaulnes put questions to him . . . It seemed to us both that we could, by ardent pressure, make our new friend say even what he pretended not to know.

'You'll see, you'll see!' replied the young fellow, rather disturbed and embarrassed. 'I've put on the plan a few indications you hadn't got . . . That's all I could do.'

Then, seeing us full of admiration and enthusiasm: 'Oh!' said he sadly but proudly, 'I'd better warn you: I'm not like other chaps. Three months ago I tried to blow my brains out, and that accounts for this bandage on my forehead like a soldier of 1870 . . .'

'And this evening, as you fought, the wound reopened,' said Meaulnes with friendliness.

But, taking no notice, the other went on in a voice slightly emphatic: 'I wanted to die. And as I didn't manage it, I shall go on living, but only for fun, like a child, like a gipsy. I've left everything behind. I have neither father, sister, home, nor sweetheart . . . Nothing left, only playfellows!'

'And these playfellows have already betrayed you,' I said.

'Yes!' he replied, with animation. 'That's because of that fellow Delouche. He guessed that I was going to side with you. He demoralised my men, whom I had so well in hand. Look at the boarding of this house last night; wasn't it well managed? Didn't it come off well? Never, since I was a child, have I organised anything so successfully . . .'

He was for a moment lost in thought; then he added, so as to leave us no illusions about himself: 'The reason I came to you both this evening is that – I was sure of it this morning – there is more fun to be got with you than with the whole gang of the others. That Delouche above all is hateful to me. Why

99

play the man at seventeen? Nothing sickens me more . . . Do you think we can catch him out again?'

'Of course,' said Meaulnes. 'But are you stopping with us long?'

'I don't know, I'd love to. I am terribly lonely. I've only Booby.'

His excitement, his gaiety suddenly vanished. For a moment he fell into the same despair in which no doubt, one day, the idea of killing himself had overcome him.

'Be my friends,' he said suddenly. 'Look: I know your secret and I've kept it from everybody. I can put you back on the track you have lost . . .'

And he added, almost solemnly: 'Be my friends in readiness for the day when I shall be again within a hairbreadth of hell, as I have already been . . . Give me your word that you will come to me if ever you hear me call – when I shall call like this – [he uttered a queer call: Hou-ou!] . . . You, Meaulnes swear to it first.'

And we swore to it because, as we were only children, all that was serious and solemn beyond reason strangely attracted us.

'In exchange,' he said, 'this is all I can tell you now: I'll tell you the house in Paris where the young lady of the manor usually goes to spend the holidays: Easter and Whitsun, the month of June and sometimes part of the winter.'

At that moment, from the big gate, an unknown voice called many times in the darkness. We guessed it was Booby, the bohemian, who dared not or did not know how to cross the playground. His insistent, anxious voice was calling, sometimes very loud, sometimes almost in whispers: 'Hou-ou! Hou-ou!'

'Tell it! Tell it quick!' called out Meaulnes to the young bohemian who had started up and was readjusting his clothes to go.

The young fellow rapidly gave us an address in Paris, which we repeated in whispers. Then, running out into the night to join his companion at the gate, he left us in a state of inexpressible agitation.

THE MAN IN SAND-SHOES

That night, about three o'clock, the innkeeper widow Delouche, who lived in the middle of the village, got up to light her fire. Her brother-in-law Dumas, who lived with her, had to start at four, and the sad-looking woman, whose right hand bore the shrivelled scar of an old burn, was hurrying to make coffee in the dark kitchen. It was cold. She threw an old shawl over her night camisole, then holding a lighted candle in one hand and with her scarred hand raising her apron to shelter the flame, she crossed the yard littered with empty bottles and packing-cases, and opened the door of the shed, which was also used as a chicken-run, to get her kindling . . . But she had hardly pushed the door ajar, when some one sprang from the darkness, extinguished the candle with a blow of his cap, and with the same blow knocked over the good woman, then took to his heels while the terrified cocks and hens set up an infernal row.

The man was carrying away in a sack – as widow Delouche realised a moment later when she regained her balance – a dozen of her finest chickens.

At the cries of his sister-in-law, Dumas ran up. He discovered that the scamp, to get in, must have opened the gate of the small yard with a skeleton key, and that he had escaped by the same way, without shutting it again. At once, being accustomed to poachers and thieves, Dumas lighted his cart-lamp and carrying it in one hand with his loaded gun in the other, proceeded to follow the track of the thief, a very faint trail – the fellow most likely wore sand-shoes – which led to the Station Road, then disappeared at the gate of a meadow. Obliged to leave his search at this, he looked up, stopped . . . and heard in the distance, on the same road, the noise of a cart going at full gallop, evidently running off . . .

For his part, Jasmin Delouche, the widow's son, had also got up, and hastening to throw his hooded cloak on his shoulders, had gone out in his slippers to inspect the village. Everything was asleep, everywhere reigned darkness and the deep silence which precede the first glimmer of dawn. Reaching the Cross-Roads he heard in the distance – as his uncle had – only the noise of a cart with the horse apparently at full gallop. The wily and cowardly boy then said to himself, as he later repeated it to us with that unbearable thick pronunciation peculiar to Montluçon: 'They've gone towards the station, but who knows if I mayn't catch others, red-handed, the other side of the village!'

And he walked back towards the church in the silence of the night. On the square, a light shone in the gipsies' caravan. Somebody must be ill. He was going to draw near and ask what had happened when a silent shadow, a shadow walking in sand-shoes, emerged from the Nookery and heeding nothing else rushed at full speed towards the steps of the van.

Jasmin, who had recognised the gait of Booby, came forth suddenly into the patch of light and asked in a low voice: 'Well! What's the matter?'

Haggard, dishevelled, toothless, the fellow stopped, looked

at Delouche with a wretched grin caused by fear and lack of breath and replied in a jerky voice: 'It is my friend who's ill . . . He had a fight last night and his wound's reopened . . . I've just been to fetch the nurse.'

As a matter of fact, about the middle of the village, as Jasmin Delouche, sorely puzzled, was going home to bed, he met a Sister of Mercy who was hurrying.

In the morning several inhabitants of Sainte-Agathe appeared on their doorsteps with heavy eyes tired by a sleepless night. There was a general cry of indignation which spread through the village like a trail of gunpowder.

At Giraudat's, a cart had stopped about 2 A.M. and had been loaded with parcels which fell in softly. There were only two women in the house and they had not dared to move. At daybreak they had realised, on opening the yard gate, that the parcels in question were rabbits and poultry. Millie, during the first recreation, found several burnt matches outside the wash-house door. We came to the conclusion that the thieves did not know our house and had not been able to break in . . . At Perreux's, at Boujardon's, and at Clément's it was at first supposed that pigs even had been stolen, but these were found during the morning busily uprooting greens in several gardens. The whole herd had seized the chance of the opened gate to take a little nocturnal outing . . . Nearly everywhere poultry had been carried away, but that was all. Madame Pignot, the baker-woman, who did not rear chickens, complained loudly during all that day, that her washing-board and a pound of rinsing blue had been stolen from her, but the deed was never proved and never entered in the records of the case . . .

This agitation, these fears, this gossip lasted the whole morning. In class, Jasmin related his night adventure.

'Ah! they're clever beggars,' he said. 'But if Uncle had met one of them, he says he'd 'ave shot him like a rabbit!'

And he added, looking at us: 'What luck it is he didn't meet Booby; he'd sure enough have fired. They all be one gang, he says, and Dessaigne said the same.'

Yet no one thought about disturbing our new friends. It was only the next day in the evening that Jasmin remarked to his uncle that Booby and their thief both wore sand-shoes. Then they agreed that this fact was worth mentioning to the police. So they decided, in great secrecy, to go, when they had a moment, to the chief town of the district and inform the head constable.

During the following days the young bohemian, still ill with his wound, did not appear. Every evening we went prowling on the church square merely to watch his lamp behind the caravan's red curtain. Feverish with anxiety we stood there, not daring to draw near this humble abode which seemed to us the magic portal of the Land to which we had lost the way.

A QUARREL BEHIND THE SCENES

The numerous disturbances and troubles of these last days prevented us from noticing that March had come and that the wind had softened. But one morning, three days after our adventure, as I went down into the playground, I suddenly realised that it was spring. A breeze, delicious as cool water, blew

over the wall; the silent rain of the night had moistened the leaves of the peonies; a rich pervasive smell rose from the freshly turned soil in the garden, and in the tree close to the window, I heard a bird which was trying to learn music . . .

Meaulnes, during the first recreation, spoke of attempting to find at once the way which the bohemian boy had outlined. With difficulty I persuaded him to wait until we had, once more, seen our friend, until the weather was really fine . . . and the plum trees in bloom at Sainte-Agathe. We talked leaning against the low wall of the narrow lane, hands in pockets, bareheaded, while the wind sometimes made us shiver with cold, and at other times, with warm puffs, awoke some deep urge within us. Ah! friend, brother, fellow-traveller, how convinced we both were that happiness was close, and that we had only to set out to reach it! . . .

At half-past twelve, during dinner, we heard the rolling of a drum at the Cross-Roads. In the twinkling of an eye, we were all at the small gate, napkins in hand . . . It was Booby announcing for that evening at eight o'clock, 'in view of the fine weather,' a great performance on the church square. At all events, 'to run no risks in case of rain,' a tent would be erected. Then followed a long programme of attractions which the wind prevented us from catching except such words as 'dumb show . . . songs . . . riding displays . . .' the whole thing punctuated by renewed rolling of the drum.

During the evening meal the big drum announced the show and thundered under our windows, making the panes rattle. Soon after, people of the village passed by, with a buzz of talk, going in small groups towards the church. And there we were both of us, forced to remain at the table, though burning with impatience!

At last, about nine, we heard a scraping of shoes and stifled laughter at the small gate: the women teachers had come to fetch us. In the pitch darkness, our little party made its way towards the show. We could see from afar, the church wall brightly lit up, as if by a big fire. Two naphtha flares swung in the wind at the door of the tent . . .

Inside, benches were arranged in tiers as at a circus. M. Seurel, the women teachers, Meaulnes and myself took our places on the lowest of these. I recall the place, which must have been rather small, as a real circus, with its wide dark stretches of rising seats, where could be seen Madame Pignot, the baker-woman; Fernande, from the grocer shop; the girls from the village; the apprentices from the forges; ladies, urchins, country folks, and every sort of people.

The show was more than half through. In the arena, a small goat was performing, standing obediently on four glasses, then on two, then on one alone. Booby was gently directing her with little taps from a switch, but all the while looking at us in a worried way, his mouth gaping, his eyes dead.

Seated on a stool, near two other flares, and at the place where the arena was connected with the caravan, was a fellow with bandaged head, wearing elegant black tights, whom we recognised as the leading man and our friend.

Scarcely were we seated when a pony, fully harnessed, pranced onto the track. He was several times led around the arena by the wounded comedian, and invariably stopped in front of one of us when asked to find the most charming person or the bravest in the audience, but always pointed to Madame Pignot when he had to spot who told the greatest lies, or was the most avaricious or 'the most in love' . . . And all round the lady, there were shrieks of laughter, screams and cackling, as when a flock of geese is chased by a spaniel! . . .

At the interval, the leading man came to have a chat with

106

M. Seurel, who could not have felt more proud had a Talma or a Léotard spoken to him; as for us, we listened with eager interest to what the comedian was saying: first about his wound – now closed up; then regarding this show – rehearsed during the long days of winter; then concerning their departure – which was not to be before the end of the month, for they meant to give other variety shows up to then.

The performance was to finish up with an elaborate dumb show.

Towards the end of the interval, our friend left us, and to reach the caravan's steps was obliged to go through a group of people who had invaded the arena, in the midst of which we suddenly noticed Jasmin Delouche. The women and the girls got out of the way. The black costume, the strange but gallant figure of the wounded man, had won their hearts. As for Jasmin, who appeared to be coming back from a long journey and was talking in a low but animated voice to Madame Pignot, he would evidently have found the local costume with the low collar, the bow of silken cord, and the elephant-like trousers, more to his taste . . . Both thumbs raised to the lapel of his jacket, he stood in a very affected and uneasy attitude. Out of spite, as the bohemian went by, he said aloud to Madame Pignot a few words I did not catch, but which were certainly an offensive remark, an insult meant for our friend. It must have been a serious and unexpected threat, for the young fellow could not help turning round and looking at the other, who, to carry it through, grinned and poked his neighbours in the ribs as if to bring them onto his side . . . All this happened in a few seconds. I was perhaps the only one on our bench to notice it.

The leading man joined his companion behind the curtain which hid the door of the caravan. All went back to their seats, thinking that the second part of the show would soon begin, and great silence ensued. Then, from behind the curtain, while the last whispered conversations were fading away, rose the noise of a quarrel. We could not hear what was being said, but we recognised the two voices as those of the tall man and the young fellow – the first explaining and justifying; the other scolding with both indignation and sadness.

'But you wretch!' the latter was saying; 'why didn't you tell me?...'

And we heard nothing further, though every one was listening. Then, suddenly, all was quiet. The dispute went on in whispers; and urchins at the top rows began to call out: 'Curtain! Curtain!' and stamped their feet.

THE BOHEMIAN TAKES OFF HIS BANDAGE

At last, peering in slowly between the curtains, a face emerged, furrowed by wrinkles, expanding in a grin both of mirth and distress, and bespeckled with black patches; there followed the figure of a lanky Pierrot made of three badly jointed parts, screwed up by some awful colic, who, with excess of caution and fear, advanced on tiptoes, his hands entangled in long dangling sleeves which swept the track.

I could not to-day reconstruct the plot of his dumb show. I remember only that, as soon as he entered the arena, in spite of vain and hopeless efforts to keep his feet, he fell. It was useless getting up again; he could not help it; he fell. He never ceased falling. He entangled himself in between four chairs all at once. He dragged after him, in his fall, a huge table which had been brought into the arena. At last he managed to measure his length beyond the barrier, at the very feet of the spectators. Two handy men, enticed with much trouble out of the audience, then dragged him by the feet and after tremendous efforts stood him up. And at each fall he uttered a little scream, each time different, a little unbearable scream, in which distress and satisfaction had an equal share. At the climax, perched on a scaffolding of chairs, he dropped in a very long slow fall, and his piercing, melancholy hoot of triumph lasted as long as the fall and was mingled with shrieks of fear from the women.

During the second part of his show, though I do not know why, I recall 'poor wobbly Pierrot' producing a little sawdust doll from his sleeves and acting with her a long tragi-comical scene. He ended it all by emptying the sawdust of her body out of her mouth. Then, with little pitiful cries, he filled her with porridge, and at the moment when all were attentive and the gaping spectators had their eyes fixed on Pierrot's daughter, bursting and sticky – suddenly catching hold of her by one arm, he hurled her flying across the audience at the face of Jasmin Delouche whose ear she missed before she landed on Madame Pignot's bosom, just under that lady's chin. The baker-woman shrieked so loud, drew herself back so sharply, and all her neighbours imitated her so well that the bench broke and the baker-woman, Fernande, sad widow Delouche, and twenty others tumbled down, legs in the air, amidst laughter, shrieks, and clapping, while the tall clown, who had fallen on his face, got up to bow and say:

'Now, Ladies and Gentlemen, we beg to thank you for your kind attention!'

But at that very moment and in the midst of the uproar, Admiral Meaulnes, who had kept silent since the beginning of the dumb show, and seemed every moment more absorbed, hastily got up and clinging to my arm, as if unable to contain himself, said aloud to me: 'Look at the bohemian! Look! Now, I recognise him.'

Even before looking, as if all the while, subconsciously, this thought had been dormant in me, only awaiting the moment to dawn, I too had guessed! Standing by one of the naphtha flares, at the door of the caravan, the young unknown actor had taken off his bandage and thrown a cloak over his shoulders. One could see by the smoking flare, as once by candlelight in the room at the manor, the clean-shaven features, very fine and aquiline. Pale, his lips half open, he was hastily turning over the leaves of a small red album, most likely a pocket atlas. Except for a scar cutting across his temple and disappearing under the mass of hair, it was, just as Admiral Meaulnes had minutely described him to me, the fiancé from the unknown manor.

It was evident that he had taken off his bandage to be recognised by us. But scarcely had Meaulnes made his gesture and uttered his cry than the young man went into the caravan after giving us a knowing look and smiling with vague sadness, as he usually smiled. 'And the other!' said Meaulnes with excitement; 'how was it I didn't recognise him straightaway! He is the Pierrot of the fête, out there . . .'

And he walked down the tiers to go towards him. But already Booby had cut off all access to the track and, one by one, was putting out the four flares; we were obliged to follow the crowd, which in the dim light, and through the narrow channels of the parallel benches, streamed slowly out while we stamped about with impatience.

When at last Admiral Meaulnes was outside, he hastened to the caravan, rushed up the steps, and knocked at the door, but all was already secured for the night. Already, no doubt, in the van with the curtains as well as in the one reserved for the pony, the goat, and the performing birds, every one was tucked up and falling asleep.

THE POLICE

We were obliged to join again the throng of people who were going through the dark streets towards the Higher Elementary School. But now we understood everything. The tall white shadow which Meaulnes had seen hurrying amongst the trees, on the last evening of the fête, was Booby, who, having rescued the disconsolate fiancé, was running away with him. The latter had accepted this wild life, full of risks, games, and adventures. It had seemed to him like starting his childhood over again . . .

Frantz de Galais had, so far, hidden his name from us and pretended not to know the way to the manor, for fear of being forced to go back home; but why had he, this evening, suddenly wished to reveal himself, letting us guess the whole truth? . . .

No end of plans went through Admiral Meaulnes' head while the crowd slowly dispersed across the village. He decided that early next day, which was a Thursday, he would go to see Frantz, and together they would start for that place! What a

lovely journey on the dewy road! Frantz would explain everything; all would be put right, and the glorious adventure
would begin again from where it left off . . .

As for me, that night, I walked with an indescribable elation
of heart. Everything contributed to my joy, from the paltry
pleasure of awaiting the Thursday holiday to the great discov-
ery we had just made and the fine piece of luck befalling us.
And I remember that, with sudden generosity of heart, I went
up to the ugliest of the notary's daughters, to whom I was often
forced to offer my arm, and spontaneously held my hand out
to her.

Bitter memories! Great hopes crushed!

The next day at eight o'clock, as we both emerged on the
church square, our shoes well polished, the buckles of our belts
shining bright, and our caps brand-new, Meaulnes, who so far
had repressed a smile whenever he looked at me, gave a shout
and rushed towards the empty square . . . At the place where
the tent and the vans had stood were only a broken jug and
some rags. The gipsies had gone! . . .

A light wind was blowing which felt icy to us. It seemed as
if at every step we were about to stumble and fall on the hard
stony ground of the square. Meaulnes, enraged, twice made as
if he would rush off, first along the road to Vieux-Nançay, then
along the road to Saint-Loup-des-Bois. One hand over his eyes,
he scanned the neighbourhood hoping our people had only
just started. But what could be done? The tracks of a dozen
vehicles were all mixed up on the square and then effaced on
the hard road. We were stuck there, powerless.

And as we were coming back across the village where the
life of a Thursday morning was beginning, four mounted
policemen, warned the evening before by Delouche, arrived
at a gallop on the square and scattered in the by-streets to block

all issues, exactly as a patrol of dragoons sent to reconnoitre a village . . . But it was too late. Booby, the chicken-snatcher, had escaped with his companion. The policemen found nobody, neither Booby himself nor the fellows who had loaded the carts with the birds he had strangled. Warned in time by the incautious remark of Jasmin, Frantz must have suddenly understood what trade kept his companion and himself alive when the cash-box was empty; full of shame and anger, he had at once mapped out the route and decided to make off before the police came. But, no longer fearing to be taken back to his father, he had shown himself to us without a bandage before he disappeared.

One thing alone remained a puzzle: how could Booby both rob the poultry-yards and at once fetch the nun for his feverish friend? But did not that sum up the whole story of the poor devil? Thief and tramp on the one hand, a kind-hearted chap on the other . . .

IN SEARCH OF THE LOST TRAIL

The sun was breaking through the morning mist on our return: housewives were shaking carpets or chatting in front of their doors: the loveliest spring morning my memory can recall was beginning in the fields and woods round the village.

All the big boys of the top form had been told to come about eight that Thursday morning to prepare, some for Matriculation, others for the Entrance Examination to Training

College. When we arrived together – Meaulnes so full of regret and uneasiness that he could not keep still, myself very depressed – the school was empty . . . A ray of bright sunlight was glinting on the dust of a worm-eaten bench and the peeling varnish of the globe.

How could we stop there in front of a book, to brood over our disappointment, when everything was calling us out-of-doors: birds chasing one another in the branches close to the windows, the other boys gone off to the woods and the fields, and above all our burning wish to try at once the incomplete route on the map approved by the bohemian – our last card, the one key left which might open the lock? . . . It was more than we could stand! Meaulnes kept walking up and down, going to the windows to look at the garden, then back again for a look towards the village, as if he was expecting some one who certainly would not come.

'I've a notion,' he said to me at last – 'I've a notion that it mayn't be as far as we think . . . Frantz struck off my plan a good bit of the road I had marked. That may mean the mare went a long way round while I was asleep . . .'

I sat idle and discouraged on the edge of a big table, one foot on the ground, the other swinging, and I remarked in a dejected way: 'Yes, but coming back, in the berlin, your journey lasted all night.'

'We left at midnight,' he replied quickly. 'They put me down at four in the morning, six kilometres west of Sainte-Agathe, whereas I'd gone by the east Station Road. So we must knock off these six kilometres from the distance between Sainte-Agathe and the Lost Land. I feel almost sure that from the wood on the Commons to what we're after, it can't be more than eight kilometres.'

'They're precisely the eight kilometres missing on your map.'

'That's true. And getting out of the wood means at least six kilometres from here; but a good walker can do it in a morning.'

Mouchebœuf came in at that moment. He had an irritating way of appearing to be a good pupil, not by working better than others, but by showing off on occasions like this.

'I knew,' he said proudly, 'I should find only you two. The others have gone to the Commons wood, under Jasmin Delouche: he knows the nests.'

And to show off his goodness, he began to relate what they had said to rag the Matric form, M. Seurel, and ourselves while planning this expedition.

'If they've gone to the wood, I shall most likely come across them,' said Meaulnes, 'as I'm going that way too. I'll be back about half-past twelve.'

Mouchebœuf was aghast.

'Aren't you coming?' said Augustin to me, stopping a moment on the step of the partly open door – and thus brought into the room a whiff of air softened by the sun, a medley of twittering, calling, and chirping, the sound of a pail on the curb of a well and the cracking of a whip in the far distance.

'No,' I replied, although the temptation was strong, 'I can't because of M. Seurel. But hurry up, I'll be on the itch to know.'

He made a vague gesture and went off quickly, full of hope.

When M. Seurel came in about ten, he had discarded his black alpaca jacket, having put on a fisherman's coat with big buttoned pockets, a straw hat, and short leather leggings to hold in his trousers. I believe he was hardly surprised at finding no one. He paid no heed to Mouchebœuf, who told him three times that the boys had said: 'Well, if he wants us, let him come and find us!'

He just said: 'Put away your things, take your caps, it's our turn to get even with them, then . . . Can you walk as far as that, François?'

I assured him I could and we started.

It was agreed that Mouchebœuf would guide M. Seurel and be his decoy-bird . . . That is to say that, knowing the thickets where the nest-hunters had gone, he would call aloud, from time to time: 'Holla! Hoa! Giraudat! Delouche! Where are you? Got any? . . . Made any finds? . . .'

As for me, to my great delight, I was told to follow the out-skirts of the wood on the east side, in case the runaways should try to escape that way.

It so happened that, on the plan as altered by the bohemian, which I had many times studied with Meaulnes, a line seemed to indicate a path, a beaten track, starting from that side in the direction of the manor. What if I should discover it this morn-ing! I began to feel certain that before midday I should find myself on the road to the Lost Land . . .

What a marvellous walk! . . . As soon as we had passed the glacis and gone round the mill, I left my two companions: M. Seurel looking as if he was off to the wars (I believe he had an old pistol in his pocket) and that traitor Mouchebœuf.

I took a cross-road and soon came to the edge of the wood – being alone in the open country for the first time in my life, and feeling like a patrol which has lost its corporal.

Here I am, I imagine, close to that mysterious happiness of which Meaulnes, one day, had a glimpse. The whole morning is mine to explore the edge of the wood – the most deliciously cool and secreted part of the district – while my big brother, too, is off on the search. It is like the old bed of a brook. I make my way under the low branches of trees unknown to me by name, but which must be alders. I have just jumped a hurdle at the end of the path, and I am under a roof of leaves in this

wide grass track, treading down nettles and crushing tall valerians.

Sometimes, for a few steps, my foot rests on a stretch of fine sand. And in the silence I hear a bird – I imagine it to be a nightingale, but most likely this is wrong, as nightingales only sing at night – a bird who persists in repeating the same phrase: the voice of the morning, a loving word under the shade of the trees, a charming invitation to a walk amongst the alders. Invisible, obstinate, he seems to follow me under the leaves.

For the first time I, too, am on the road of adventure. I am no longer hunting for shells of bygone streams, under M. Seurel's guidance, nor orchids unknown to the school-master, nor even, as often before, for the deep and dried-up spring in Father Martin's field, with a grating so well hidden by weeds and grass that to rediscover it gave us each time greater trouble . . . I am searching for something far more mysterious. It is the path told of in books, the ancient obstructed path, the path to which the weary prince could find no entrance. It is found at last at the most forlorn hour of the morning, when you have long since forgotten that eleven or twelve is about to strike . . . And suddenly, as one thrusts aside bushes and brier, with a movement of hesitating hands unevenly raised level to the face, it appears in sight as a long shadowy avenue, the outlet of which is a small round patch of light.

But while I hope thus and am enraptured, I unexpectedly come out into a clearing, which is simply a meadow. Without giving it a thought, I have reached the other side of the Commons, which I had always imagined a very long way off. And there, on my right, in between stacks of logs, and astir with life in the shade, stands the forester's house. Two pairs of stockings are drying on the window-sill. In previous years, whenever we had reached the entrance of the wood, we used to point to a patch of light at the end of a long, dark avenue and say: 'That house out there, that's the forester's cottage, Baladier's.' But we had never pushed on as far as that. We had often heard people say, as if referring to some extraordinary venture, 'He's been as far as the forester's cottage! . . .'

This time, I have been as far as Baladier's cottage, and I found nothing.

I was just beginning to feel my tired legs and the heat, which I had not so far noticed; I was fearing the return journey all by myself, when close at hand I heard the voice of M. Seurel's decoy-bird, Mouchebœuf, then other voices calling me . . .

I saw a group of six big lads, amongst whom Mouchebœuf the traitor was the only one triumphant. There were Giraudat, Auberger, Delage, and others . . . Thanks to the decoy, they had been caught, some up a mulberry tree that stood solitary in the clearing, others in the act of robbing a woodpecker's nest. That fool of a Giraudat, with his swollen eyes and greasy overall, had hidden the little ones against his stomach, in between his shirt and his skin. Two of their companions had run off at M. Seurel's approach: probably Delouche and the little Coffin. At first they had answered Mouchebœuf by jokes on his name, which the echoes of the wood repeated, and he, believing he had caught them, had replied stupidly in a temper: 'You'd better come down from there, you know! M. Seurel's here . . .'

Then the noise had stopped at once. There had been a silent flight across the wood. As they knew it thoroughly, it was useless to think of catching them. On the other hand, no one knew what had become of Admiral Meaulnes. His voice had not been heard, and we had to give up looking for him.

It was past midday when we slowly started back towards Sainte-Agathe, with drooping heads, tired and muddy. On coming out of the wood, where we scraped and stamped the mud from our shoes on the dry road, the sun began to strike fiercely down. Already it was no longer the fresh and bright morning of spring. The noises of the afternoon had started. Now and again, a cock set up a melancholy crowing in the deserted farms by the roadside. At the descent of the glacis we stopped a moment to chat with some farmhands back at their work after lunch. They were resting with their elbows on the stile, and M. Seurel was saying to them: 'Ah! the rascals! Here, look at Giraudat. He's put the brood inside his shirt. They've done in there what they liked. It's *all* right! . . .'

It seemed to me the men were laughing at my disaster, too. They laughed and shook their heads, but did not altogether blame the youngsters, whom they knew well. They even confided to us, while M. Seurel was starting off again at the head of our party: 'There was another chap as went by. That tall fellow, you know . . . On the way back he must've met the cart from the Barns and been given a lift. He was put down here, at the entrance of the lane to the Barns, covered with mud and ragged. We told him as we'd seen you go by, this morning, but that you were not back yet. He slowly set off for Sainte-Agathe.'

In fact Admiral Meaulnes was waiting for us, seated on a pier of the glacis bridge and looking worn out with fatigue. He said, in answer to M. Seurel's questions, that he also had gone to look for the truants. But to the question I put to him in whispers, he shook his head and only said with disappointment: 'No! Nothing! Nothing at all like it!'

After lunch, he sat at one of the big tables in the classroom – stuffy, dark, and empty amidst the glorious countryside – and burying his head in his arms, fell into a long sleep, sullen and heavy. Towards evening he wrote a letter to his mother, after having been a long time lost in thought, and as if coming to an important decision. And that is all I can remember of that melancholy ending to a great day of defeat.

WASHING-DAY

We had reckoned too soon on the coming of spring. On Monday evening we decided to do our home work immediately after four as in the summer, and to get a better light, we dragged two big tables into the playground. But the sky became suddenly cloudy; a drop of rain fell on an exercise-book; we hastened to go in. And we silently watched, out of the large windows of the big classroom now so dark, the flight of the clouds in the grey sky.

Then Meaulnes, who was at the window with us, one hand on the handle, could not refrain from saying, as if he were angry to feel so much regret rise up in him: 'Ah! the clouds rolled along better than this when I was on the road, in the Fair Star cart.'

'On what road?' asked Jasmin.

But Meaulnes made no reply.

'As for me,' I said, to create a diversion, 'I should have loved travelling that way in a carriage, with the rain pouring down, sheltered under a big umbrella.'

'And reading all the while during the journey, as if you were indoors,' added another.

'It was not raining and I had no longing to read,' replied Meaulnes. 'I thought only of looking at the countryside.'

But when in his turn Giraudat asked him of what country he spoke, Meaulnes again kept silent. And Jasmin said: 'I know . . . Always that famous adventure! . . .'

He had said these words in conciliatory and important tones, as if he was himself a little in the secret. It was trouble lost; his advances met with no response; and as night was falling, every one raced off through the cold downpour, his overall wrapped over his head.

The rain continued until the following Thursday. And that Thursday was even gloomier than the last. The whole country-side was bathed in a sort of icy mist as in the worst days of winter.

Millie, led astray by the beautiful sun of the week before, had had the washing done, but there could be no question of hang-ing it out to dry on the garden hedges, nor even on lines in the lumber-rooms, as the air was so damp and cold.

Discussing the matter with M. Seurel, she conceived the idea, as it was Thursday, of spreading the washing in the classrooms and of heating the stove red-hot. Meals were to be cooked on the stove to dispense with fires in the kitchen and in the dining-room, and we were to spend the day in the top-form classroom.

At first – I was so young! – I regarded this novelty as a treat. A dreary treat! . . . All the heat of the stove was taken by the washing; it was extremely cold. In the playground a fine wintry rain fell softly and endlessly. Yet it was there that at nine o'clock in the morning, bored to death, I discovered Admiral Meaulnes. Through the bars of the tall gate against which we silently rested our heads, we looked towards the top of the village and watched a funeral procession which had come from remote parts of the country and had stopped at the Cross-Roads. The coffin, brought on an ox wagon, was lowered and placed on a flagstone at the foot of the tall cross where the butcher, one night, had noticed the bohemian's sentries! Where was he now, the young captain who could so well fake the boarding of a ship? . . . The vicar and the choir boys, as was the custom, walked up to the coffin and their mournful chants reached us. This, as we knew, would be the only sight the whole day, which would pass like muddy water along the gutter.

'And now,' said Meaulnes suddenly, 'I am going to pack. I must tell you, Seurel: I wrote to my mother last Thursday asking her to let me complete my studies in Paris. I am leaving to-day.'

He continued looking towards the village, his hands against the bars, level with his face. No use asking if his mother, who was rich and indulged all his whims, had allowed this one. No use either to ask why he suddenly wanted to go to Paris! . . .

But certainly there was regret in him, and fear at leaving this dear land of Sainte-Agathe from which he had set out on his adventure. As for me, a heavy distress rose in my heart which I had not felt at first.

'Easter is coming!' he said with a sigh, by way of explanation.

'As soon as you find her, out there, you will write, won't you?' I asked.

'Of course, that's agreed. Aren't you my friend and my brother? . . .'

And he placed his hand on my shoulder.

Little by little I understood that all was at an end, now that he wanted to complete his studies in Paris; never again should I have my big brother with me!

Our one hope of coming together again was that house in Paris where the trail of our forlorn adventure might be rediscovered . . . But with Meaulnes himself so sad, what a poor hope was that for me!

My parents were told the news: M. Seurel showed great surprise, but soon yielded to Augustin's reasons; Millie, the good housewife, was most upset at the idea that Meaulnes' mother would see our house in a state of unusual untidiness . . . The trunk, alas! was soon packed. We sought out his Sunday shoes from under the stairs; a few underclothes from the cupboard; then his papers and schoolbooks – all that a boy of eighteen possesses in the world.

Mme. Meaulnes arrived at midday with her carriage. She lunched with Augustin at the Café Daniel and took him away with hardly a word of explanation, as soon as the horse had been fed and harnessed. We said good-bye to them on the threshold; and the carriage disappeared at the turning of the Cross-Roads.

Millie rubbed her shoes in front of the door and went back into the cold dining-room, to tidy what had been disarranged. As for me, I found myself obliged, the first time for months, to face alone a long Thursday evening – with the clear feeling that the old carriage had borne away my youth forever.

I BETRAY HIM

What was I to do!

The weather was clearing a little. It seemed as if the sun would come through. Occasionally a door banged in the big house. Then silence returned once more. From time to time my father crossed the playground to fetch a scuttle of coal to feed the stove. I saw the white washing hanging on the lines, and I had no wish to go back to the sad room, changed to a drying-room, in order to face my last task of the year, the preparation for the Training College Entrance Exam, which, however, ought to have been my only thought.

A queer thing: a feeling akin to freedom was blended with the boredom which tortured me. Meaulnes gone, the whole adventure ended in failure, I seemed at any rate free from that strange longing, that mysterious preoccupation which kept me from behaving like every one else. Meaulnes gone, I was no longer the fellow-adventurer, no longer the brother on the trail; I became a boy again like other village boys. And this was easy, for I had only to follow my natural inclination.

The youngest of the brothers Roy passed along the muddy street; he was swinging at the end of a string, then flinging into the air three horse-chestnuts which fell into the playground. I was at such a loose end that three or four times I quite liked throwing back the chestnuts to him over the wall.

Suddenly I saw him give up this childish game and run towards a cart which was coming along the Old Plank Road. To climb in at the back of the cart without it stopping was quickly done. I recognised Delouche's horse and cart. Jasmin was driving and the big Boujardon was standing up in it. They were coming back from the meadow.

'Come with us, François!' called out Jasmin, who must already have known that Meaulnes had gone.

And indeed, without a word to a soul, I clambered up into the jolting cart and stood like the others with my back against the tall uprights. It took us to the house of the widow Delouche.

We are now in the back parlour of the good woman who keeps what is both an inn and a grocer's shop. A white ray of sunlight glints in at the low window, onto the tin boxes and a barrel of vinegar. Big Boujardon sits down on the window-sill, and the huge fellow munches Savoy biscuits, facing us with a fat smile. The biscuit tin, opened on a barrel within reach, is half empty. The young Roy screams with delight. There is a kind of intimacy of the wrong sort between us. Jasmin and Boujardon are to be my friends, now, I see. The course of my life has suddenly changed. It seems to me that Meaulnes has been gone a very long time and that his adventure is an old sad story, but finished.

Young Roy has discovered on a shelf a half-empty bottle of liqueur. Delouche offers us each a drink, but, as there is only one glass, we all drink out of it. They help me first, with slight condescension, as if I were not one of themselves, not a sportsman, not a peasant. This rather annoys me. And when Meaulnes is spoken of I become anxious to show that I know his story and to tell some of it, just to scatter my annoyance and regain my composure. In what way could this hurt him since all his adventures here are now finished? . . .

Am I telling this story badly? It does not produce the effect which I was expecting.

My companions, like good country folk whom nothing surprises, remain unimpressed by such trifles.

'Only a wedding! What!' says Boujardon. 'Delouche has seen one at Preveranges which was still more peculiar.'

The mansion? Oh, there would be in the neighbourhood people who'd heard of it, right enough.

The girl? Meaulnes would marry her when once he had served his year as a soldier. 'He should have spoken to us about it,' adds one of them, 'and shown us his plan, instead of confiding in a gipsy!'

I am caught in failure; here is my chance to quicken their curiosity: I decide to explain who this gipsy was, where he came from; his strange fate . . . Boujardon and Delouche do not care to listen.

'That fellow's done it all. It's him who made Meaulnes unsociable. Meaulnes who used to be such a jolly chap! It's him who started that silly nonsense about boarding ships and night attacks, making us into a kind of school brigade . . .'

'You know,' said Jasmin, looking at Boujardon and shaking his head in repeated nods, 'it was a jolly good job I reported him to the police. That chap did a lot of mischief in these parts and would have done more! . . .'

And I almost agree with them. The whole affair would have taken a different turn if we had not come to look upon it as so mysterious and tragic. The influence of that Frantz spoiled everything . . .

But suddenly, while I am absorbed in these thoughts, a noise is heard in the shop. Jasmin Delouche quickly hides the bottle of liqueur behind a barrel; the fat Boujardon climbs down from his window, places his foot on an empty and dusty bottle which rolls away, and twice he nearly topples over. Young Roy, half choking with laughter, pushes us all from behind to hurry us out.

126

Without quite understanding what is happening, I run away with them; we cross the yard and by means of a ladder we climb into a hayloft. I hear the voice of a woman calling us good-for-nothings.

'I should never have thought she would be back so soon,' says Jasmin in a whisper.

Only then do I understand that we were there for no good, but to steal biscuits and liqueur. I am as much disappointed as that wrecked mariner who, fancying he was talking with a man, suddenly found himself conversing with a monkey. I think only of leaving the loft, these adventures displease me so much. Besides, night is falling . . . My companions make me go by back ways, then across two gardens, and round a pond, until I find myself back in a muddy wet street in which the lights of the Café Daniel are reflected.

I am not proud of the way I have spent my evening. I soon find myself at the Cross-Roads. Suddenly, against my will, at the bend of the road, I seem to see, once more, the clean-cut face of a brother smiling at me; a last waving of the hand and the carriage disappearing . . .

A cold wind, getting into my overall, makes it flap, a wind similar to those of that memorable winter so tragic and so fine. Already everything appears to me less easy. In the big class-room, where my parents await me for dinner, sudden draughts mingle with the feeble heat of the stove. I shiver, while I am being reproached for my afternoon of idle roaming. Though the very thing that might help me would be to resume my old regular life, I am even deprived, that evening, of the consolation of sitting at my usual place at dinner. The table has not been laid; we all eat off our knees, each settling where best he can in the dark classroom. I eat in silence the thin cake which has been cooked on the top of the stove and which, intended as a reward for a Thursday of diligent work, has been left to burn on the red-hot rings.

In the evening, alone in my room, I hasten to bed to stifle the remorse which I feel surging up from the depths of my grief. But twice I awoke during the night, fancying at first that I heard the creaking of the bed in which Meaulnes used to turn over, all of a heap, and the second time listening for the light steps of the hunter upon the watch, in the dim distance of the lumber-rooms . . .

THE THREE LETTERS
FROM MEAULNES

In all my life I have received only three letters from Meaulnes. They are still at home in a chest of drawers. Each time I read them again, I feel the same sadness as of old.

The first arrived two days after he had left.

MY DEAR FRANÇOIS,

To-day, as soon as I got to Paris, I went in front of the house mentioned. I saw nothing. There was no one there. No one will ever be there.

The building mentioned by Frantz is a private house one storey high. Mademoiselle de Galais' room must be on the first floor. The top windows are the most hidden by the trees, but one sees them quite well from the pavement, as one walks by.

128

All the curtains have been drawn and it would be mad to hope that, one day, Yvonne de Galais' face would appear from behind the drawn curtains.

The house stands on a boulevard . . . It was raining a little on trees already green. You could hear the sharp clanging of the tramcars always going by.

I walked up and down, underneath the windows, for nearly two hours. I went in for a drink at a bar close by, so as not to be taken for a burglar up to some mischief. Then I returned to my hopeless watch.

Night came. Windows lit up nearly everywhere, but not in that house. There is certainly no one there. And yet Easter is approaching.

Just as I was about to leave, a girl or a young woman – I don't know which – came and sat on one of the rain-soaked benches. She was dressed in black with a small white collar. When I left, she was still there, not having stirred in spite of the cold of the evening, and waiting, goodness knows for what or for whom. You see, Paris is full of fools like me.

AUGUSTIN

Time passed. I waited in vain for a word from Meaulnes all Easter Monday and the following days – days so calm after the Easter fever that just to wait for summer seemed the only thing to be done. June brought examinations and a terrible heat, a suffocating haze hovering over the countryside, without a breath of wind to dispel it. Night afforded no coolness and consequently no respite from this torture. It was during this unbearable month of June that I received the second letter from Admiral Meaulnes.

June, 189 . .

MY DEAR CHAP,

This time all hope is gone. I have known it since yesterday evening. My grief, which I hardly felt at first, has been increasing ever since.

Every evening I went and sat on that bench, watching, pondering, hoping in spite of all.

Yesterday, after dinner, the night was dark and stifling. People were talking on the pavement, under the trees. Above the dark leaves – toned to green by the lights – flats were lit up on the second and third storeys. Here and there, summer had forced a window to be thrown wide open . . . The lamp could be seen standing alight on the table, scarcely changing the sultry obscurity of June; you could see almost to the other end of the room . . . Ah! if the dark window of Yvonne de Galais had suddenly lit up as the others, I believe I should have found courage to go up the stairs, to knock and enter . . .

The girl of whom I spoke to you was still waiting there, like me. I came to think that she might know the house, and I asked her.

'I know,' she said, 'that at one time, in this house, a girl and her brother used to come for the holidays. But I learned that the brother had run away from his parents' country-house and was never found again, and that the girl had married. That explains why the house is shut up.'

I walked off. Ten steps farther, I stumbled against the curb of the pavement and nearly fell. During the night – it was last night – when the women and the children left off their noise in the back yards, and I might have gone to sleep, I began to hear the cabs rolling by in the street. They passed only now and then. But no sooner had one gone by than, in spite of myself,

I waited for the next: the horse's bell, his hoofs clinking on the asphalt . . . And it went on repeating: empty town, your poor love gone, eternal night, summer, fever . . .

Seurel, dear man, I am in great distress.

AUGUSTIN

Few confidences in these letters, whatever you may think! Meaulnes did not tell me either why he had remained silent so long, or what he now intended to do. I had the impression that he was breaking with me, his adventure over, as he was breaking with his past. It was no good my writing to him; I received no reply. Only a word of congratulation when I passed my preliminary Matriculation. In September I heard through a school friend that he had been for his holidays to his mother's at La Ferté d'Angillon. But, that year, invited by my Uncle Florentin, we had spent the holidays at Vieux-Nançay. And Meaulnes went back to Paris without my having a chance to see him.

I received the last of the three letters I ever received from Meaulnes, on my return to school, at the end of November, while I was working with melancholy zeal for my final Matriculation, hoping in the following year to secure a teacher's post without going through Bourges Training College.

'I still go under that window,' he wrote. 'I still wait, not that there is any hope: just sheer madness. At the end of these cold autumn Sundays, about the time when night comes, I cannot decide to go home and close the shutters of my room without returning to stand there in the chilly street.

'I am like the mad woman of Sainte-Agathe who would go to her front door every minute and look towards the station, one hand raised above her eyes, to see if her dead son were coming home.

'Seated on a bench, shivering and wretched, I take pleasure in imagining that some one is going to take me gently by the arm . . . I should turn round. It would be she. "I am a little late," she would simply say. And all suffering and all madness vanish away. We enter our home. Her furs are cold, her veil damp; she brings in with her a flavour of the outside mist; and as she draws near the fire, I see the flaxen fairness of her hair and the soft outlines of her beautiful face bent towards the flame . . .

'Alas! the pane remains white, with the curtain drawn across it. And should the girl from the Lost Land draw it aside, I have no longer anything to tell her.

'Our adventure is at an end. Winter, this year, is as dead as the grave. Perhaps when we die, perhaps death alone will give us the key, the sequence and the end of this adventure that failed.

'Seurel, the other day, I asked you to think of me. Now, on the contrary, it is better to forget me. It would be better to forget everything.

.   .   .   .

'A. M.'

And this new winter proved as dead as the preceding one had been alive with mysterious life: the church square without gipsies; the playground which the boys deserted on the stroke of four . . . the classroom where I studied alone and without pleasure . . . In February, for the first time that winter, snow fell, definitely burying the tale of our adventures, blurring every trail, blotting out the last traces. And I tried, as Meaulnes had asked me in his letter, to forget everything.

Third Part

BATHING

The bad lads of the countryside thought it a lark to smoke cigarettes, to put sugar and water on their hair to make it curl, to kiss girls from the Continuation School in the street, and to call out from behind a hedge, 'Pokebonnet,' to rag a passing nun. At twenty, however, bad lads of that kind can very well improve and become often most sensible fellows. The problem is graver when the bad lad's appearance is wizened and old, when his mind is occupied with low tales of the women roundabout, when he is always making stupid remarks about Gilberte Poquelin for the other boys to laugh. But even so there is still room for hope . . .

That was the case with Jasmin Delouche. He continued, I do not know why, but certainly from no wish to pass exams, to study with the top form when every one would rather he gave it up. Between whiles, too, he learned the plasterer's trade with his Uncle Dumas. And soon this Jasmin Delouche and Boujardon and a softish fellow called Denis, son of the deputy mayor, were the only big boys with whom I cared to associate, because they belonged to 'Meaulnes' time.'

Besides, Delouche was genuinely keen to be my friend. To tell the truth, though he had been Admiral Meaulnes' enemy, he wanted to be the Admiral Meaulnes of the school: at any rate, he regretted perhaps not having been his lieutenant. Less thick than Boujardon, he had felt I believe, what an extraordinary event Meaulnes had been in our life. And I often heard him repeat: 'Ah! that's what he used to say, Admiral Meaulnes . . .' or again, 'Just as Admiral Meaulnes would've said . . .'

This old-looking fellow, besides being more of a man than we were, got hold of ripping things which gave him a pull over us: a mongrel with long white hair who answered to the irritating name of Bécali and fetched stones thrown ever so far, without being much good for anything else; a second-hand bicycle which Jasmin let us ride sometimes in the evening after school, but on which he preferred to exercise the village girls; last but not least, a white donkey, quite blind, which could be harnessed to any vehicle.

It was Dumas' donkey, but, in the summer, it was lent to Jasmin whenever we went bathing in the Cher. His mother, at such times, always gave him a bottle of lemonade which we placed under the driver's seat, amongst the stiff, dry bathing-drawers. And we set out, eight to ten big boys from the top form, going with M. Seurel, some on foot, others hoisted in the donkey cart which we left behind at Deep Waters Farm, where the path along the Cher became like a ravine.

I have good reason to remember in all its minute details one outing of this kind, when Jasmin's donkey took to the Cher the slips, luggage, lemonade, and M. Seurel, while we followed on foot. It was during the month of August. We had just finished examinations. We were care-free, and the whole summer, all happiness, seemed to belong to us; so, early that fine Thursday afternoon, we marched along the road singing, not knowing what we sang or why we sang it.

On the way, only one shadow fell on this innocent picture. We noticed Gilberte Poquelin ahead of us. She walked alluringly, in a rather short skirt and high-heeled shoes; she had the sweet yet bold air of a girl who was nearly a woman. She left the road for a by-lane, no doubt on her way to fetch milk. Little Coffin at once proposed to Jasmin to follow her.

'It wouldn't be the first time I'd kissed her either . . .' said the other. And he began to relate several risky stories concerning her and her girl friends, while, by way of bragging, our little troop took to the lane and left M. Seurel on the road forging ahead in the donkey cart. Once in the lane, however, our band began to scatter. Even Delouche, in our presence, did not appear over-anxious to approach the girl who hurried on, and he did not come nearer than fifty yards. There was a display of cock-crowing and hen-clucking, a few enticing little bursts of whistling; then we walked back the way we had come, feeling uncomfortable and thwarted. Back on the road, we had to run, under the blazing sun, too. We no longer sang.

We undressed and dressed again in the parched willow-ground bordering the Cher. The willows sheltered us from on-lookers, but not from the sun. Our feet were on sand and dry mud; our one thought was for the bottle of widow Delouche's

137

lemonade being kept cool in the pool at Deep Waters, a pool hollowed out in the very bank of the Cher.

There were always pale-greenish weeds to be found at the bottom, and two or three creatures which looked like wood-lice; but the water was so clear, so transparent, that fishermen never hesitated to kneel and drink at it, one hand placed on either bank.

Alas! it happened that day as it always did . . . Once we were dressed and, squatting on our heels in a circle, were ready to share the cool lemonade out of two tumblers, after inviting M. Seurel to take his share, there came to each of us scarcely more than a little froth which grated on the throat and only aggravated one's thirst. So finally, as his turn came, each of us went to the pool we had at first despised and slowly lowered his face to the level of the clear water. But we were not all used to these peasants' ways. Several of us, myself included, never managed to quench our thirst: some because they did not like water; others because their throats contracted at the fear of swallowing a woodlouse; others again, deceived by the trans-parency of the still water and unable to estimate the exact dis-tance to its surface, pushed half of their faces in with their lips and drew in through the nose stinging water which seemed quite hot; others for all these reasons put together . . . What did it matter! It always seemed to us, there on the parched banks of the Cher, that the whole fresh beauty of nature was enclosed in that spot. And even now, whenever I hear the word pool anywhere, it is of that one pool I lovingly think.

We came back at dusk with the same care-free spirit as when we went. The Deep Waters' track, leading up to the road, was a brook in the winter, but in the summer a ravine unfit for traffic, obstructed by holes and big roots and leading uphill between tall rows of shady trees. Some of the bathers went

138

that way, just for fun. But with M. Seurel, Jasmin, and several other boys, we followed an easy sandy path running parallel to the first and bordering a neighbouring farm. We could hear the others talk and laugh close to us, down below, hidden from sight in the shady path, while Delouche told his mannish tales ... At the top of the tall row of trees, evening insects were droning and could be seen against the clear sky, as they moved around the lacework of the leaves. Sometimes, one suddenly tumbled down, its hum fizzling out all at once ... A beautiful quiet summer evening! ... A peaceful homecoming, void of hope, but also of longing, after an ordinary little country outing ... Once again, without realising it, Jasmin came to disturb this peacefulness ...

Just as we reached the top of the hill, at the place where two huge ancient stones stand – they are rumoured to be the remains of a fortress – he began to speak of the estates he had visited, above all of one half forsaken in the neighbourhood of Vieux-Nançay: the Sand Pit Manor. With his Allier accent, which shows affectation in rounding off some words and in shortening others, he related having seen, some years previously, in the tumble-down chapel of the old manor, a tombstone on which were carved the words:

HERE LIES
SIR GALOIS, KNIGHT,
FAITHFUL TO HIS GOD, HIS KING
AND HIS LOVE.

'Well! I never!' said M. Seurel, slightly shrugging his shoulders, ill at ease at the turn the conversation had taken, yet anxious nevertheless to let us talk like men.

Then Jasmin went on describing the manor house as if he had spent his life there.

On their way home from Vieux-Nançay, he and Dumas had more than once been puzzled by the old grey tower which could be seen above the firs. There, in the middle of the woods, you came to a maze of decrepit buildings which you could visit when the owners were away. One of the keepers of the place, to whom they had given a lift, had once taken them to the mysterious manor. But since then everything had been razed to the ground; there only remained, people said, the farm and a small country-house. The occupiers were still the same: an old naval officer, in reduced circumstances, and his daughter.

He went on talking . . . talking . . . I listened attentively, feeling, without being aware of it, that all this concerned facts well known to me, when suddenly, in the simple way extraordinary things do happen, Jasmin turned to me and touched me on the arm as if struck by an idea which had never occurred to him.

'My goodness, now I come to think of it,' he said, 'it must have been there Meaulnes – you know, Admiral Meaulnes? – went.

'Of course,' he went on, for I did not answer him, 'and I remember that the keeper used to speak of the son of the place, a queer fellow who had very weird ideas . . .'

I no longer listened to him, convinced as I was from the first that he had guessed right and that in front of me, far from Meaulnes, far from all hope, there had just opened out, as clear and easy as a familiar road, a path to the manor without a name.

AT FLORENTIN'S

Just as far as I had been an unhappy child, dreamy and retiring, so I now became resolute and as we say at home 'determined,' when I felt that upon me depended the outcome of this high adventure.

From that evening, I believe, my knee definitely ceased to hurt me.

Vieux-Nançay was the parish to which the Sand Pit estate belonged and where all M. Seurel's relatives lived, and in particular my Uncle Florentin, a tradesman with whom we often spent the end of September. Free as I was from examinations, I did not want to wait, and was granted permission to go at once to my uncle. But I decided to say nothing to Meaulnes as long as I could not be certain of having good news to impart. For, indeed, what was the good of drawing him out of his despair, to plunge him back into it, perhaps more deeply, afterwards?

Vieux-Nançay was for many years my favourite place in the world, the place that meant holidays, where we only went on rare occasions, when a carriage could be hired to take us. There had formerly been some disagreement with the branch of the family living there, and no doubt this explains why one had each time to beg Millie so hard to get her to come. But I cared little about these squabbles! . . . No sooner was I there than I became lost in the crowd of uncles and cousins, boys and girls, and enjoyed a life crammed with jolly doings.

We used to live with Uncle Florentin and Aunt Julie. They had a boy of my age, Cousin Firmin, and eight daughters, the two eldest of whom, Marie-Louise and Charlotte, might have been seventeen and fifteen. They kept a large shop in front of the church, at the entrance to this small town in Sologne – a sort of general store, the shopping centre for all the neighbouring gentry and sportsmen living in lonely places in the remote country, often thirty kilometres from any station.

This shop, with its grocery and drapery counters, had numerous windows looking on the road and a glass door opening on the church square. But a strange thing, though quite ordinary in this poor district, the floor of the shop was of trodden earth.

At the back of the premises were six rooms, each stocked with a different kind of goods: the room with hats, the room with garden tools, the room with lamps ... goodness knows what! When, as a child, I used to go through this maze of a store, it seemed as if my eyes would never exhaust all its marvels. And even at that time I still thought that there could be no real holidays in any other place.

The family lived in the big kitchen, the door of which opened on the shop, and in this kitchen, at the end of September, huge fires were blazing by the side of which the gamekeepers and poachers who sold game to Florentin often came for a drink quite early in the morning, while the little girls, who were already up, went all over the place, making much noise, or smoothed one another's hair with 'some nice-smelling stuff.' On the walls some old photographs, yellowish groups of schoolboys, depicted my father – after one had taken some time to recognise him in his uniform – amidst his Training College friends ...

The mornings were always spent there; or in the yard where Florentin grew dahlias and reared guinea-fowls; here, seated on soap chests, you set about roasting coffee, or unpacking crates filled with all kinds of carefully wrapped things, the name of which we did not always know . . .

All day long the shop was invaded by peasants or by the coachmen of the neighbouring gentry. Carts, coming from far out in the country and dripping with the September fog, would pull up and stop in front of the glass door. And from the kitchen we listened to the peasant-women's talk, curious to hear all their stories . . .

But in the evening, after eight o'clock, when we went out with lanterns to take hay to the horses whose reeking skins filled the stables with steam, the whole of the shop belonged to us!

Marie-Louise, the eldest of my cousins, though one of the smallest, was still in the shop, folding and putting away rolls of cloth and coaxing us to come and cheer her up. So Firmin and I with all the girls burst into the huge shop, under the overhead porcelain lamps, and coffee-grinders were set turning and acrobatic stunts performed on the counters; sometimes Firmin brought out from the attics some old trombone covered with verdigris, for the trodden earth floor was good to dance on . . .

I still blush at the idea that, at any moment in those previous years, Mlle. de Galais might have come in and caught us at these childish games . . . But it was just before nightfall, one evening of that month of August, while I was quietly talking with Marie-Louise and Firmin, that I saw her for the first time . . .

The very first evening of my arrival at Vieux-Nançay I had questioned my Uncle Florentin concerning the Sand Pit estate.

'It is no longer an estate,' he told me. 'Everything has been sold, and the buyers, sportsmen, have pulled down the old buildings to enlarge their shoot; the great courtyard is by now just a waste land of heather and broom. The former owners have only kept a one-storey shack and the farm. You'll often have a chance of seeing Mademoiselle de Galais here; it's she does all the shopping, coming sometimes on horseback, sometimes driving, but always, the same old horse, old Bélisaire . . . It's a funny turn-out!'

I was so upset that I no longer knew what question to ask so as to learn more.

'But surely they were rich?'

'Yes. M. de Galais used to give parties to amuse his son, a strange boy, full of queer ideas. To give him a good time, the father always thought of some grand new thing. They had girls come from Paris . . . fellows from Paris and elsewhere . . .

'The Sand Pit was all falling to ruins, Mme. de Galais was near her end, they were still trying to amuse him, putting up with all his whims. 'Twas last winter – no, the winter before, they gave their biggest fancy-dress fête. Half of their guests were from Paris, others were country folk. They had bought or hired any amount of marvellous fancy costumes, games, horses, boats. Always to amuse Frantz de Galais. It was said that he was about to marry, and that it was his betrothal party. But he was much too young. And it was all broken off suddenly; he ran away and he's never been seen since . . . After the lady's death, Mademoiselle de Galais was suddenly left alone with her father, the old sea captain.'

'Isn't she married?' I asked at last.

'No,' he said, 'I've heard nothing of it. Might you be a suitor?'

Very much put out, I confessed to him, as briefly and as discreetly as possible, that my best friend, Augustin Meaulnes, would perhaps be one.

'Ah!' said Florentin, smiling, 'if he's not particular as to money, it is a good match . . . Should I say a word about it to M. de Galais? He still comes here sometimes to get small shot for game. I always give him a taste of my old brandy.'

But I begged him to do nothing of the sort, to wait. And on my part, I delayed to inform Meaulnes. Such an accumulation of lucky circumstances made me feel rather anxious. And this anxiety forced me not to inform Meaulnes of anything before I had at least seen the girl.

I had not long to wait. The next day, a little before dinner, night began to fall, and with it came a fresh mist, more like September than August. Firmin and I, guessing the shop would be empty of customers at the moment, had come to talk to Marie-Louise and Charlotte. I had confided to them the secret which had brought me to Vieux-Nançay earlier than usual. Elbows on the counter or seated with both hands stretched out flat on the polished wood, we were telling one another all we knew about the mysterious girl – and that was precious little – when a noise of wheels made us turn round.

'There she is, that's her,' they whispered.

A few seconds later the queer equipage stopped in front of the glass door. An old farm carriage with rounded panels and small moulded cornices, the like of which I had never seen before in that district; an old white horse which always seemed to want to graze along the road, so low did he bend his head as he walked; and on the box – I say it in all simplicity of heart, but knowing well what I say – the most beautiful girl the world may ever have held.

I never saw so much grace combined with so much gravity. Her costume gave her so slender a waist that she seemed fragile. A long brown cloak, which she took off as she came in, was thrown on her shoulders. She was the gravest of girls, the

145

frailest of women. A mass of fair hair weighed on her forehead and over her face which was delicate in outline and delicate in moulding. On her pure complexion summer had placed two freckles . . . I detected only one defect in so much beauty: in moments of sadness, discouragement, or simply deep thought, this pure face was slightly dappled with red, as happens to people suffering from some serious and unsuspected complaint. Then one's admiration on looking at her was replaced by a kind of pity, the more heart-rending because the more surprising.

At least this is what I seemed to discover as she slowly got down from the carriage, and Marie-Louise, with complete ease, at last introduced me and encouraged me to speak.

They offered her a polished chair, and she sat down, her back resting against the counter, while we remained standing. She appeared to know the shop well and to be fond of it. Aunt Julie, being at once informed, came in, and talked quietly, with her hands crossed over her stomach and her peasant shopkeeper's white cap nodding gently. And thus the moment when conversation would begin on my part – which I rather dreaded – was postponed . . .

It came very simply.

'And so,' said Mademoiselle de Galais, 'you will soon be a teacher?'

Aunt Julie was then lighting over our heads the porcelain lamp which gave dim light to the shop; I saw the girl's sweet childlike face, her candid blue eyes, and was all the more surprised at her clear and serious voice. Whenever she stopped talking, her gaze settled away from the listener, not moving while she awaited the answer, and she slightly bit her lip.

'I should also be teaching,' she said, 'if only M. de Galais would let me! I would teach little boys, like your mother . . .'

146

And she smiled, showing me thus that my cousins had spoken to her of me.

'You see,' she went on, 'the village people are always very polite and kind and obliging to me. And I am very fond of them. But then, what credit can there be in my loving them? . . . While, with a school teacher, they are apt to be rather cross and critical, don't you think? There are endless tales of lost pencils, exercise-books too dear, and of children who do not learn . . . Well, I would fight it out with them and they would like me nevertheless. It would be far more difficult . . .'

And, without a smile, she dropped back into her thoughtful and childlike attitude, with her motionless blue gaze.

We were, the three of us, embarrassed by that ease in speaking of delicate things, of what is secret and subtle, and only comes off well in books. There was a moment's silence; and slowly a long discussion began . . .

But with a sort of regret and of animosity against I know not what essence of mystery in her life, the girl went on:

'And then I would teach the boys to be wise with a wisdom I know. I would not put into their hearts any longing to go about the world, as you will most likely do, M. Seurel, when you are an assistant master. I would teach them to find the happiness which is quite close to them, though it does not appear so . . .'

Marie-Louise and Firmin were as much confused as I was. We stood there, not saying a word. She felt our embarrassment, stopped, and bit her lip, and lowered her head, then she smiled as if she was making fun of us.

'For instance,' she said, 'there is perhaps some big silly boy who is looking for me at the other end of the world, while I am here, in Madame Florentin's shop, under this lamp, and my old horse is waiting at the door. If the young man did see me, he most likely would not believe his eyes? . . .'

147

To see her smile, daring seized me, and I felt that it was time to say, while I also laughed: 'And it may be that I know him, that big silly boy?'

She quickly looked up at me.

At that moment there was a ring at the shop door; two country women entered carrying baskets.

'Come in the "dining-room," you will be in peace,' said my aunt, as she pushed open the kitchen door.

And, as Mademoiselle de Galais was refusing and wanted to go at once, my aunt added: 'M. de Galais is there, chatting with Florentin by the fire.'

There was always, even in the month of August, the habitual fir-faggot crackling and blazing in the big kitchen. There also a porcelain lamp was lit and an old man with a kind, wrinkled face entirely shaven – the type of man nearly always silent like one burdened with age and memories – was seated close to Florentin in front of two glasses of brandy.

Florentin greeted me.

'François!' he called out in his strong huckster's voice, as if there was a river between us or many acres of land, 'I have just arranged an afternoon's outing on the banks of the Cher for next Thursday. Those who like can shoot game, others can fish, or dance, or bathe! . . . Mademoiselle, you will come on horseback; that's agreed with M. de Galais. I've arranged everything . . .

'And François!' he added, as if he had only just thought of it, 'you might bring your friend, Monsieur Meaulnes . . . It's Meaulnes he is called, isn't it?'

Mlle. de Galais had stood up, suddenly growing very pale. And at that precise moment, it came back to my mind that one day, at the mysterious manor, by the side of the lake, Meaulnes had told her his name . . .

148

When she held out her hand to me at the moment of leaving, there was between us, more clearly than if we had spoken many words, a secret understanding which death alone was to break, and a friendship more moving than a great passion.

. . . At four o'clock next morning, Firmin knocked at the door of the little room which I occupied in the guinea-fowls' yard. It was still night and I had great trouble in finding my belongings on the table, amongst the brass candlesticks and the brand-new statuettes of saints which had been chosen out of the shop to decorate my dwelling on the day before my arrival. In the yard, I heard Firmin pumping up my bicycle tyres, and in the kitchen Aunt Julie using the bellows to make up the fire. The sun was hardly risen when I left. But my day was to be long: I was first going to lunch at Sainte-Agathe to explain my prolonged absence, then, continuing my way, I meant, before the evening, to reach La Ferté d'Angillon and the home of my friend Augustin Meaulnes.

THE GHOST

I had never been for a really long ride on a bicycle. This was my first. But for a long time Jasmin had been secretly teaching me how to ride in spite of my bad knee. A bicycle is fairly good fun for any ordinary fellow: what should it not mean to a poor chap like me, who, only a short time back, dragged his leg wretchedly along, sweating after a mile or two? To sweep down hills and plunge into the valley hollows; to cover as on wings the far stretches of the road ahead and to find them in bloom at your approach; to pass through a village in a moment, and to take it all with you in one glance . . . in dreams only, till then, had I known such a delightful, such an easy way of getting about. I tackled even the hills with zest. For I must own, it was the road leading to Meaulnes' village I was thus eating up . . .

'A little before you reach the place,' Meaulnes had once said to me, describing his village, 'you see a great wheel with arms which the wind turns . . .' He did not know what it was used for, or perhaps pretended not to know to arouse my curiosity the more.

It was only when this August day was drawing to its close that I noticed, turning to the wind in a huge meadow, the big wheel which must have served to bring up water to a small farm near by. The first dwellings could be seen behind poplars in the meadow. Gradually, as I made my way along the curve where the road turns to follow the brook, the view expanded and opened out . . . On reaching the bridge, I discovered at last the village High Street.

In the meadow, cows were grazing, hidden by the reeds, and I heard their bells while, having dismounted from my bicycle, and my hands on the handlebar, I surveyed the country into which I was bringing tidings of such gravity. Houses with approaches over a small wooden bridge were lined up by the side of a ditch which ran down the street and looked like fishing boats at anchor on a peaceful evening with their sails clewed up. It was the time of day when a fire is being lighted in every kitchen.

Then it was that fear, and a kind of vague reluctance at coming to disturb so much peace, began to sap my courage. To increase my sudden weakness, I recalled that my Aunt Moinel lived there, on the small square of La Ferté d'Angillon.

She was one of my great-aunts. All her children were dead, but I had known Ernest well, the youngest of all, a tall boy who was to be a teacher. My great-uncle Moinel, the old registry clerk, had soon followed him, and my aunt had remained alone in her queer little house, with the rugs all of patchwork, the tables full of paper cocks, hens, and cats, and the walls decked with old diplomas, portraits of the dear defunct, and lockets containing dead hair.

With all her griefs and mourning, Aunt Moinel was the soul of oddness and good temper. When once I had found the little square where her house stood, I called her loudly through the half-open door, and from the other end of her three rooms leading out of each other, I heard her utter a shrill little cry: 'Well! Good Heavens!'

She spilled her coffee into the fire – how could she be making coffee at this time of day? – and she appeared . . . shoulders well thrown back, and on her head, something which might have been either hat, bonnet, or hood, perched high up over a huge bumpy forehead, suggesting a cross between a Mongol and a Hottentot: and she laughed with little jerks, showing what remained of her small teeth.

But while I kissed her, she clumsily and hastily took hold of the hand which was behind my back. With an air of great mystery – perfectly out of place, as we were quite alone – she squeezed into my palm a small coin which I dared not look at, but guessed to be a franc. Then, as I made a pretence at asking explanations and thanking her, she gave me a poke in the ribs, exclaiming loudly: 'Oh! go on! As if I didn't know all about it!'

She had always been poor, always borrowing, always spending. 'I have always been stupid, always unfortunate,' she would say without bitterness, in her high-pitched voice.

Feeling sure that I worried over pennies as she did, the dear woman had not waited for me to take breath before pressing into my hand her scanty savings of the day. And, in later days, too, this was always how she welcomed me.

Dinner was as strange as the greeting – both melancholy and queer at the same time. She always had a candle within reach of her hand: sometimes she carried it off and left me in the dark: sometimes she put it on the little table which was littered with chipped and cracked dishes and vases.

'The Prussians,' she said, 'broke the handles off this one in 1870, as they couldn't take it away.'

It was only then I remembered, on seeing once again this tall vase with its tragic history, that we had once dined and slept there in former days. Father was taking me to the Yonne to see a specialist who was to cure my knee. We had had to take a fast train which started before daybreak . . . That melancholy dinner now came back to my mind, and all the stories related by the old clerk as he rested his elbows on the table before his rose-coloured drink.

And I was reminded also of my fears . . . After dinner, sitting by the fire, my aunt had taken Father aside to tell him ghost stories: 'I turn round . . . Ah! my dear Louis what do I see? A little grey woman . . .'

Her head was known to be packed with terrifying nonsense of this kind.

And this very evening when dinner was over and, tired out with my bicycle ride, I had gone to bed in one of Uncle Moinel's check nightshirts, she came and sat at the foot of my bed and began to talk in the shrillest, most mysterious voice.

'Poor François, I must tell you something I've not told a soul.'

I thought: 'Now I'm in for it. Here's for another night of terror, like ten years ago! . . .'

And I listened. She nodded her head, looking straight in front of her as if she were relating the story to herself:

'I was coming back from a party with Moinel. It was the first wedding we'd been to together since poor Ernest's death; and I met my sister Adèle there, whom I'd not seen for four years. An old friend of Moinel, a very rich man, had invited us to his son's wedding at his place, the Sand Pit. We'd hired a carriage. That had cost us a good bit of money. We were making our way along the road about seven in the morning, in the middle of winter. The sun was just rising. There was no one about. But what do you think I saw all at once, right in front of us, there on the road? A little fellow posted there, a small young man, as handsome as the day, not moving, but looking at us coming. As we got nearer, we could make out his pretty face – so white and so pretty that it gave one a turn! . . .

'I clung to Moinel's arm; I was shaking like a leaf; I thought it was God himself! . . . I said to Moinel: "Look! A ghost!"

'He replied in whispers, quite furious: "Well! I saw it. You'd better shut up, you old chatterbox . . ."

'He didn't know what to do, when suddenly the horse stopped . . . At close quarters, it showed a pale face, a forehead covered with beads of sweat, a dirty tammy and long trousers. We heard its sweet voice saying: "I am not a man, I am a girl. I ran away, and I am tired out. Could you take me in your carriage, please, kind people?"

'At once we got her in. No sooner was she seated than she fainted. And guess who that was we'd come across? It was

153

Frantz de Galais' sweetheart, the young man at the Sand Pit, where we'd been invited to the wedding!'

'But there could've been no wedding,' I said, 'as the fiancée had run off!'

'Well, of course not,' she went on, looking at me quite dejectedly. 'There'd been no wedding, on account of that poor silly girl having got into her head a thousand mad notions that she explained to us. She was one of the daughters of a poor weaver. She firmly believed that so much happiness was impossible; that the young fellow was too young for her; that all the marvels he'd told her about were imagination; so when at last Frantz came to fetch her, Valentine took fright. He used to walk with her in the garden of the Archbishop's Palace at Bourges, not minding the cold or the wind. The young fellow – out of delicacy, of course, and because he loved the younger sister – was full of attention to the elder. So, my silly girl must needs get notions. She said she wanted to go home and fetch a shawl; but once there, to make sure no one would come after her, she put on man's clothes and set off on foot along the road to Paris. Her young man got a letter from her in which she said she was off to Paris to join a fellow she was in love with. But that wasn't true . . .

'"I'm happier in my sacrifice," she said to me, "than if I were his wife." Yes, poor idiot, but as a matter of fact he had never thought for a second of marrying the sister; he blew out his brains; his blood was seen in the wood, but his body was never found.'

'And what did you do with that wretched girl?'

'First of all we brought her round with a drop of brandy. Then we gave her something to eat, and we no sooner got home than she fell asleep by the fire. She stayed with us a good bit of the winter. All day long, while it was light, she

154

stitched, making dresses, trimming hats, or else she cleaned the house in a sort of rage. She it was who stuck back that wall-paper you see there. But in the evening, at nightfall, when her work was done, she would always find some excuse for going into the yard, or into the garden, or just outside the front door, even when it was cold enough to freeze one to death. And there she would be found weeping fit to break her heart.

'"Well, what's the matter now? Tell us!"

'"Nothing, Madame Moinel!"

'And she would go in.

'The neighbours used to say: "What a pretty little servant you've found, Madame Moinel!"

'In spite of all we could say, when March came she made up her mind to go on to Paris; I gave her some old dresses which she altered, Moinel paid for her ticket at the station and gave her a little money. She's not forgotten us; she's now doing dressmaking in Paris, close to Notre-Dame; she still writes at times to ask if we know anything about the Sand Pit. Once and for all, to free her of these thoughts, I replied that the estate had been sold, the buildings pulled down, the young man gone forever, and the girl married. All this is true, I should think. Since then, dear Valentine has written far less often . . .'

It was not a ghost story Aunt Moinel was relating in her thin piercing voice, so well fitted for such stories. Yet I was feeling utterly wretched. For we had sworn to Frantz, the bohemian, always to help him as brothers, and now the chance had come . . .

But was it the moment to spoil the joy I was to bring to Meaulnes the next morning, by telling him what I had just learned? What would be the good of putting him on such an impossible job? True, we had the address of the girl; but where could we find the bohemian who was always on the move? . . . Better let mad people alone, I thought. Delouche and Boujardon were quite right. How much harm this romantic Frantz had done us! And I resolved to say nothing until I had witnessed the marriage of Augustin Meaulnes with Mademoiselle de Galais.

After making this decision, a painful feeling of ill omen persisted in my mind – a stupid feeling which I quickly brushed aside.

The candle was almost out; a mosquito hummed; but Aunt Moinel, with her elbows on her knees and her head on one side under the velvet bonnet which she never took off except when she went to bed, began her story over again . . . From time to time she sharply raised her head to observe what my feelings were or perhaps to see if I was still awake. At last, cunningly, with my head on the pillow, I closed my eyes pretending to be dozing . . .

'There! You are asleep . . .' she said in a deeper voice and slightly disappointed.

I took pity on her and I protested: 'Oh, no, Auntie, I assure you . . .'

'Oh! but you are,' she said; 'besides, I quite understand that all this can hardly interest you. I am talking of people you've never known . . .'

And this time, like a coward, I made no reply.

GREAT NEWS

Next morning, when I reached the High Street, it was such fine holiday weather, it was so still, and so many peaceful and familiar sounds rose from all over the village, that the happy confidence of a bearer of good news came back to me.

Augustin and his mother lived in the old schoolhouse. On the death of his father – retired long before this and enriched by a legacy – Meaulnes had pressed his mother to buy the school in which the old schoolmaster had taught for twenty years and where he himself had learned to read. Not that it was a pleasant house to look at: it was a big square building like a little town hall, which indeed it had once been; the ground-floor windows opened on the street and were so high that no one ever looked in through them; and the yard at the back, where no tree grew and a high shelter blocked any view of the countryside, was certainly the most denuded and the most forlorn of all the forsaken playgrounds I have ever seen.

In the odd-shaped hall on which four doors opened, I found Meaulnes' mother bringing back from the garden a huge bundle of clothes which she must have put to dry at a very early hour of this long holiday morning. Her grey hair was carelessly twisted up; wisps of it fell across her face; her regular features, under her old-fashioned cap, looked tired and her eyes heavy, as if after a sleepless night, and she kept her head lowered sadly in a dreamy way.

But suddenly she saw me, and recognising me she smiled.

'You come just in time,' she said. 'Look! I was bringing in the clothes I'd put out to dry for Augustin's journey. I've spent the night looking over his accounts and getting his things together. The train leaves at five, but we shall manage to get everything ready.'

You would have said – for she showed such assurance – that she had herself taken this decision. Yet it is likely she did not even know where Meaulnes intended to go.

'Upstairs,' she said, 'you will find him busy writing in the town hall.'

I climbed up the stairs, opened the door on the right, over which the words 'Town Hall' still remained on a board, and found myself in a big room with four windows – two opening on the village, two on the country; the walls were decorated with faded portraits of the Presidents Grévy and Carnot. The chairs of the town councillors still stood in front of a table with a green baize cover, on a long platform which filled the back of the room. And there, seated in the centre of the room in the mayor's old armchair, was Meaulnes, busy writing, dipping his pen in an old-fashioned inkstand shaped like a heart. This place, which seemed meant for some well-to-do villager, was the room where Meaulnes liked to retire during the holidays, whenever he was not roaming about the country . . .

As soon as he had recognized me, he got up, but not with the eagerness I had pictured in my mind.

'Seurel!' he merely said in astonishment.

He was still the same tall youth, with marked bony features and closely cropped hair. An untrimmed moustache was beginning to droop over his lips. Always the same loyal look . . . But something like a veil of mist covered the ardour of the past, though every now and then his old passion dispelled it.

He appeared very upset to see me. At one bound I was on the platform. But, strange to say, he did not even think of holding out his hand. He turned towards me, both hands behind

158

his back, and seeming very ill at ease. And already, looking at me without seeing me, he was absorbed in what he was going to say to me. Slow to break into speech, then and always, like men who live alone – hunters and adventurers – he had come to a decision without bothering about the words required to explain it. And only now that I was in front of him did he begin painfully to seek the necessary words.

However, I gaily related to him how I had come, where I had spent the night, and that I was very surprised to see Madame Meaulnes preparing for her son's departure.

'Ah! so she's told you? . . .' he asked.

'Yes. You're not going far, I hope?'

'Yes, very far.'

Out of countenance for a moment, I no longer dared to say nytahing and did not know where to begin with my message, for I felt that presently, by a mere word, I was going to wipe out this decision which I did not understand.

But he himself spoke at last like some one who wishes to justify himself.

'Seurel,' he said, 'you know what the strange adventure of Sainte-Agathe meant to me. It was all I lived and hoped for. With that hope lost, what was to become of me? . . . How could I live like other people?

'Well, I tried to live out there in Paris, when I saw that all was finished and that it was scarcely worth while even looking for the Lost Land . . . But how could a man, who had once leapt at one bound into Paradise, get used to living like everybody else? What means happiness for others appeared to me absurd. And the day when I sincerely and deliberately decided to behave as others do, I piled up remorse for a long time to come . . .'

I sat on one of the platform chairs with my eyes on the

ground and listened without looking at him; I could not tell what to think of these obscure explanations.

'Come on, Meaulnes,' I said, 'explain yourself more clearly! Why this long journey? Have you made a mistake you must make amends for? a promise you must keep?'

'That's just it,' he replied. 'You remember that promise I made to Franz? . . .'

'Ah!' I said, relieved, 'is that all?'

'That's all. But perhaps also a fault to make good. Both things at once . . .'

There followed a moment of silence during which I decided to begin speaking and prepared my words . . .

'There's only one explanation, so I've come to believe,' he said again. 'Of course, I would have liked, once more, to see Mademoiselle de Galais, simply to see her once more . . . But I am convinced, now, that when I discovered the nameless manor, I was at the height of what stands for perfection and pure motive in any one's heart, a height I shall never reach again. In death alone, as I once wrote to you, I may hope to find again the beauty of that day . . .'

He changed his tone only to begin again with strange animation, while he came nearer to me.

'But listen, Seurel! This new intrigue and this long journey, this mistake I made and must make amends for, it is all, in a way, my old adventure still going on . . .'

A pause, during which he painfully tried to grasp once more the events of the past. I had missed the previous opportunity. For nothing on earth would I let this chance slip; and this time I spoke – too hastily, for later I bitterly regretted not having waited for his confession.

So I uttered the sentence which I had prepared for the previous occasion, and which no longer seemed to work. I said,

160

without a gesture, and scarcely raising my head: 'But what if I came to tell you that all hope is not lost?'

He looked at me; then, suddenly taking his eyes away, blushed as I have never seen any one blush: a rush of blood which must have beat hard against his temples . . .

'What do you mean?' he asked at last, indistinctly.

Then, in one gush, I related what I knew, what I had done, and how, the appearance of things having altered, it seemed almost as if it were Yvonne de Galais who had sent me to him.

He was now dreadfully pale.

During all this narrative – which he listened to in silence, with head sunk between his shoulders in the attitude of one who is taken by surprise and cannot tell how to defend himself, whether to hide or run away – I remember that he interrupted me only once. I was telling him, amongst other things, that all the Sand Pit had been pulled down and that the old manor no longer existed.

'Ah!' he said, 'there you are' (as if he had watched for a chance of justifying his behaviour and the despair into which he had sunk). 'There you are: there is nothing left . . .'

To end my tale, as I felt convinced that the assurance of such an easy course would sweep away what remained of his grief, I told him that a country outing had been arranged by my Uncle Florentin, that Mademoiselle de Galais was coming to it on horseback, and that he himself was invited . . . But he appeared completely put out and continued silent.

'You must at once cancel your journey,' I said with impatience. 'Let's go and tell your mother.'

And, as we were going downstairs together, 'That country outing? . . .' he asked with some hesitation. 'Must I really come? . . .'

'My dear good chap,' I replied, 'what a question to ask!'

He looked like a man who is pushed forward against his will.

Downstairs, Augustin gave Madame Meaulnes to understand that I would stay for lunch, dinner, and the night, and that he himself would hire a bicycle next day and go with me to Vieux-Nançay.

'Oh! very well,' she said with a nod, as if this news confirmed all she thought.

I sat down in the little dining-room under the illustrated calendars, the chiselled daggers, and the leather bottles from the Sudan which a brother of M. Meaulnes, who had been in the marines, had brought home from his distant travels . . .

Augustin left me there alone for a moment before the meal, and in the next room, where his mother had prepared his luggage, I heard him tell her, in a slightly lowered voice, not to unpack his trunk – as his journey was perhaps only delayed . . .

THE COUNTRY OUTING

I had trouble to keep up with Meaulnes along the road to Vieux-Nançay. He rode like a racer. He did not push up any of the hills. His unaccountable hesitation of the previous day was followed by a feverish nervousness and an eagerness to hasten our arrival which rather frightened me. At my uncle's he showed the same impatience and seemed unable to be interested in anything until about ten next morning, when settled in the carriage, we were ready to start for the river.

It was the end of August; the summer was drawing to a close; the empty sheaths of the yellowing chestnut trees were beginning to litter the white roads. The drive was not long. The Guelders, the farm close to the spot we were making for on the banks of the Cher, was scarcely more than two kilometres beyond the Sand Pit. Now and again we came across other guests also driving, and even young fellows on horseback, whom Florentin had boldly invited in M. de Galais' name . . . An attempt had been made, as of old, to bring rich and poor together, squires and peasants. Thus it was we noticed Jasmin Delouche coming on his bicycle, for he had, some time back, made the acquaintance of my uncle through Baladier the forester.

'There's the fellow,' said Meaulnes, spotting him, 'who had the key of the whole thing while we were searching as far as Paris. It is maddening!'

And each time he looked at him his bitterness increased. Delouche, who on the contrary considered he deserved our full gratitude, rode very near to our carriage as escort, right to the end. He had clearly taken pains with his toilet, without much result, and the end of his threadbare jacket rubbed the mudguard of his machine.

But in spite of the constraint he put upon himself to be agreeable, his old-looking face never succeeded in pleasing. It made me feel a kind of vague pity for him. But on whom would I not have had pity that day? . . .

I never recall that country outing without an obscure regret – a stifling uneasiness. I had looked forward to the day with so much joy . . . Everything appeared so perfectly contrived to make us happy. But so little happiness came of it! . . .

Yet how beautiful were the banks of the Cher! Where we

stopped, the hill sloped gently down to the riverside, and the land was divided into small green meadows and willow groves separated by fences like so many tiny gardens. On the other side, the river had steep banks cut out of rugged grey hills; and on the most distant of these you could make out romantic country seats, each with a turret rising from the firs. Now and again, in the far distance, was heard the barking of the pack of hounds at the Chateau de Préveranges.

We had reached this spot through intricate little lanes thick with sharp flints or else full of sand – lanes which, near the river, springs changed into streams. As we went by, wild brambles caught at our sleeves. And at one moment we plunged into the cool darkness at the bottom of ravines, while the next, owing to a break in the hedges, we were bathed in the clear light of the whole valley. Then, farther out on the other bank, as we approached, a man hanging onto the rock was with slow movements setting ground lines for fishing. Heavens! what a beautiful day it was!

We settled on a grass plot, a clearing in a copse of silver birches. It was like a wide lawn of fine turf and seemed to offer room for endless games.

The horses were unharnessed and taken to the farm. Then we began to unpack the food – right in the wood – and to set up on the grass the small folding tables my uncle had brought.

Just then volunteers were required to go to the entrance of the adjoining road to keep watch for the late comers and show them where we were. I at once offered myself; Meaulnes followed me, and we posted ourselves by the suspension bridge at the junction of many lanes and the road leading from the Sand Pit.

There we had to wait, walking up and down talking of the past, trying as best we could to divert our thoughts. One more

164

carriage arrived from Vieux-Nançay with some unknown peasants and a tall girl decked with ribbons. Then nothing more, or
rather three children in a donkey cart, the children of the former
gardener at the Sand Pit.

'I seem to recognise them,' said Meaulnes. 'I feel sure these
are the kids who got hold of my hands, that first evening of the
fête, and took me in to dinner . . .'

But at that moment the donkey refused to go and the children
jumped down to pull at the beast, poking and whacking him as
hard as they could; then Meaulnes, much put out, pretended he
had made a mistake . . .

I asked them if they had come across Monsieur and Mademoiselle de Galais on the road. One replied that he did not
know; the other, 'I believe so, sir.' So we were no better off.

At last they walked down towards the lawn, some pulling
the donkey by the bridle, others pushing behind. And we turned
back to wait. Meaulnes kept his eyes fixed on the bend of the
Sand Pit road, watching with a sort of terror for the approaching vision of the girl he had once so much sought. A strange
and almost ludicrous nervousness clutched at him and vented
itself on Jasmin. From the small hillock on which we had
climbed to survey the road, we could see, on the lawn down
below, a group of guests amongst whom Delouche was trying
to cut a fine figure.

'Look at that idiot holding forth!' Meaulnes said to me.

And I replied, 'Leave him alone. He does the best he can,
poor chap.'

Meaulnes would not stop. Some distance away a hare or a
squirrel must have come out of the thicket. Jasmin, to show off,
pretended to chase it.

'Look at that! He's running now! . . .' said Meaulnes, as if
that beat everything in cheek.

And this time I could not keep from laughing; Meaulnes, too, but only for a moment.

After another quarter of an hour:

'Suppose she does not come? . . .' he asked.

I replied, 'But she promised. Try and be patient!'

He resumed his watch. But at last, unable to put up any longer with this unbearable delay, he said:

'Listen. I'm going down to the others. I don't know what fate is now against me; but if I stay here, I feel sure she will never come – that it is utterly impossible she will presently appear at the end of this road.'

And he went away towards the lawn, leaving me alone. I walked some hundred yards along the road to kill time. And at the first bend I saw Yvonne de Galais riding side-saddle on an old white horse, so frisky this morning that she was obliged to pull the reins to prevent him trotting. M. de Galais, in silence, painfully walked on foot by the horse's head. On the way they had most likely taken turns in using the old mount.

Seeing me alone, the girl smiled, jumped nimbly to the ground, and, giving the reins to her father, came towards me while I hurried up to her.

'I am pleased at finding you alone,' she said. 'For I wouldn't show old Bélisaire to any one but you, and I don't want to put him with the other horses. He's too ugly and too old, for one thing, then I always fear he might get hurt by the others. Yet he's the only one I dare to ride, and when he's dead, I shall never go on horseback . . .'

In Mademoiselle de Galais as in Meaulnes I felt, beneath this charming animation and this grace which seemed so peaceful, something impatient and almost anxious. She talked faster than usual. In spite of a rosy flush on her cheeks, there was an

166

intense pallor here and there round her eyes, on her forehead, in which all her trouble was manifest.

We agreed to tie Bélisaire to a tree, in the little wood near the road. Old M. de Galais, still not saying a word, produced the halter from the holster and tied up the animal – rather low, so it seemed to me. I promised to send presently from the farm hay and oats and straw . . .

And Mademoiselle de Galais arrived on the lawn just as I picture her in former days, walking towards the shore of the lake, when Meaulnes saw her for the first time.

Taking her father's arm and with her left hand holding aside the flap of the long cloak that wrapped her round, she drew near the guests with her usual expression, at once so serious and so childlike. I walked by her. All the guests, who had scattered about or were playing farther out, stood up and gathered to welcome her. There was a brief moment of silence while every one gazed as she approached.

Meaulnes had mingled with the group of young men and nothing marked him out from amongst his companions except his height; yet there were others almost as tall. He did nothing to draw attention to himself, making no gesture, taking no step forward. I could see him, dressed in grey, standing motionless, and, like every one else, keeping his eyes fixed on the beautiful girl advancing. At last, however, with an unconscious and uneasy gesture, his hand went over his bare head as if amongst the well-brushed heads of his companions, to hide his own, so rough, and with hair cropped like a peasant's.

Then the group gathered round Mademoiselle de Galais. She was introduced to the girls and boys she did not know . . . My friend's turn was soon to come and I felt as anxious as he could be. I was preparing to make the introduction myself.

But, before I could say anything, the girl advanced towards him, with surprising assurance and gravity:

'I recognise Augustin Meaulnes,' she said.

And she held out her hand to him.

THE COUNTRY OUTING
(*concluded*)

Newcomers drew near almost at once to greet Yvonne de Galais and the two young people found themselves parted. By some wretched accident they were not put together for lunch at the same little table. Yet Meaulnes seemed to have recovered confidence and courage. I was isolated between Delouche and M. de Galais and more than once from this distance I saw my friend wave his hand to me.

It was only towards the end of the evening, after boating on the neighbouring pond, games, bathing, and chatting had started everywhere, that Meaulnes found himself again in the girl's presence. We were sitting on some garden chairs which we had brought, talking with Delouche, when Mademoiselle de Galais, deliberately leaving a group of young people amongst whom she seemed bored, made her way towards us. I remember that she asked us why we were not boating on The Guelders lake as the others were.

'We had a few goes this afternoon,' I replied; 'but it's rather dull and we soon tired of it.'

'Well! why shouldn't you go on the river?' she said.

'The current's too strong, we might get carried away.'

'We want a motor-boat,' said Meaulnes, 'or that steamboat there used to be.'

'We no longer have it,' she said in a rather low voice. 'We've sold it.

And there was a moment's awkward silence.

Jasmin seized this opportunity to declare that he was going to join M. de Galais.

'I shall manage to find him,' he said.

Strangeness of fate! These two, so completely different, were delighted with each other, and had hardly parted company since the morning. M. de Galais took me aside for a moment, towards evening, to tell me that I had in Delouche a friend full of tact, deference, and fine qualities. He had even perhaps entrusted to him the secret of old Bélisaire's existence and of the horse's hiding-place.

I was planning also to withdraw, but I felt the two young people so ill at ease, so worried in each other's presence, that I thought it prudent to remain.

But all this discretion on Jasmin's part, all this precaution on mine, served little purpose. These two talked, but invariably, with an obstinacy of which he must have been unaware, Meaulnes always came back to the marvels of the old days. And each time the poor tortured girl had to repeat to him that everything was gone: the old queer and oddly shaped house rased to the ground; the lake drained and filled with earth; and the children in their charming costumes dispersed for ever . . .

'Ah!' Meaulnes would simply say with despair and as if each of these disappearances showed him to be right and the girl or myself wrong . . .

We were walking side by side . . . I vainly tried to create a

169

diversion from the sadness which was coming over all three of us. For again Meaulnes, with one abrupt question, would give way to his haunting idea. He asked information about everything he had seen of old: the little girls, the driver of the old berlin, the ponies of the race.

'. . . Are the ponies also sold? So, there are no longer horses on the estate? . . .'

She replied that there were none. She did not speak of Bélisaire.

Then he conjured up the things in his bedroom; the chandeliers, the tall tooking-glass, the old broken lute . . . He inquired about all this with unwonted eagerness, as if he wanted to convince himself that nothing survived of his fine adventure, and that the girl would not bring back to him one piece of wreckage which could prove that they had not both lived in a dream – as the diver brings up from the bottom of the sea mere pebbles and seaweeds . . .

Mademoiselle de Galais and I could not refrain from smiling sadly; then she decided to explain to him:

'You will never see again the beautiful mansion that M. de Galais and I had arranged for our poor Frantz. We spent our lives doing as he wished us. He was such a strange, charming boy. But everything vanished with him on that evening of the betrothal that never came off. M. de Galais had then already lost his fortune without our knowing. Frantz was in debt and his former friends – getting news of his disappearance – at once brought us their claims. We became poor. Madame de Galais died, and in a few days we lost all our friends. Could Frantz come back – if he is not dead – and find again his friends and his fiancée, and the interrupted wedding take place – then perhaps everything would be as of old! But can the past come to life again?'

'Who knows?' said Meaulnes thoughtfully. And he put no more questions.

We were walking, all three of us, without noise on grass that was short and ever so slightly touched with yellow. Augustin had close to him on his right the girl whom he had thought forever lost. Whenever he asked one of his cruel questions, her charming and troubled face would slowly turn towards him as she answered; and once, while speaking, she gently placed her hand on his arm in a gesture full of trust and surrender. Why was Admiral Meaulnes there like a stranger, like some one who has not found what he was looking for and for whom nothing else has any interest? Three years earlier he might not have been able to bear this happiness without terror, without madness, perhaps. But whence came this emptiness, this remoteness, this powerlessness to be happy which now possessed him?

We were approaching the little wood where M. de Galais had that morning tied up Bélisaire; the sun, now declining, lengthened our shadows upon the grass. On the far end of the lawn we heard the voices of the little girls and others playing games – voices mellowed by distance to a happy buzz; and we remained silent in the marvellous quiet; then we heard some one singing on the other side of the wood, from the direction of The Guelders, the farm by the river. The voice was young and distant, and belonged to some one taking cattle to water: the tune was rhythmic as a dance, but the man sang it with a drawl and dragged it as though it were some old sad ballad:

> *My shoes are red . . .*
> *Good-bye, my lover!*
> *My shoes are red . . .*
> *Good-bye for ever! . . .*

Meaulnes had raised his head to listen. It was actually one of the tunes which the belated peasants had sung that last evening of the fête at the nameless manor, when everything had fallen to pieces. Nothing but a memory – the most wretched memory – of those beautiful days which would return no more.

'Do you hear that?' said Meaulnes in a subdued voice. 'Oh! I am going to see who it is.' And thereupon he dashed into the little wood. Almost at once the voice was silent; one heard for a moment longer the man whistling to his beast still farther away – then nothing more . . .

I looked at the girl. Pensive and dismayed, she kept her eyes fixed on the copse where Meaulnes had just disappeared. How many times, in later days, was she not to look thus pensively at the gap through which Admiral Meaulnes was vanishing for ever!

She turned towards me.

'He's not happy,' she said sorrowfully.

She added: 'And perhaps I can't do anything for him? . . .'

I hesitated to reply, fearing that Meaulnes, who must have reached the farm in an instant and was now coming back through the wood, might hear what we were saying. I was, however, on the point of encouraging her; of advising her not to mind being rather blunt with the tall boy; that most likely some secret tormented him which he could never confide to her or any one of his own accord – when suddenly a cry came from the other side of the wood; then we heard a thudding, as of a horse furiously pawing the ground, and the noise of wrangling in broken sentences . . . I understood at once that an accident had happened to old Bélisaire and I ran towards the place whence the uproar came. Mademoiselle de Galais followed me from afar. At the other end of the lawn our movement must have been noticed, for directly I entered the copse, I heard the shouts of people hurrying to meet us.

Old Bélisaire, tied up too low, had caught one of his forefeet in the halter; he had not moved until M. de Galais and Delouche, in the course of their walk, had come near him, then frightened, upset by the unusual oats given him, he had begun to struggle furiously; the two men had tried to free him, but so clumsily that they had only succeeded in further entangling him, at the risk, too, of dangerous kicks. It was then that Meaulnes, on his way back from The Guelders, had chanced upon the group. Furious at so much bungling, he had pushed the two men aside, almost knocking them into a bush. He had freed Bélisaire cautiously but very deftly. Too late, though; the damage was done; the horse appeared to have strained a tendon or else to have broken something, for he drooped his head dismally and kept one of his legs held up under his belly; he was trembling all over; his saddle, too, was half off his back. Meaulnes was stooping to feel the leg and examine it and said nothing.

When he looked up, nearly every one had gathered around, but he saw no one. He was red with anger.

'I would like to know,' he called out, 'who tied him up like this! And left his saddle on all day! And who dared to saddle so old a horse, scarcely fit for the lightest gig.'

Delouche was about to say something – to take the blame upon himself.

'Shut up! It's your fault. I saw you tugging at his halter like a fool to get him loose.'

And bending down again he began rubbing the horse's leg with the palm of his hand.

M. de Galais, who so far had said nothing, made the mistake of attempting to come out of his reserve. He stammered:

'Naval officers are accustomed to . . . My horse.'

'Oh! He's yours, is he?' said Meaulnes, a little calmer, but very red, turning his head towards the old man.

I thought he was going to change his tone, to apologise. He paused a moment. And then I saw that he took a bitter, despairing pleasure in aggravating the situation, in smashing everything for ever, as he said with insolence:

'Well, I shouldn't boast of it, if I were you!'

Some one suggested: 'Perhaps cold water . . . If we bathed it at the ford.'

'This horse must be taken away at once,' said Meaulnes, without replying, 'while he can still walk – and there's no time to be lost! He should be put in the stable and never taken out again.'

Several young fellows immediately offered themselves. But Mademoiselle de Galais at once thanked them. Her face on fire and ready to burst into tears, she said good-bye to every one and even to Meaulnes, who, utterly abashed, dared not look at her. She took the animal by the reins as one catches hold of somebody's hand, more to feel close to him than to lead him . . . The late summer wind was so mild on the Sand Pit road that it seemed like May, and the leaves in the hedges quivered in the south wind . . . We saw her set off thus, her arm partly out of her cloak, and holding in her slim hand the thick leather rein. Her father walked painfully by her side . . .

Sad end to the evening! Little by little everybody picked up his belongings and the picnic things; chairs were folded, tables taken down; the carriages, loaded with luggage and guests, went away one by one while hats were raised and handkerchiefs waved. We were the last to go with my Uncle Florentin who, like us, was silently brooding over his sad and great disappointment.

Then we drove swiftly off in our well-hung carriage behind

174

our beautiful chestnut. The wheels grated on the sand as we took the corner, and soon Meaulnes and I, who sat at the back, saw the cross-road which old Bélisaire and his owners had taken slowly disappear.

Then my friend, the last person in the world to cry, turned suddenly towards me and his face was twisted by the coming of irresistible tears.

'Stop, will you?' he said, placing a hand on Florentin's shoulder. 'Don't bother about me. I'll come back by myself on foot.'

He put a hand on the mud-guard of the carriage and vaulted to the ground at one leap. He turned back, to our consternation, and started running: he ran right back to the lane we had just passed, the lane leading to the Sand Pit. He must have reached the manor by the avenue of firs he had followed in the old days when, like a tramp hiding in the thicket, he had heard the mysterious conversation of the unknown beautiful children.

And this was the evening on which, sobbing, he asked Mademoiselle de Galais to marry him.

THE WEDDING DAY

A Thursday, early in February, a fine icy Thursday evening with a high wind blowing, somewhere about half-past three or four . . . Near the villages, clothes have been hung on hedges since midday and are drying in the strong breeze. Children, tired of playing, sit by their mothers asking for the story of their wedding days. In every house the dining-room fire brightly lights up what seems an altar of shining toys.

Any one who does not wish to be happy has only to climb up to the attics to hear till evening the whistle and moan of shipwrecks; or he can go out on the road for the wind to flap back his scarf on his mouth as in a sudden warm kiss which will make him weep. But for him who loves happiness there stands, by the side of a muddy lane, the Sand Pit house which my friend Meaulnes has just entered with Yvonne de Galais who has been his wife since midday.

The engagement had lasted five months. It had been a peaceful time, as peaceful as the first meeting had been full of excitement. Meaulnes had often come to the Sand Pit during those days, either on his bicycle or driving. At least twice a week, as she sat sewing or reading by the window overlooking the moor and the firs, Mademoiselle de Galais would suddenly see his tall hurrying shadow move behind the curtain, for he always comes that roundabout way, up the drive he once came by. But this is the only allusion – a tacit one – which he makes to the past. Happiness seems to have lulled his strange anguish.

Some trivial happenings have marked these five quiet months. I have been appointed teacher at the little hamlet of Saint-Benoist-des-Champs. Saint-Benoist is not a village, but only a few farms scattered about the countryside, with the school-house standing completely isolated on the side of the road some way up a hill. I lead a very solitary life; but going across the fields it takes me only three quarters of an hour to reach the Sand Pit.

Delouche lives now with his uncle who is a builder at Vieux-Nançay. He will soon be the head man. He often comes to see

me. Meaulnes, at the request of Mademoiselle de Galais, is now very nice to him.

All this explains why we are there rambling about together, towards four in the afternoon, when all the wedding people have already left.

The ceremony was held at midday as quietly as possible, in the old chapel of the Sand Pit, which was not pulled down and stands partly hidden by firs, on the slope of the adjoining hill. Meaulnes' mother, M. Seurel and Millie, Florentin and the others went off in their carriages after a hurried lunch. Jasmin and I alone remained.

We are taking a stroll along the woods behind the Sand Pit house, by the side of a wide expanse of land, the site of the manor now destroyed. Without owning to it and without knowing why, we are filled with anxiety. We try in vain to divert our thoughts and beguile our uneasiness during this wandering walk, by attracting one another's attention to the forms of hares and the small sandy furrows where rabbits have been scratching . . . to a trap set in the wood . . . or to the trail of a poacher . . . But we always come back hauntingly to the edge of the copse from where the silent and closed house can be seen . . .

The wide window which looks on the firs opens onto a wooden balcony invaded by unruly grass bending under the wind. A light, as of a burning fire, is reflected on the panes of the window where from time to time a shadow is seen to pass. Silence and solitude are all around: in the neighbouring fields, in the kitchen garden, in the farm which alone remains of the old outhouses. The farm hands have gone to the village to celebrate the happiness of their master and mistress. From time to time the wind, heavy with a mist which feels almost like rain, comes to damp our faces, and brings us the remote phrases of a piano. Out there, in the closed house, some one is playing. I stopped a moment to listen in silence. It is at first like a trembling voice which, from afar, scarcely dares to sing its joy . . . It is like the laughter of a little girl who, in her room, fetches all her toys out and displays them to her sweetheart . . . It also brings to my mind the shy pleasure of a woman who, having gone to put on a beautiful dress, comes back to show it and is not yet sure it will please . . . This air which I do not know is also a prayer, an entreaty to happiness not to be too cruel, a bowing of the head and as it were a falling on the knees before happiness . . .

The thought comes to me: 'At last they are happy. Meaulnes is there close to her . . .'

And to know this, to feel sure of it, is sufficient to bring perfect satisfaction to the simple child that I am.

But just then, while thus dreaming, and my face wet from the wind crossing the moor as if by sea-spray, I feel some one touch me on the shoulder.

'Listen!' says Jasmin in a low voice.

I look at him. He beckons to me not to move; and he too, with bent head and knitted brow, stands listening.

FRANTZ'S CALL

Hou-ou!

This time I have heard. It is a signal – a call on two notes, high and low – which I once heard of old . . . Ah! I remember: it is the cry of the tall comedian as he hailed his young companion from the school gate. It is the call to which Frantz made us swear to answer no matter where or when it came. But what can he be wanting here to-day, that fellow?

'It comes from the big fir wood on the left,' I say in half whispers. 'Most likely a poacher.'

Jasmin shakes his head: 'You know quite well it's not,' he says.

Then lower: 'They have both been in these parts ever since this morning. About eleven I came unawares upon Booby keeping a lookout in a field close to the chapel. He took to his heels when he spotted me. Perhaps they've come a long way on their bikes, for he was covered with mud halfway up his back . . .'

'What are they after, I wonder?'

'I don't know. But we must certainly send them off. They must not be left to prowl about here. Else all the mad tricks will begin again.'

I am of the same opinion without owning to it.

'The best would be to join them,' I say, 'to see what they want, to make them listen to reason . . .'

So, stooping under the branches, we slowly and silently make our way across the copse as far as the big fir wood from where, at regular intervals, rises this prolonged cry, which is not in itself uncanny, yet seems to us an evil omen.

In this part of the wood where the eye roams between regular rows of trees, it is difficult to take any one by surprise or walk any distance without being seen. We make no attempt at it. I post myself at one corner of the wood, Jasmin goes to the opposite corner, thus allowing each of us to command, from the outside, a view on two sides of a rectangle and to let neither of the bohemians escape without hailing him. These arrangements being made, I begin to play my part of peace messenger

179

and call out: 'Frantz!... Frantz! Have no fear. It's only me, Seurel; I want to talk to you...'

There is a moment's silence; I am about to call again when from the very heart of the wood and rather too far for my eyes to reach, a voice orders: 'Stay where you are; he'll come to you.'

Gradually from between the tall firs, which in the distance look closely set together, I discern the outline of the young man approaching. He seems to be covered with mud and is badly dressed; trouser clips are tight round his ankles, an old midshipman's cap fits closely on his hair which is too long. I can now see his face, so much thinner... He looks as if he had been crying.

Coming towards me resolutely: 'What is it you want?' he asks insolently.

'And yourself, Frantz, what are you doing about here? Why come and disturb those who are happy? What are you asking for? Tell me.'

Questioned thus point-blank, he blushes slightly, stammers, and only replies: 'But *I* am not happy; I am so wretched.'

Then he breaks into bitter sobs, his head in the bend of one arm; he is leaning against a tree. We had taken a few steps in the wood; the spot is perfectly quiet. Even the sound of the wind is hushed by the tall firs bordering the wood. Amongst the rows of trunks the noise of the stifled sobbing of the young man echoes and dies out.

I wait until he grows calmer, and, placing a hand on his shoulders, say:

'Frantz, you'd better come with me. I'll take you to them. They'll welcome you as a lost child now found, and all this will be at an end.'

But he would hear nothing; in a voice subdued by tears, miserable, angry, obstinate, he started once again: 'And so

180

Meaulnes won't be bothered with me? Why does he not answer when I call? Why can't he keep his word?'

'Oh! come on, Frantz,' I replied, 'these fantastic childlike days are over. Don't disturb with mad whims the happiness of those you love; of your sister and Augustin Meaulnes.'

'But he alone can save me, you know that well. He alone can find again the trail I am looking for. These last three years, now, Booby and I have been knocking about France without any success. My one hope left was in your friend. And he does not answer my call. Hasn't he got his love back? Why can't he think of me? He must begin to think of me. Yvonne will let him go . . . She's never refused me anything.'

He turned towards me a face where tears had traced dirty streaks in dust and grime, the face of an old-looking child, worn-out and beaten. His eyes were circled with freckles, his chin badly shaved; his hair, too long, trailed over his dirty collar; with hands in his pockets he stood shivering. He no longer was, as of old, a princely child dressed in tatters. Yet at heart, most likely, he was more of a child than ever: fantastically imperious and then all at once in despair. But these childish ways were now intolerable in a young man already looking more than grown up . . . Formerly there was so much youthful pride about him that all the madness in the world was right for him. But now one was at first tempted to pity him for having failed in life, then to reproach him for absurdly acting the romantic young hero, as I saw that he persisted in doing . . . And finally I could not help thinking that our handsome Frantz with the beautiful love story had most likely taken to stealing for a living, just like his companion Booby . . . So much pride had ended in this!

'What if I promise,' I said at last, having thought it out, 'that in a few days Meaulnes shall start on a search all for your sake?'

'He will be successful, won't he? You are sure of it?' he asked with chattering teeth.

'I believe so. Everything comes easy to him now!'

'And how shall I know? Who will tell me?'

'You will come back here in exactly a year from today, at this same time: you will then find the girl you love.'

And saying this I am thinking not of disturbing the newly married couple, but of making inquiries through Aunt Moinel and myself hastening to find the girl.

The bohemian looked straight at me with really wonderful trustfulness. Just as if he were fifteen! – the age one could easily have taken us to be at Sainte-Agathe, on the evening of the sweeping of the classrooms, when we three took that terrible childlike oath.

Despair gripped him once more when he felt obliged to say: 'Very well, we must go.'

He looked with an evident pang at the surrounding woods which he was about to leave again.

'In three days from now,' he said, 'we shall be on the roads of Germany. We've left our caravans a long way off. And for the last thirty hours we've ridden without a stop. We thought to get here in time to take Meaulnes away before the wedding and search with him for my fiancée, as he once looked for the Sand Pit Manor.'

Then again, falling back to his terrible childishness: 'Call your Delouche back,' he said, going away; 'meeting him would really be too dreadful.'

Gradually, in between the firs, I watched until I saw his grey outline disappear. I called Jasmin and we resumed our watch. But almost at once, farther out, we spotted Augustin closing the shutters of the house, and we were struck by his strange behaviour.

HAPPY PEOPLE

Later on I came to know in minute detail what had happened out there . . .

From early in the afternoon Meaulnes and his wife, whom I still call Mademoiselle de Galais, had been left entirely by themselves in the drawing-room at the Sand Pit. All the guests having gone, M. de Galais had opened the door, letting the high wind moan for a second all through the house, then he had set off towards Vieux-Nançay, not to be back until dinner, in time for locking up and giving orders at the farm. No noise from outside now reaches the young people, only the leafless branch of a rose tree tapping against the window-pane on the side of the moor. Like two passengers in a drifting boat, the two lovers, in the winter gale, are left alone with happiness.

'The fire is almost going out,' said Mademoiselle de Galais, and she tried to take a log out of the chest.

But Meaulnes hurried to put the wood on the fire himself. He then took the hand the girl had put out, and they stood there facing one another as if stifled by some great news which could not be uttered.

The wind swirled by with the noise of an overflowing river. From time to time, as on the window of a train, a drop of rain left a slanting streak across the pane.

Then the girl suddenly stole away. She opened the passage door and disappeared with a mysterious smile. Augustin was for a moment left alone in semi-darkness . . . The tick-tick of a small clock recalled the dining-room at Sainte-Agathe . . . He no doubt thought: 'So this is the house so much sought after; the passage once so full of whispers and strange encounters . . .'

It is at this moment that he must have heard – Mademoiselle de Galais told me later that she also heard it – the first call of Frantz close to the house.

It was in vain then that the young woman showed him all the marvels with which she was burdened: the toys she had played with as a little girl; all the photographs of herself as a child; as a *vivandière*, herself and Frantz on their mother's knee, and such a pretty mother . . . then all that was left of her sedate little dresses of childhood; 'even this one which I was still wearing just before you came to know me, at the time, so I believe, you must have arrived at the Higher Elementary School at Sainte-Agathe . . .' Meaulnes no longer saw anything or heard anything.

Once, however, he appeared to grasp again the idea of his extraordinary, inconceivable happiness.

'You are here,' he said dully, as if merely to say it made him dizzy – 'you are moving close to the table and your hand for a moment rests on it . . .'

And again: 'Mother, when she was young, would lean forward slightly like you, when speaking to me . . . And when she sat at the piano . . .'

Then Mademoiselle de Galais proposed to play before night came. But it was growing dark in that corner of the drawing-room and they had to light a candle. The pink lamp-shade accentuated the rosy flush which on the girl's face was a sign of great anxiety.

Out there, at the edge of the wood, I began to hear the trembling song brought by the wind, but soon broken into by the second call of the two mad fellows who had come nearer to us through the firs.

For a long time Meaulnes listened to the girl, while he looked silently out of the window. More than once he turned towards the sweet face, now so frail and anxious. Then he came near to Yvonne de Galais and lightly placed one hand on her shoulder. She felt, close to her neck, the gentle pressure of the caress to which she should have been able to respond.

'Night is falling,' he said at last. 'I am going to close the shutters. But do not stop playing . . .'

What took place then in that mysterious and wild heart? I often wondered and only came to know when it was too late. Unknown remorse? Inexplicable misgivings? Fear of seeing this unheard-of happiness, to which he clung so closely, soon vanish from between his hands? And then the terrible temptation at once and for ever to dash to the ground this marvel he had conquered? . . .

He went out slowly and silently after having once more looked at his young wife. From the edge of the wood we saw him first close with some hesitation one of the shutters, then look vaguely our way, close another, and suddenly run off at full speed in our direction. He reached us before we could think of better concealment. He noticed us as he was going to jump over a small hedge recently planted and enclosing a meadow. He changed his course. I recall that he looked haggard, like a hunted beast . . . He attempted to retrace his steps and climb over the hedge on the side of the brook.

I called him: 'Meaulnes! . . . Augustin! . . .'

But he never even turned his head. Then, feeling sure that this alone could hold him back: 'Frantz is here,' I called out. 'Stop!'

He at last stopped. Out of breath and without giving me time to be ready with what I ought to say: 'He's here!' he said. 'What's he wanting?'

'He's wretched,' I replied. 'He came to ask your help in looking for what he has lost.'

'Ah!' said he, lowering his head. 'I guessed that much. I tried in vain to drown that thought . . . But where is he? Tell me quick.'

I told him that Frantz had just gone and that he certainly could not be caught now. It was a great shock to Meaulnes. He hesitated, walked ahead two or three steps, then stopped. He appeared in the depths of uncertainty and grief. I related to him what I had promised in his name to Frantz. I said that I had arranged a meeting with him a year hence at the same place.

Augustin, so calm usually, was now in an extraordinary state of impatience and agitation.

'Ah! why did you do that!' he said. 'Of course I can save him. But it must be at once. I must see him, speak to him; he must forgive me, that I may make amends for all . . . Otherwise I can no longer show my face out there . . .'

And he looked towards the Sand Pit house.

'Well,' I said, 'just for a childish promise you made you are now going to wreck your happiness.'

'Ah! if it were only that promise!' he exclaimed. And thus I knew that something else was binding the two men together, though I could not guess what it was.

'In any case,' I said, 'it's now too late. They are on their way to Germany.'

He was about to reply when a face, dishevelled, tortured, haggard, appeared between us. It was Mademoiselle de Galais. She must have run, for her face was wet with drops of sweat. She must have fallen and hurt herself, for her forehead was scratched above the right eye and blood was caked in her hair.

It has sometimes happened to me, in the poor districts of

Paris, to witness a couple which one thought happy, united, and honest, suddenly bring their quarrel into the street to be separated by the intervention of the police. The scandal had broken out all at once, no matter when, just as they sat down at dinner, before the Sunday walk, when keeping the little boy's birthday . . . and now everything is forgotten and smashed. The man and the woman in their quarrel are no more than two pitiful fiends, while the children in tears rush up to them, hugging them closely, begging them to keep quiet and not to fight.

Mademoiselle de Galais, coming thus close to Meaulnes, put me in mind of one of those children, those poor distracted children. I believe that, had all her friends, all the village, all the world been looking on, she would have rushed forward all the same, she would have dropped on us in the same way, dishevelled, tearful, her face dirty.

But when she once understood that Meaulnes was really there, that this time, at all events, he would not forsake her, she placed her arm under his and could not help laughing amidst her tears as would a child. They said not a word to each other. But, as she had pulled out her handkerchief, Meaulnes took it gently from her hands; with care and precaution he wiped away the blood from the girl's hair.

'We must now go in,' he said.

And in the bracing high wind which lashed at their faces that wintry evening I left them to go back together, he helping her by the hand at awkward places, she smiling and hastening – towards the home they had for a moment forsaken.

FRANTZ'S HOUSE

I had to remain shut up in the school during the whole of the following day, a prey to dull anxiety, feeling but little re-assured by the happy ending to yesterday's scene. Immediately after the hour of 'private study' which follows afternoon school, I made my way to the Sand Pit. Night was falling when I reached the avenue of firs leading to the house. The shutters were already closed. I feared to intrude by coming at so late an hour the day after a wedding. So I prowled about close to the edge of the garden and in the neighbouring fields for a long while, hoping all the time to see some one come out of the closed house . . . But my hopes were in vain. Nothing stirred, not even in the adjoining farm. And I had to go home, haunted by the gloomiest forebodings.

This uncertainty lasted on next day, a Saturday. In the evening I made haste to get my cape, my stick, a piece of bread to eat on the way, and reached the Sand Pit to find everything closed up there just as the day before . . . A little light on the first floor; but not noise, not a movement . . . At the farmhouse, however, I now noticed, from the yard, the front door left open, the fire burning in the great kitchen, and I heard a noise of voices and footsteps as is usual at supper time. This reassured me without telling me much. I could not say anything to these people nor ask them anything. And I went back to resume my watch, to wait in vain, thinking at any moment to see the door open and the tall form of Meaulnes emerge.

It was only on Sunday, during the afternoon, that I resolved to pull the bell at the Sand Pit. While I was making my way up the bare hills, I heard in the distance the church bells ringing

for vespers on that winter Sunday. I felt lonely and distressed. I do not know what sad foreboding overwhelmed me. And I was only partly surprised when, in answer to my ring. M. de Galais appeared alone and spoke to me almost in whispers: Yvonne de Galais was in bed with a high fever; Meaulnes had been obliged to leave on Friday morning to go on a long journey; no one knew when he would come back . . .

And as the old man, very embarrassed, very sad, did not ask me to come in, I at once said good-bye to him. The door shut and I remained on the doorstep for a moment, my heart torn, my mind in chaos, watching, without knowing why, a branch of dead wistaria which the wind swayed in a beam of sunshine.

Thus the secret remorse, which Meaulnes had carried within him since his stay in Paris, had ended by proving too strong. My big friend had been forced in the end to let go of the happiness to which he had clung so obstinately.

Every Thursday and Sunday I came to ask news of Yvonne de Galais until the evening when at last, being convalescent, she sent word for me to come in. I found her sitting by the fire in the drawing-room with its low wide window looking on the grounds and the woods. She was not pale as I had imagined she would be, but on the contrary feverish, with bright red patches under her eyes and in a state of extreme agitation. Though she still seemed very weak, she was fully dressed. She hardly spoke, but said each sentence with extraordinary animation as though she were longing to convince herself that happiness had not yet vanished . . . I have no memory of what we said. I remember only that, with some hesitation, I came to ask when Meaulnes would be back.

'I don't know when he will come back,' she replied quickly.

There was entreaty in her eyes and I refrained from asking more.

189

I often went to see her. I often talked to her by the fire in that low drawing-room where night came quicker than anywhere else. She never spoke about herself or her hidden grief. But she never tired of making me relate in all its details our schoolboy life at Sainte-Agathe.

She listened to the tale of our youthful troubles with a grave, tender interest, almost maternal. She showed no surprise at anything, not even at our most daring, most dangerous childish pranks. This thoughtful tenderness which she had inherited from M. de Galais, had not been exhausted by her brother's deplorable adventures. The only lament to which the past prompted her was, I think, at not having been enough her brother's true friend, for on the day of his great disaster he had not dared to tell her more than any one else, and he had thought himself for ever lost. And, after all, it was indeed a heavy task the young woman had assumed – a perilous task that of seconding a mind as madly fantastic as was her brother's; an overwhelming task when it was a matter of joining one's lot with so adventurous a spirit as my friend Admiral Meaulnes.

One day she gave me the most touching, I could almost say the most mysterious proof of this faith she kept in her brother's childish dreams, and the care she took to preserve at least some fragments of the dream in which he had lived up to his twentieth year.

It was during a desolate evening of April, very much like autumn. For nearly a month we had enjoyed a softly premature spring and, accompanied by M. de Galais, the dear woman had again resumed the long walks she was fond of. But that day, the old man being tired and myself free, she asked me to go with her in spite of the threatening weather. The storm – rain and hail – caught us more than two kilometres away from the Sand

Pit as we walked by the lake. Under the shed where we sought shelter from the never-ending shower, the wind was icy cold, and we stood close to one another, lost in thought in front of the darkened landscape. I still picture her, wearing a soft neat dress and looking pale and worried.

'We must go back,' she kept saying. 'We've been gone so long. What might not have happened?'

But to my surprise, when at last it became possible to leave our shelter, the young woman, instead of turning back towards the Sand Pit, went on her way and asked me to follow her. After a long walk we reached a house I did not know, standing by itself at the side of a rutted lane which must have led towards Préveranges. It was a small private house with a slate roof, only marked out from the type usual in the district by its isolation and remoteness.

Any one watching Yvonne de Galais would have believed the house belonged to us and that we had left it during a long absence. She stooped to open the small iron gate, and she made haste to inspect anxiously the lonely spot. A big yard, overgrown by weeds where children seemed to have come to play during the long dragging evenings at the end of winter, was hollowed out by the rain. A hoop was soaking in a puddle. The heavy shower had left only trails of white gravel in the small gardens which the children had bestrewed with flowers and peas. And we at last discovered, huddled together against the step of one of the damp doors, a whole brood of chickens quite drenched. Most of them were dead under the stiffened wings and the crumpled feathers of the mother.

The dear woman, fronted by so pitiful a sight, gave a stifled cry. She bent down, disregarding water and mud, pulled out the live chickens from the dead, and wrapped them in a fold of her cloak. Then we went into the house, of which she had the key. Four doors opened out of a narrow passage into which swept a gust of wind. Yvonne de Galais opened the first door on our right and made me go into a dark room, where, after a moment of uncertainty, I made out a tall looking-glass and a small bed covered with a red silk eiderdown, in peasant fashion. As for her, having for a moment searched in other parts of the dwelling, she came back with a flat basket filled with down, which she delicately slipped under the eiderdown. And while a languid ray of sunshine, the first and last of the day, made both our faces paler and the dusk more gloomy, we stood there, frozen and worried, in this strange house!

From time to time she would look inside the feverish nest, taking away another dead chicken to prevent it causing the death of the others. And each time it seemed to us that something, perhaps a gust of wind through the broken panes of the attic, perhaps the mysterious sorrow of unknown children, was silently lamenting.

'This was Frantz's house when he was little,' my companion at last said to me. 'He'd wanted a house all his own, far from every one, in which he could go to play, enjoy himself and live just as he pleased. Father had found this fancy so extraordinary, so funny, that he hadn't refused. And whenever it pleased him, on a Thursday or Sunday, no matter when, Frantz would go and live at his house like a man. Children of the neighbouring farms used to come to play with him, help him with housekeeping, work in the garden. It was a wonderful game! And at night time he was not afraid of sleeping alone. As for us, we admired him so much, we never once thought of being anxious.

'Now, the house is empty,' she went on with a sigh; 'it has been so for a long time. M. de Galais, altered by age and grief,

192

has never done anything to trace my brother or call him back. And what could he have done? But I often pass this way. Little peasant children, from hereabout, come to play in the yard as in the old days. It pleases me to pretend they are Frantz's old friends; that he himself is still but a child and that he will soon come back with the fiancée of his choice. These children know me so well. I play with them. That brood of chicks was ours . . .'

It had needed this shower and this childlike dismay to induce her to confide to me the great grief of which she had never spoken, her deep regret at having lost a brother so mad, so charming, so much admired.

And I listened to her, not knowing what to reply, my heart heavy with suppressed sobs . . .

Then, having closed the doors and the gate and replaced the chickens in their wooden hutch at the back of the house, she sadly took my arm and I led her home.

Weeks and months went by. Days now of the past! Lost happiness! This girl who had been the fairy, the princess, the mysterious love dream of our youth, it was now my lot to take by the arm, finding the necessary words to soften her grief, while my friend had run away. What can I now say of these days, of these evening talks after school-hours on the hill of Saint-Benoist-des-Champs, of these walks during which the one thing we ought to have discussed was the only one concerning which we were resolved to keep silent? The only memory I have preserved, though already dimmed, is that of a beautiful face grown thinner, of two eyes whose lids slowly lower when they look at me, as if already they contemplate only an inner world.

And I remained her faithful companion – in this long wait we never spoke of – during a whole spring and a whole summer such as will never be again. Many a time we went back to Frantz's house during an afternoon. She would open the doors to air the rooms, so that nothing should be mouldy on the young couple's return. She tended the partly wild fowls which had their home in the poultry-yard. And on Thursdays and Sundays we helped to keep going the games of the neighbouring village children, whose laughter and shouts in this lonely spot made the small forsaken house appear more empty, more deserted than ever.

A TALK IN THE RAIN

August, the holiday month, took me away from the Sand Pit and the dear woman. I was booked to go to Sainte-Agathe for my two months' leave. I once again saw the bare playground, the shelter, the empty classroom . . . Everything spoke of Admiral Meaulnes and was filled with the memory of our youth now past. During those long mellowing days, I shut myself in the record room or the deserted classroom as I used to before Meaulnes' arrival. There I read, wrote, and recalled the past . . . Father was often away jack-fishing. Millie, in the drawing-room, played the piano or sewed as of old. . . . In the absolute silence of the classroom torn green paper wreaths, jackets off prize books, clean blackboards, reminded me that the year was over, that the prizes were given, and that everything awaited

194

autumn, the new school year and fresh endeavour – and here I kept brooding over the fact that our youth was likewise ended and that happiness had failed; and I awaited the return of the school year at the Sand Pit and Augustin's home-coming which perhaps would never be . . .

There was, however, one piece of good news I could tell Millie when she insisted on questioning me about the bride. I dreaded her questions, and her way, at once very innocent and very shrewd, of causing you sudden embarrassment by putting her finger on your most secret thoughts. So I checked all inquiry by announcing that the young wife of my friend Meaulnes was expecting to become a mother in October.

As for me, I recalled the day when Yvonne de Galais had made me understand this great news. There had been a moment of silence; I had felt a youth's uneasiness, and to be rid of it, I had said at once without thinking – realising only too late all the tragedy I was thus stirring up, 'You must be very happy?'

But she, without reservation or regret, neither remorse nor ill-will, had replied with a beautiful smile, 'Yes, very happy.'

This last week of the holidays, which was usually the best and most romantic, a week of heavy rain when fires begin to be lit and which I generally spent shooting at Vieux-Nançay, in the black damp fir woods, I made ready to return directly to Saint-Benoist-des-Champs. Firmin, Aunt Julie, and my girl cousins at Vieux-Nançay would have asked too many questions to which I did not want to reply. So I gave up, for once, the joy of spending eight good days shooting in the country, and went back to my school-house four days before term began.

I arrived before night in the playground, which was littered with brown leaves. My driver went away and I entered the stuffy, echoing dining-room, where I sadly undid the parcel of provisions Mother had prepared for me . . . Then, restless and anxious, I hurried through a light meal, took my cape and started on a feverish walk which led me straight to the boundaries of the Sand Pit.

I had no wish to intrude on the very first evening of my arrival. Yet, more daring than in February, after a walk around the estate, where Yvonne de Galais' window alone showed a light, I climbed over the garden fence at the back of the house and in the gathering dusk sat on a bench near the hedge, happy merely to be so close to what thrilled and troubled me more than anything else in the world.

Night approached. Fine rain began to fall. With bowed head I watched my shoes getting wet in the rain and shining – paying them no heed. Darkness slowly enclosed me, and the cool of night, without troubling my reverie. I dreamed sadly and tenderly of the muddy lanes at Sainte-Agathe on such a September evening; I pictured the square full of mist, the butcher boy whistling on his way to the pump, the lights of the café, the waggonette and its merry occupants under a shield of open umbrellas, arriving at Uncle Florentin's at the end of the holidays . . . And I was sadly saying to myself, 'What good is all this happiness if my friend Meaulnes cannot be there, nor his young wife . . .'

It was then I raised my head and saw her two steps away. Her shoes made on the sand a slight noise which I had mistaken for raindrops from the hedge. Her head and shoulders were wrapped in a big shawl of black wool and the fine rain was like powder on the hair over her forehead. She must have seen me from her bedroom window, which looked onto the garden, and had come down to me. In the old days Mother used thus to worry about me, hunting me up to say, 'You must come in,' but beginning herself to enjoy the night walk in the rain, she would only say, very gently, 'You will catch cold!' and remain by me for a long talk . . .

Yvonne de Galais held out a burning hand; then she gave up the idea of taking me indoors, and sat down on the mossy, rusted bench at the end which was not too wet, while I remained standing, one knee on the bench, and stooped to catch what she was saying.

She at first scolded me in a friendly way for having thus shortened my holidays.

'But I had to come back as soon as I could,' I replied, 'to keep you company.'

'The fact is,' she said, almost in whispers and with a sigh, 'I am still alone. Augustin has not come back . . .'

Taking this sigh to express regret, an implied reproach, I began slowly to say: 'So many mad schemes in so beautiful a mind! Perhaps the love of adventure stronger than anything . . .'

But she interrupted me. And it was there, that very evening, that for the first and last time she spoke to me of Meaulnes.

'Do not talk like this, François Seurel,' she said gently, 'you are my friend. It is only we – it is only me, who am guilty. Think what we did . . . We've said to him: 'Here's happiness; here's what you've looked for during all your youth; here's the girl who was the aim of all your dreams!" How could anyone thus pushed into happiness not be seized with misgiving, then fear, then terror! How could he have resisted the temptation of running away!'

'Yvonne,' I said softly, 'you knew quite well you were that very happiness, that very girl . . .'

'Ah!' she sighed. 'How could such an arrogant thought ever have entered my head? It is that thought caused all the trouble. I had said to you, "Perhaps I can't do anything for him." And in my heart I was thinking, "He has searched for me so long and I love him so, I am bound to make him happy." But when I saw him by my side, with all this fever and anxiety, his mysterious remorse, I understood that I was but a helpless woman like others. "I am not worthy of you," he kept repeating when daylight came at the end of our wedding night. And I tried to comfort him, to reassure him. But nothing could quiet his anguish. Then I said: "If you must go, if I have come to you at a moment when nothing can make you happy, if you must leave me for a time so as to come back later, after having found peace, I myself ask you to go . . ."'

In the dusk I saw that she had raised her eyes towards me. It was a sort of confession she had made to me and she was anxiously waiting for my approval or condemnation. But what could I say? Certainly, within me, I pictured the Admiral Meaulnes of old, so clumsy, so awkwardly shy, that he would rather be punished than make excuses for himself or ask permission which would naturally have been granted. No doubt Yvonne de Galais should have shaken him out of this, and, taking his head in her hands, have said to him: 'What do I care what you did! I love you; are not all men sinners?' No doubt, with all her generosity and her willingness to sacrifice herself, she had been greatly in the wrong in thus throwing him back on the road to adventure . . . But how could I condemn so much kindness, so much love! . . .

There was a long moment of silence during which, both deeply stirred, we could hear the rain drip in the hedges and beneath the branches of the trees.

'So he went away in the morning,' she went on. 'There was no longer anything separating us. And he kissed me, like a husband leaving his young wife for a long journey . . .'

She got up. I took her feverish hand in mine, then her arm,

198

and we walked up the avenue, now plunged in darkness.

'Yet, did he ever write to you?' I asked.

'Never,' she replied.

And then the thought came to us both of the adventurous life he was at this moment leading on the roads of France or Germany; so we began to speak of him as we had never done before. Forgotten details, old recollections came back to our minds while we slowly walked to the house, at each step coming to a long stop, the better to exchange our memories . . . And for a long time – as far as the garden-gate – I heard in the night the gentle, low voice of the young wife; and I too was caught up in my old enthusiasm and never wearied of talking to her, with deep friendship, of the one who had forsaken us . . .

THE BURDEN

School was to begin again on the Monday. On Saturday evening about five, a woman from the farm appeared in the playground where I was busy sawing wood for the winter. She came to tell me that a little girl was born at the Sand Pit. The confinement had been difficult. At nine in the evening, the midwife from Préveranges had been called. At midnight the horse had been once more harnessed to fetch the Vierzon doctor. He had had to use forceps. The little girl's head was injured and she screamed much, but appeared likely to live. Yvonne de

Galais was at present prostrate, but she had suffered and struggled through with extraordinary courage.

Immediately, I left my job, ran in to change my coat, and, content on the whole with the news, followed the good woman as far as the Sand Pit. With great care I climbed up the narrow wooden stairs leading to the first floor, anxious not to wake either of the patients. And there M. de Galais, tired but happy, made me go into the room where the cradle, draped in curtains, had been provisionally installed.

I had never been in a house on the very day a baby had been born. How quaint, mysterious, and good it seemed to me! It was such a beautiful evening – a true summer evening – that M. de Galais had not hesitated to open the window which looked on the yard. He leaned by my side on the window-sill and told me the story of the night in full detail but happily, and as I listened I became vaguely conscious of someone from a strange country now present in the room with us . . .

Then under the curtains the stranger began to cry, a shrill, prolonged cry . . . And M. de Galais said in a soft voice, 'It's that wound on the head makes her cry.'

Mechanically he began to rock the bundle of curtains, and you felt he had been doing this ever since morning, acquiring the habit at once.

'She has already laughed,' he said, 'and she takes hold of one's finger. But you've not seen her yet?'

He opened the curtains and I saw a little face, red and puffed, the top of the head was pear-shaped and deformed by the forceps.

'That's nothing,' said M. de Galais; 'the doctor says it will set itself right . . . Give her your finger, she'll hold on to it.'

I was there, discovering an unknown world. My heart was full of a strange joy I had never felt before.

M. de Galais cautiously peeped in at the young mother's door. She was not asleep.

'You can come in,' he said.

She lay prostrate, her feverish face in the midst of her unloosened fair hair. She held out her hand to me, smiling in a tired way. I congratulated her on her daughter. And in a voice that was a little hoarse and unusually harsh – the harshness of one just back from a fight, 'Yes, but they have injured her so!'

I had to go soon after, not to tire her.

The next day was a Sunday, and in the afternoon I hurried almost cheerfully to the Sand Pit. On the front door was pinned a notice which stopped my hand on its way to the bell:

Please

do not ring

I did not guess what it referred to. I knocked quite loud. I heard, inside, muffled steps hastening. Someone I did not know – it was the doctor from Vierzon – opened the door.

'Well! What's the matter?' I said quickly.

'Hush! Hush!' he replied in a low voice, and troubled. 'The little girl nearly died last night. And the mother's very ill.'

Completely disconcerted, I followed him on tiptoe up to the first floor. The little girl, asleep in her cradle, was dreadfully pale and white, like a little dead child. The doctor thought he would save her. As for the mother, he could not tell . . . He gave me long explanations as to the one friend of the family. He spoke of congestion of the lungs, embolism. He was doubtful, he could not be sure . . . M. de Galais came in, frightfully aged in two days, haggard and trembling.

201

He took me into the bedroom, scarcely knowing what he was doing:

'She must not be alarmed,' he said in a low voice; 'the doctor says we must assure her that all is well.'

Extremely flushed, Yvonne de Galais lay with her head thrown back as on the previous day. Her cheeks and forehead were dark red; at times her eyes became distended as happens to one who is suffocating; she was fighting death with untold courage and sweetness.

She could not speak, but she held out a burning hand with such friendliness that I nearly burst into tears.

'Well, now! Well, now!' said M. de Galais loudly, with terrible cheerfulness that resembled madness. 'You see, she doesn't look too bad for an invalid!'

And I did not know what to reply, but kept in mine the hand, so terribly hot, of the dying young woman . . .

She tried to make an effort to say something, to ask me I know not what; she turned her eyes to me, then towards the window as if to make me understand I must go and fetch someone . . . But then a dreadful fit of suffocation came upon her. Her beautiful blue eyes, which but a moment before had called me so tragically, distended, her cheeks and forehead darkened, and she struggled gently, endeavouring to the end to restrain her terror and despair. Doctors and women hurried to her help with a flask of oxygen, towels, and bottles, while the old man bending over her was shouting in his rough and shaky voice – shouting as if she was already far away from him: 'Don't be frightened, Yvonne. It's nothing. No need to be afraid!'

Then the crisis passed. She managed to breathe a little, yet she continued to be half suffocated, her eyes white, her head thrown back, still struggling, but unable, even for a moment, to look at me or to speak, to emerge from the abyss into which she had already sunk.

... And as I was entirely useless, I made up my mind to go. I could no doubt have stayed a moment longer, and at this thought I feel overwhelmed by terrible remorse. But how could one tell? I still hoped. Still tried to convince myself death could not be so near.

When I reached the edge of the firs, behind the house, that last look of Yvonne de Galais towards the window came back to my mind, and I scanned with the attention of a sentry or a man-hunter the depths of that wood from which Augustin had come in former days and into which he had fled this last winter. Alas, nothing stirred. Not one suspicious shadow; not a branch that moved. But at length, out there, towards the lane coming from Préveranges, I heard the faint sound of a bell; soon a child in a red *calotte* and black overall appeared at the bend, a priest was following him ... And I walked away fighting back my tears.

School was to start next day. At seven o'clock there were already two or three boys in the playground. I hesitated a long while before coming down, before showing myself. And when I appeared at last, unlocking the door of the mouldy classroom which had been closed for two months, what I most dreaded happened: I saw the biggest of the boys leave a group of young-sters playing under the shelter and advance towards me. He came to tell me that 'the young lady at the Sand Pit had died at nightfall on the previous evening.'

Everything turns to confusion, everything mingles with this grief. It seems to me now that never again shall I have the courage to start school. Only to cross the playground is an effort which will break me up. Everything is painful, everything is bitter, now that she is dead. The world is empty, holidays ended. Ended the long country drives, ended the mysterious fête . . . Life is again the burden it was of old.

I tell the children there will be no school this morning. They go away in small groups to carry the news to others about the country-side. As for me, I take my black hat, a mourning coat I have, and start wretchedly towards the Sand Pit.

I am in front of the house we had sought three years ago! It is in this house that Yvonne de Galais, Augustin Meaulnes' wife, died yesterday evening. A stranger would take it for a chapel, so great is the silence which has settled since yesterday on this desolate spot.

So this is what this fine morning of the new school year, this treacherous autumn sun which glides under the branches, had in store for us. How could I fight against hideous revolt and a blinding flood of tears! We had again found the beautiful girl. We had won her. She was my friend's wife and I myself loved her with that deep, secret friendship which is never told. I used to look at her and be happy like a little child. I might one day have married another girl, and she would have been the first to whom I should have confided the great secret news . . .

Yesterday's notice has been left close to the bell on one side of the door. The coffin has already been brought into the hall downstairs. In the room on the first floor, it is the child's nurse who greets me, relates to me the end, and gently pushes the door ajar . . . She is there. No more fever nor struggle. No more flush nor waiting. Nothing but silence, and, framed in cotton wool, a hard face, unsensitive and white, a dead forehead from which the hair rises thick and stiff.

M. de Galais, crouched in one corner with his back to us, is there in his socks, searching with tragic obstinacy amongst

a confusion of drawers he has pulled out of a cupboard. Now and again he takes out of them some old and already faded photographs of his daughter, and sobs shake his shoulders like a burst of laughter.

The funeral is for midday. The doctor fears the rapid decomposition which sometimes follows on an embolism. This is why the face, as well as the whole body, is surrounded by cotton wool soaked in carbolic.

The last toilet has been made – she had been dressed in her beautiful frock of dark blue velvet bespangled with little silver stars, its fine but old-fashioned leg-of-mutton sleeves flattened and folded under; but at the moment of bringing up the coffin it is found that there is not room to turn it in the very narrow corridor. It will have to be hauled up through the window from the outside, by means of a rope, and be lowered again in the same way . . . It is then that M. de Galais, still bent over these ancient things amidst which he searches for some lost tokens, suddenly steps in with terrifying impetuosity.

'Rather than allow such a dreadful thing to be done,' he says, in a voice broken by tears and anger, 'I will take her myself in my arms and carry her down . . .'

And he would do as he says at the risk of fainting halfway and crashing down with her!

Then I offer myself, deciding on the only possible course of action; with the help of a doctor and a nurse, placing one arm under the back of the stretched-out dead woman, the other under her legs, I gather her against my breast. Seated on my left arm, her shoulders resting on the right one, her drooping head uplifted under my chin, she weighs terribly against my heart. I walk down slowly step after step along the stiff flight of stairs, while in the room below all is being prepared.

My arms soon ache with fatigue. At each step, with this load on my breast, I am more out of breath. Clinging to the inert and heavy body, I lower my head towards the head of her I carry. I breathe heavily and her fair hair enters my mouth, dead hair with a taste of the earth. This taste of earth and of death, this weight on my heart, that is all that is left to me of the great adventure and of you, Yvonne de Galais, the woman so long sought – so loved . . .

THE COMPOSITION TEST BOOK

Not long afterwards, old M. de Galais took to his bed in the house full of sad memories, where women spent the day rocking and soothing a small ailing baby. He passed away peacefully in the first severe weather, and I found it hard to keep back my tears at the bedside of this charming old man whose kindly indulgence and fantastic whims, joined to those of his son, had caused our whole adventure. He fortunately died in complete oblivion of all that had happened, and indeed in almost absolute silence. As for a long time he had had neither relatives nor friends in this part of France, he chose me for his sole legatee until the return of Meaulnes to whom I was to account for everything, if he ever came back . . . And so I lived henceforth at the Sand Pit. I no longer went to Saint-Benoist except for school, starting early in the morning, eating at midday a lunch prepared at the farm, which I warmed up on my stove, and coming back in the evening after 'private study.'

I was thus able to keep by my side the child whom the maids from the farm tended. Above all I added to my chance of not missing Meaulnes if ever one day he returned to the Sand Pit.

Besides, I had not lost hope of finding at last, in a piece of furniture or a drawer at the house, some paper, some indication, which would convey intelligence of his movements during his long silence of the previous years – and perhaps thus I might be able to grasp the reason of his flight or at all events to find some trace of him . . . I had already searched in vain through innumerable closets and cupboards; I had opened in the storerooms quantities of boxes of all shapes, which I found full of bundles of old letters and yellowish photographs of the Galais family, or else overflowing with various millinery trimmings: flowers, aigrettes, feathers, and old-fashioned birds. Out of these boxes came a strange faint perfume, the scent of faded things, which would suddenly awaken in me, for the whole day, memories and regrets, and stop my search . . .

At last, home from school one day, I unearthed in the attic a small old-fashioned trunk, very low and long in shape, covered with pig-hide half eaten through, which I recognised as Augustin's school trunk. I upbraided myself for not having begun my search there. I easily forced the rusted lock. The trunk was crammed full of books and exercise-books from Sainte-Agathe. Arithmetics, studies in literature, sum-books, goodness knows what! . . . Greatly moved rather than curious, I began to rummage amongst all this, reading over again the dictations I still knew by heart, as we had recopied them so many times: 'The Aqueduct,' by Rousseau; 'An Adventure in Calabria,' by P. L. Courier; 'A Letter of George Sand to her Son.'

There was also a 'Composition Test Book.' This surprised me a little, as such books usually remained at school, the pupils never taking them home. It was a green exercise-book, faded at the edges. The name of the pupil, Augustin Meaulnes, was written on the cover in a beautiful round hand. I opened it. By the date of the tests, April, 189 – I realized that Meaulnes had started it only a few days before leaving Sainte-Agathe. The first pages were kept with religious care, as was the rule when one set work down in the composition book. But there were only three pages written, the others were blank, and this explained why Meaulnes had taken it away.

I was there on my knees, brooding over these practices and petty rules which had loomed so large during our youth, while my thumb skimmed the pages of the unfinished book causing them to open. And it was thus I discovered writing on other sheets. After four blank pages it started again.

It was still Meaulnes' writing, but a hurried hand, ill-shaped, scarcely legible, forming small, unequal paragraphs separated by blank lines. In places there was only an unfinished sentence. Sometimes a date. From the first line I came to the conclusion that there might be information concerning Meaulnes' past life in Paris, indications of the trail I was looking for, and I went down into the diningroom to use the daylight in perusing this strange document. It was a clear rough winter day. Sometimes the bright sun would cast the shadows of the crossbars of the window on the white curtains, then a sudden squall would throw an icy shower against the panes. And it was at this window, in front of the fire, that I read these lines which explained so many things to me and of which I give here the exact copy . . .

THE SECRET

I passed once more under her window. The panes are always dusty and whitened by the double curtain behind. Should Yvonne de Galais open it now, I have no longer anything to tell her, since she is married . . . What's to be done now? How live? . . .

'*Saturday, February 13.* I met by the river that girl who gave me news in the month of June and who used, like me, to wait before the closed house . . . I spoke to her. While she walked, I noticed, from the side, the slight blemishes in her face: a little line by the lips, a little hollowness in the cheeks, and powder a little thick on her nostrils. Turning suddenly, she looked me full in the face, perhaps because her full-face was prettier than her profile, and said abruptly: "You do amuse me. You remind me of a young man who made love to me once at Bourges. I was engaged to him . . ."

'Moreover, at night, on the deserted wet pavement reflecting the light of a street lamp, she suddenly came close and asked me to take her with her sister to the theatre that evening. For the first time I observed that she was dressed in mourning, in a woman's hat far too old for her young face, and that she carried a long thin umbrella like a cane. And as I was quite close to her my nails got caught in the front of her dress . . . I do not jump at her suggestion. She is cross and immediately wants to go away. And now it is I who hold her back and beg her. Then a workman, passing in the dim light, says in a low voice, bantering: "Don't you go, little girl. He'll do you a mischief!"

'And we stopped there, both of us, embarrassed.

'*At the theatre*. The two girls – my friend, whose name is Valentine Blondeau, and her sister – have come in cheap scarves.

'Valentine is in front of me. Every moment she turns round, restlessly as though inquiring what I want of her. I, near her – well, I feel almost happy; each time I reply with a smile.

'All round us there were women wearing dresses that were too low. And we joked about them. She smiled at first, then said, "I must not laugh at them: my dress is too low, too." And she wrapped her scarf round her. As a matter of fact, under the square of black lace, you could see that in her hurry to change her dress she had rolled back the top of her simple chemise that was working up.

'There is something poverty-stricken and childish about her. She has a curious suffering and adventurous look which attracts me. Near her, the only person in the world who could give me news of the people of the manor, I never stop brooding on my strange past adventure . . . I wanted to ask fresh questions about the little house in the boulevard. But she, in her turn, put such troublesome questions to me that I did not know how to reply. I feel that henceforth we shall, both of us, be dumb on that subject. And yet I know, too, that I shall see her again. What's the good? Why? . . . Am I now doomed to dog the steps of every person who carries with him the faintest, most distant whiff of my foiled adventure? . . .

'At midnight, alone in the deserted street, I ask myself what meaning this new strange story has for me. I walk by houses like cardboard boxes in a row, in which a whole people sleep. And all of a sudden I remember a decision I had taken a month

or so ago: I had resolved to go there by night, about one in the morning to go right round the house, to open the garden-gate, to enter like a thief and to search for some indication which would help me to find the lost manor, to see her again, merely to see her again . . . But I am tired, I am hungry. I, too, hurried to dress for the theatre and I have had no dinner . . . However, I remain a long time seated, much disturbed in mind, on the edge of my bed before lying down, a prey to vague remorse. Why?

'They did not want me either to see them home or to know where they lived. But I followed them long enough to know. I know they live in a little street which leads into the neighborhood of Notre-Dame. But at what number? . . . I guessed they were dressmakers or milliners.

'Valentine, without telling her sister, made a plan to meet me on Thursday at four in front of the theatre we had been to.

' "If I'm not there to-morrow," she said, "come on Friday at the same time, and Saturday, and so on, every day."

'*Thursday, February 18*. I went to wait for her, in a high wind foretelling rain. You said to yourself all the time, "It'll end by raining." . . .

'I walk along in the twilight of the streets with a weight on my heart. A drop falls. I fear a downpour: a storm would keep her from coming. But the wind rises again and the rain still keeps off. Above in the grey afternoon sky – now grey and now ablaze with light – a great cloud must have yielded to the wind. And I am here on the earth, miserably waiting . . .

'*In front of the theatre*. I am certain, after a quarter of an hour, that she won't come. From where I stand on the embankment I keep watch on the stream of people passing over the bridge, the way she ought to be coming. I follow with my eyes all young women in mourning whom I see approach and almost feel a kind of gratitude for those who, when nearest to me, have resembled her the longest and made me hope . . .

'*An hour's wait*. I am tired. At nightfall a policeman takes a rough to the station near by and the rough hurls all the filthy insults he knows at him. The policeman is furious, pale, dumb . . . In the passage he begins to strike, then he closes the door to beat the wretched man in peace . . . This terrible thought comes to me: "I have renounced paradise and am now stamping my feet at the gates of hell."

'To ease my restless mind, I leave the place and make for the little narrow street, between the Seine and Notre-Dame, where I almost know where they live. I walk to and fro alone. Now and again a servant or housewife comes out in the fine rain to shop before night . . . Nothing here for me and I go away . . . I walk through the clear rain which keeps the night back, up to the square where we ought to meet. There are more people than before – a black crowd . . .

'Suppositions – despair – fatigue – I cling to the thought of to-morrow. To-morrow at the same time I shall come back and wait for her. And I am in a great hurry for to-morrow to come. I look forward with weariness to the evening to-day and then to the next morning which I must go through somehow with nothing to do . . . But surely this day anyhow is practically over? . . . By the fire, in my room, I hear them shout the evening papers. Without any doubt, from her house hidden somewhere in the town near Notre-Dame, she is hearing them cried, too.

'She . . . I mean: Valentine.

'That evening, which I wanted to skip, weighs strangely up-

on me. While the hours advance, while the day is soon to end –
and I should like it ended – there exist men who have trusted
all their hope to it, all their love and their last strength. There
are dying men, others threatened by ruin, who would all like
to-morrow never to come. There are others for whom remorse
will dawn with to-morrow. Others who are so tired that this
night will never be long enough to give them the rest they
need. And I, I who have wasted to-day, how dare I summon
to-morrow?

'*Friday evening.* I had thought to write, "I have not seen her
again." And everything would have been finished.

'But when I reached the corner of the theatre at four o'clock –
there she was! Slight and solemn, wearing black, but with powder on her face and a little collar which made her look like a
naughty Pierrot. A look at once doleful and malicious.

'She comes to tell me that she wants to leave me at once,
that she will never come any more . . .

'And yet at nightfall here we still are, the two of us, slowly
walking, one close to the other, on the gravel path of the
Tuileries. She tells me her story, but tells it in so involved a
manner that I understand it badly. She says "my lover" in speaking of the man to whom she had been engaged, but whom she
did not marry. She does so purposely, I think, to shock me and
to keep me from attaching myself to her.

'Here are some of her phrases which I write down against
my will:

' "Don't you trust me an atom," she says; "I always get into
scrapes."

' "I've seen a good bit of life, quite on my own."

' "I upset the man I was engaged to. I left him because he

admired me too much; he saw me only in imagination, never as I was. I'm full of faults. We should have been very unhappy."

'Every moment I catch her trying to make herself out worse than she is. I think that she wants to prove to herself that she was right in doing the stupid thing she speaks of, that she has nothing to regret and is not worthy of the happiness which was offered her.

'Another time:
' "What I like about you," she said, giving me a long look – "what I like about you – and I can't know why – are my memories . . ."

'Another time:
' "I still love him," she said, "more than you think."
'And then suddenly, abruptly, sadly: "Well, what do *you* want? Do *you* love me? Are *you* going to propose to me?"
'I muttered something. I don't know what I replied. As likely as not I said, "Yes." '

Here this sort of journal stopped. There began rough drafts of letters, illegible, scribbled, scratched out. Precarious betrothal! . . . The girl, at Meaulnes' request, had left her job. He had busied himself with preparations for the wedding. But for ever clutched at by the desire to continue the search, to set out again on the tracks of his lost love, he must doubtless have disappeared on several occasions; and in his letters, with tragic embarrassment, he tried to justify himself to Valentine.

THE SECRET
(continued)

Then the journal began again.

He had noted memories of a stay they had both made some-where in the country, I do not know where. But, strange to say, from this moment, perhaps from a feeling of secret mod-esty, the journal had been kept in such a broken, irregular man-ner, scribbled down so hurriedly, that I have been obliged to go over it again myself and rewrite all this part of his story.

June 14. When he awoke early in the morning in the bedroom of the inn, the sun lit up the black curtain's red design. Farm labourers were drinking their morning coffee in the inn par-lour and talking in loud voices. They were put out, in a rude and kindly way, about one of their employers. Doubtless Meaul-nes had been hearing this restful noise for a long time in his sleep, for he took no notice at first. The curtain figured with grapes reddened by the sun, the morning voices rising to the silent bedroom, all this mingled with the one impression of waking up in the country at the beginning of delightful sum-mer holidays.

He got up, knocked lightly on the door into the next room without obtaining a reply and opened it a little, noiselessly. Then he saw Valentine and understood where his feeling of peace and happiness came from. She was asleep, quite still and silent; you could not hear her breathe; she slept as a bird might sleep. For a long time he watched this child's face with the shut eyes, this child's face that was so peaceful you could not wish it to waken or ever be troubled.

She made no other movement to show she was no longer asleep than to open her eyes and look at him.

As soon as he was dressed, Meaulnes came back to the girl. 'We are late,' she said.

And she immediately became like a housewife in her home.

She tidied the rooms, brushed the clothes which Meaulnes had worn the day before and, when she came to the trousers, was quite upset. The bottoms of the legs were covered with thick mud. She hesitated, and then, with careful precaution before brushing them, began to scrape off the first coat of mud with a knife.

'That's just what the boys do at Sainte-Agathe,' Meaulnes said, 'when they have taken a toss in the mud.'

'Oh! Mother taught me that,' Valentine said.

. . . And such was exactly the helpmate that the sportsman and peasant which Admiral Meaulnes was might have wished for previous to his mysterious adventure.

June 15. At the dinner at the farm where they were invited, much to their annoyance (thanks to friends who introduced them as husband and wife), she behaved as shyly as a young bride.

Candles had been lighted in two stands, and one was put at each end of the white linen-covered table, as at a quiet country wedding. Faces in that dim light, when people looked down, were hidden in shadow.

On the right of Patrice (the farmer's son) sat Valentine, then Meaulnes, who remained gloomy and silent to the end of dinner, though he was the one they generally addressed. Ever since he had resolved, in order to check gossip, to pass Valentine

216

off for his wife in this deserted village, regret and remorse tore at him. And while Patrice was playing the host like a proper squire, Meaulnes kept thinking: 'By rights, I should be presiding at my own wedding feast this evening, in a low dining-room like this, a lovely room I know well.'

Valentine close to him, timidly refused everything that was offered her. You would have said she was a peasant girl. At each fresh offer she looked at her friend and seemed to want to hide against him. Patrice had been vainly insisting for a long time that she should empty her glass, until at last Meaulnes leaned towards her and said gently: 'You must drink, dear little Valentine.'

Then she meekly drank. And Patrice smilingly congratulated the young man on having such an obedient wife.

But both of them, Valentine and Meaulnes, remained silent and thoughtful. For one thing, they were tired; their feet were soaked in the mud of their walk and felt frozen on the newly washed kitchen flagstones. And then the young man was forced from time to time to say: 'My wife, Valentine, my wife . . .'

And every time he heavily pronounced the word, before these unknown peasants in this dark room, he felt that he was doing a wrong.

June 17. The afternoon of this last day began badly.

Patrice and his wife went for a walk with them. Little by little the two couples became separated, among the rough slopes covered with heather. Meaulnes and Valentine sat down in a little copse amongst some junipers.

The wind brought drops of rain: the weather was lowering. The evening, it seemed, had a bitter taste, the taste of such gloom as love itself could not dispel.

217

They stopped there, for a long time, in their hiding-place, crouched under branches, talking little. Then the weather lifted. It became fine. They believed, now, that all would be well.

And they began to speak of love. Valentine talked and talked . . .

'This,' she said, 'is what the man I was engaged to promised me, like the child he was: we should immediately have a home like a thatched cottage hidden away in the country. It was all ready, he said. We were to arrive as though returning from a long journey on the evening of our wedding day, about the time that night comes. And along the roads and in the court-yard, and hidden in bushes, unknown children would have a fête to welcome us, shouting, "Long life to the bride!" What nonsense, isn't it?'

Meaulnes listened, speechless and anxious. There came back to him the echo of sounds once heard before. And in the voice of the girl as she told this story, there seemed the tone of vague regret.

But she feared that she had hurt him. She turned towards him with warmth and kindness: 'All I have I want to give to you,' she said, 'something which has been more precious to me than anything . . . and you shall burn it!'

Then, looking straight at him, anxiously, she produced a small packet of letters from her pocket and handed them to him, letters from the man to whom she had been engaged.

Ah! instantly he recognized the fine handwriting. Why had it not occurred to him sooner! It was the handwriting of Frantz, the bohemian, which he had once seen on the despairing note left in the bedroom at the manor . . .

Now they were walking along a narrow lane, between daisies and grasses lit by the slanting rays of the sun at five in the afternoon. Meaulnes was so stupefied that he could not yet grasp the extent of the disaster which all this meant to him. He read because she asked him to read. Childish, sentimental pathetic words and phrases . . . Such as, in the last letter:

'. . . *Ah! you have lost that little heart, unforgivable little Valentine. What's going to happen to us? At any rate I am not superstitious . . .*'

Meaulnes read, half blinded by regret and anger, his face motionless but pale, and he shuddered. Valentine, uneasy to see him like this, looked to find what page he was at and what so bothered him.

'Oh! that's a jewel,' she explained quickly – 'a jewel he gave me and made me swear to keep always. That was one of his mad ideas.'

But she managed only to exasperate Meaulnes.

'Mad!' he said, putting the letters in his pocket. 'Why repeat that word? Why not have wanted to believe in him? I knew him; he was the most wonderful fellow in the world!'

'You knew him!' she cried at the pitch of excitement. 'You knew Frantz de Galais!'

'He was my best friend; he was my brother-in-arms, and now I've taken the girl he was engaged to from him! – Ah!' he went on, in fury, 'what mischief you've done us, you who would believe in nothing! You're the cause of it all. It's you who've mucked it all, mucked it all . . .'

She wanted to speak to him, wanted to take his hand, but he repulsed her brutally.

'Go away! Let me be!'

'All right,' she said, her face hot, stammering and half crying, 'if that's it, I shall indeed go. – Make my way back to Bourges with my sister. And if you don't come and find me – you know, don't you, that father's too poor to keep me – well, I shall go right back to Paris. I shall tramp the streets as I've done once already; and I shall become a bad girl for certain, I know I shall, as I've no job any more . . .'

And she went off to find her belongings to catch the train, while Meaulnes, not even watching her go off, kept walking on anywhere.

The journal broke off again.

Rough drafts of letters followed once more, the letters of a man undecided and at his wit's end. Back at La Ferté d'Angillon Meaulnes wrote to Valentine, apparently to reaffirm his resolve never to see her again and to give her the precise reasons for it, but in reality perhaps, so that she could reply. In one of these letters he asked her what, in his first distress, he had not even dreamed of asking her: Did she know where the manor was, the manor that had been so searched for? . . . In another, he begged her to make it up with Frantz de Galais. He would set himself to find him again . . . All the letters of which I saw the rough drafts could not have been sent. But he must have written two or three times without receiving any reply. It must have been a time of fierce and miserable struggle for him, in complete isolation. As the hope of ever seeing Yvonne de Galais again had vanished, he must have felt his great resolution weaken little by little. And from the pages which I shall presently give – the last in the journal – I imagine that he must have hired a bicycle one fine morning at the beginning of the holidays and gone to Bourges to visit the cathedral.

He started out early by the lovely road through the woods, inventing, as he went along, any number of reasons for appearing before the girl he had thrown over, without loss of dignity and without asking her to make it up.

The last four pages which I have been able to put together give the narrative of this journey and of this last mistake . . .

THE SECRET
(concluded)

August 25. After a long search he found the house of Valentine Blondeau on the other side of Bourges, at the far end of the new suburbs. A woman on the doorstep – Valentine's mother – seemed to be waiting for him. She was a good housewife in appearance, heavy, shabby, but still good-looking. She watched him come with curiosity and when he asked, 'Are the Misses Blondeau at home?' she explained gently and kindly that they had gone to Paris on August 15. 'They forbade me to say where they were going,' she added, 'but their letters will be forwarded from their old address.'

As he pushed his bicycle back along the little garden, he thought: 'She's gone . . . All is over as I wanted . . . I've driven her to this. "I shall become a bad girl for certain," she said. And I've pushed her into it! I've ruined the girl Frantz was engaged to!'

And he kept saying to himself in a low voice like a madman, 'So much the better! So much the better!' knowing quite well that it was really 'So much the worse!' and that under the eyes of that woman, before reaching the gate, he was going to stumble and fall on his knees.

221

He never thought of luncheon, but stopped at a café in which he wrote a long letter to Valentine, only to cry aloud, only to get rid of the despairing cry which choked him. His letter kept repeating endlessly: 'You could! . . . You could! . . . You could stoop to this! . . . You could ruin yourself like this!'

Officers were drinking near him. One of them was noisily telling a story about a woman which could be heard in snatches: 'I said to her . . . you ought to know me . . . I play with your husband every evening!' The others laughed and turning round spat behind the benches. Meaulnes, pale and dusty, watched them as a beggar might. He imagined them holding Valentine on their knees.

For a long time he rode round the cathedral on his bicycle muttering, 'As a matter of fact, I really came to see the cathedral.' You could see it rise on the deserted square, enormous and indifferent, at the end of every street. These streets were narrow and filthy as the alleys that surround village churches. Here and there hung a red lantern, sign of a house of ill fame . . . Meaulnes felt his utter misery in this unclean, vicious quarter, nestling, as in old times, under the buttressed walls of the cathedral. There came over him a peasant's fear, a loathing for this church of the town, where vices are sculptured on the cornices, which is built among evil places and has no remedy for the purest sorrows of love.

Two girls passed, street walkers, their arms round one another's waists, and looked at him boldly. From disgust or for fun, to avenge his love or to destroy it, Meaulnes followed them slowly on his bicycle, and one of them, a wretched girl whose thin yellow hair was held up at the back in a false chignon, gave him a rendezvous for six o'clock in the Garden of the Archbishop's Palace – the very garden in which Frantz in one of his letters had arranged to meet poor Valentine.

He did not say no, realising that he would have left the town far behind by that time. And she stopped a long while at her low window over the sloping street, making vague signs to him.

He hurried to regain the road.

Before leaving, he could not resist the mournful wish to pass for the last time before Valentine's house. He gazed at it and was able to gather food for sorrow. It was one of the last houses in the suburb and the street became a road from that place . . . In front a sort of empty plot made something like a little square. No one was at any of the windows, no one in the yard or anywhere. Only a dirty powdered girl passed along the wall, dragging two little boys in rags.

There had Valentine passed her childhood, there she had begun to look at the world with her confident, wise eyes. She had worked, stitching, behind those windows. And Frantz had gone by to see her, to smile at her, along this very street. But now nothing remained, nothing . . . The sad afternoon dragged on and Meaulnes knew only that somewhere, this very day, the melancholy place she would never come to again was passing before the mind's eye of Valentine, now ruined.

The long ride ahead of him must have remained the last succour against his woe, his last enforced distraction before being plunged into its depths.

He went away. By the side of the road, and amongst the trees at the edge of the water along the valley, delicious farmhouses showed their pointed gables with green trellises. Down there, no doubt, on the lawns, girls were pensively talking of love. You could imagine souls down there, beautiful souls . . .

But for Meaulnes at that moment there existed but one love, that unsatisfying love which had just been buffeted so cruelly, and the girl among all girls whom he ought to have protected and kept safe was precisely the girl whom he had just sent to her ruin.

A few hurried lines of the journal informed me that he had planned to find Valentine again, at all costs, before it was too late. A date, in the corner of one page, led me to believe that this was the long journey for which Madame Meaulnes was making preparations when I came to La Ferté d'Angillon to upset everything. Meaulnes was noting down his memories and projects in the deserted 'Town Hall' one fine morning at the end of August – when I had pushed open the door and brought him the great news which he had ceased to expect. He had been caught, checked by his old adventure, without daring to do anything or confess anything. Then remorse began and regret and grief, sometimes stifled, sometimes emerging in triumph, until his wedding day on which the cry of the bohemian in the fir wood reminded him dramatically of his young manhood's first oath.

He had hastily scribbled in this same composition test book a few words, at dawn, before going away (with her permission – but forever) from Yvonne de Galais, his wife since the previous day:

'I am going. I must follow the tracks of the two bohemians who came yesterday to the fir wood and have gone on bicycles toward the east. I shall not come near Yvonne de Galais again until I can bring back with me and install in "Frantz's house," Frantz and Valentine married.

'This manuscript, which I began as a secret journal and which has become my confession, is to be the property, if I do not come back, of my friend François Seurel.'

He must have hastily slipped the exercise-book under the others, relocked his old small schoolboy trunk and disappeared.

Epilogue

*T*ime passed on. I lost hope of ever seeing my friend again, and the days went by mournfully in the village school and sadly in the deserted house. Frantz never came to meet me at the place I had arranged, and anyhow Aunt Moinel had long since forgotten where Valentine lived.

The only happiness of the people at the Sand Pit soon became the little girl whom they had been able to save. At the end of September, she showed herself to be a sturdy and pretty child. She was nearly a year old. She pushed chairs along quite by herself, gripping the rungs, and trying to walk, not minding tumbles, and she made a clatter which woke long remote echoes in the empty house. When I held her in my arms, she would never let me give her a kiss. She had a shy, and at the same time charming way of wriggling to get free and pushing my face away with her little open hand, while shouting with laughter. With all her gaiety, with all her childish violence, you would have said that she was on the way to scatter the gloom which had weighed on the house since her birth. I would sometimes say to myself, 'Without any doubt, in spite of this shyness, she will be a little my child.' But once again Providence decided otherwise.

One Sunday morning at the end of September, I got up very early, even before the woman who was the little girl's nurse. I was to go fishing by the Cher, with two men from Saint-Benoist and Jasmin Delouche. Villagers from the neighbourhood often met me in this way for poaching expeditions, tickling trout at night, fishing with nets in prohibited waters . . . On holidays all through the summer time we left at dawn, and did not come back till noon. It was the way most of these men gained a living. As for me, it was my one pastime, the only adventure which recalled the doings of our set in former days. And I ended by really liking these jaunts, these long hours of fishing by the riverside or amongst the reeds of the pond.

That morning, then, I was down at five-thirty, in front of the house in a little shed that leaned against the wall which separated the English garden of the Sand Pit from the kitchen garden of the Farm. I was busy disentangling my nets which I had thrown down in a heap the previous Thursday.

It was not quite day: it was the dawn of a beautiful morning in September; and the shed from which I was hurriedly getting my tackle was half in darkness.

There I was silent and busy when suddenly I heard the iron gate opening and a footfall on the gravel path.

'Ha! ha!' said I to myself. 'Here come these fellows sooner than I thought. And here am I, not ready yet! . . .'

But the man who came into the courtyard was unknown to me. He was, so far as I could distinguish, a great bearded fellow dressed like a sportsman or a poacher. Instead of coming to find me where the others knew that I always was at the time we had arranged to meet, he went straight to the front door.

'Good!' I thought; 'it's a friend of theirs whom they've invited without telling me and they've sent him on ahead to explain.'

The man gently played with the latch of the door, making no noise. But on coming out I had fastened the door behind me. He behaved in the same way at the kitchen door. Then he hesitated a moment and turned towards me a troubled face, made clear in the half-light. And it was only then that I recognised Admiral Meaulnes.

For a long moment I remained where I was, terrified, in despair, suddenly gripped again by all the grief which his return awakened. He had disappeared behind the house, had walked round it, and returned, hesitating.

Then I approached him and without saying a word I threw my arms round him, sobbing. Immediately he understood:

'Ah!' he said in an abrupt voice. 'She's dead, is that not so?'

And he stood where he was, upright, deaf, motionless, and terrible. I took him by the arm and gently led him towards the house. It was day now. At once, so that the hardest task should be accomplished, I made him mount the stairs which led to the death chamber. As soon as he was in, he fell on his knees by the bed and for a long time kept his head buried in his arms.

At last he rose with bewildered eyes, swaying, not knowing where he was. And still guiding him by the arm, I opened the door by which this room communicated with that of the little girl. She had awakened of her own accord – while her nurse was downstairs – and had boldly sat up in her cot. One could just see her surprised face turned towards us.

'Here is your daughter,' I said.

He started and looked at me.

Then he seized her and lifted her up in his arms. He could not see her well at first because he was crying. Then, a little to divert this great emotion and this flood of weeping, holding her tightly against him all the while on his right arm, he turned his lowered head to me and said:

'I've brought them back, the other two . . . You must go and see them in their house.'

And indeed, when I went early in the morning, thoughtful and almost happy towards the house of Frantz which Yvonne de Galais had once shown me empty, I saw from the distance, sweeping the doorstep, a sort of young housewife with a turned-down collar, an object of curiosity and excitement to several little cowherds in their Sunday clothes on the way to mass.

Meanwhile the little girl became annoyed at being squeezed up, and as Augustin, his head on one side to conceal and check his tears, continued not to look at her, she gave him a great slap with her little hand on his bearded, wet mouth.

This time the father lifted his daughter on high, jumped her up on his outstretched arms, and looked at her with a kind of smile. She was pleased and clapped her hands . . .

I had stepped back a little to see them better. Rather let down and yet wonder-struck, I realised that the little girl had at last found in him the playfellow she had been dimly expecting . . . Admiral Meaulnes had left me one joy; I felt that he had come back to take it away from me. And already I could imagine him at night, wrapping his daughter in his cloak and setting out with her for new adventures.